JUL - - 2022

SOUND OF DARKNESS

SOUND OF DARKNESS

HEATHER GRAHAM

THORNDIKE PRESS
A part of Gale, a Cengage Company

Copyright © 2022 by Heather Graham Pozzessere.
Krewe of Hunters.
Thorndike Press, a part of Gale, a Cengage Company.

Thorndike Press® Large Print Core.
The text of this Large Print edition is unabridged.
Other aspects of the book may vary from the original edition.
Set in 16 pt. Plantin.

LIBRARY OF CONGRESS CIP DATA ON FILE.
CATALOGUING IN PUBLICATION FOR THIS BOOK
IS AVAILABLE FROM THE LIBRARY OF CONGRESS.

ISBN-13: 978-1-4328-9642-3 (hardcover alk. paper)

Published in 2022 by arrangement with Harlequin Enterprises ULC.

Printed in Mexico
Print Number: 01   Print Year: 2022

With lots of love and all best wishes for Gysselle Escobar-Leon, Ray, Jeff, Zohe, Koralis and Emily.

PROLOGUE

Orlando, ten years ago

"Help me!"

Colleen Law heard the call as clearly as if the person had shouted in her ear.

But she was nowhere near anyone.

"Help, me! Oh, please . . . help!"

She was in the playground in her neighborhood, a quiet residential area just east of Celebration in Orlando, Florida.

It was a pleasant, middle-class place, with a low crime rate. While Central Florida might be theme-park-ville, she knew her parents had chosen a home with a high safety rate for children.

What else did one prioritize when they had three children, triplets no less?

But now, someone was screaming for help.

She leapt out of the swing where she had been sitting, playing games on her phone, and raced across the street to her house where her father had been working in the yard, pruning the hibiscus bush that grew around the house.

"Dad!" she cried.

"What?" he asked, perplexed.

"Don't you hear that? Someone is screaming for help!"

He frowned, casting his head to the side. She loved her father; he was a good dad and a good man. But he was now looking at her as if she were crazy.

"Honey, I don't hear anything. What did you hear?"

Before she could answer, she heard the cry again, now more like a sob of someone who had lost hope.

This time, she had a direction.

It was coming from a car parked in front of the Clancy house just down the street.

"Dad, there's someone in that car who needs help!"

"Colleen, are you sure? That car has been parked there for a few hours —"

He clearly wasn't listening. She had heard the cries plain as day. She looked at her father in frustration and raced down to the car. A quick glance assured her there was no one in it, but it also showed her the keys had been dropped on the floor near the gas pedal below the driver's seat.

She knew she had to grab the keys quickly,

aware her father had frantically chased after her; he probably thought she was breaking into someone's private property.

She was, of course. Though was it breaking in if the door was unlocked?

It wasn't. But there was a loose rock from the small coral stone wall that surrounded the Clancy property and she swept it up quickly, thinking of just how long she was going to be grounded if she was wrong and there was no one in the trunk.

But she knew she had heard the cries!

The coral rock smashed the window with a shattering sound. She unlocked the door and grabbed the keys as she heard her father yelling, "Colleen! Have you lost your mind?"

He was almost upon her. She studied the keys as quickly as she could, shaking.

She found the key fob, which held buttons to lock and unlock the car, and open the trunk.

She hit the one for the trunk, opening it.

It lifted just as her father reached the passenger's side of the car, and she raced to the rear.

Then she screamed.

There was a woman in the trunk. She was bound, gagged, and beaten badly.

Her father came around and saw the woman; a dark look came over his face as he reached into his pocket for his cell phone. He called the police, describing the situation and demanding they get an ambulance out to them fast.

"Dad! We can't wait! We have to help her!" Colleen said, reaching into the car. She couldn't believe she was doing so. The woman was covered in blood, but there was duct tape covering her mouth, and though her eyes were closed, Colleen refused to believe she was dead.

She ripped off the duct tape.

"Oh, God, Colleen," her father warned. "You shouldn't . . . We don't know if she's . . ."

Alive! Colleen thought.

But her father suddenly came to that realization and reached into the car, lifting the woman out. He was a strong man; she knew he had kept fit chasing after her and her siblings. He was able to lift the woman cleanly from the trunk, not bumping her head or body into anything.

He laid her on the ground, pulled a Swiss Army knife out of his pocket, and sliced through the ropes that tied her wrists and ankles. He had her stretched out on the lawn, and he quickly began artificial respiration. They could hear sirens in the distance, drawing closer.

As the first police car and ambulance pulled to a halt, Colleen saw the woman cough and gasp and take her first breath.

She was alive.

Colleen looked at her father. "Dad," she whispered, almost crying she was so relieved. "You saved her!"

Her father looked at her strangely.

"No, Colleen," he said softly. "You saved her. I don't know how . . . but you saved her."

CHAPTER ONE

Mark Gallagher spoke softly to his dog as he pulled his phone from his pants pocket to call his partner, Ragnar Johansen, who was sitting at a bus stop within shouting distance.

"Act chill for a minute, Red," he told the dog.

Red was a big Labrador mix, a good hundred pounds.

"He found it?" Ragnar asked over the phone.

"Hey! Yeah!" Mark said loudly for anyone who might have been watching or in earshot.

Red sat for a moment at his feet. He had already indicated the house where the young woman was being held.

"He found it, and we can move," Ragnar said. "Red is one damned cool canine."

It wasn't Red's size that made him so unique. The Krewe members all called him

"Special Agent Red" since he was a service dog in many ways, but he was highly trained in other areas.

Red was excellent at finding people — both the living and the dead.

"He found this house, and hopefully Sally. Alive," Mark said softly.

The young woman had gone missing, and according to her parents and friends, she wasn't the type to just disappear. And while a dozen possibilities could be considered in any disappearance, they'd been immediately concerned.

Two women from areas just outside of DC had also recently disappeared.

Only they were later found — dead.

"Heading around the back now. It's number 1405. I checked with Angela. The house has been rented by an Alex Grant. Angela says it's a pseudonym."

"So, it's really Carver," Ragnar said. "But this is your plan. Um, I'll take the front. I'll come up with a ruse — selling Girl Scout Cookies won't work."

"I don't think so," Mark said dryly. His partner not only had a Scandinavian name — he looked as if he'd stepped off the set of a Viking movie.

"Maybe I'll be selling life insurance."

"I know you'll make something work.

We'll go," Mark told him, and ended the call.

It was going to be tricky; the man could be holding a young woman. The young woman could die. But they didn't have a search warrant and the laws weren't always on their side.

But right now, life came first.

"Now, boy, if you will," Mark said softly to the dog.

Red let out a woof and took off at a dead run. Mark pretended to lose the leash, running after the dog into the yard.

He was grateful there was no fence.

Red went around to the back. Mark, following after him, heard the doorbell ring, and he knew his partner was at the front. He gave the bell a minute to be answered, and then nodded at Red, who loped to the back door, throwing himself against it.

"Red, hey boy, stop, please!" Mark said. Of course, the dog knew to keep going.

It worked as he had hoped. Their suspect, Jim Carver, after answering the doorbell and hearing the ruckus in the other room, was soon at the back door, swearing. But as planned, Ragnar had taken the opportunity to enter the house after Carver had answered the ringing doorbell.

Red pushed his way into the house, barking furiously at Carver.

"What the hell?" Carver yelled furiously. "I'm going to have this animal put to sleep — and you!" He stopped, staring at Ragnar. "What the hell?" he repeated. "I said you could come into the foyer, and now, you're in my house! Get the hell out!"

"I heard someone screaming," Ragnar said.

"What? You didn't hear anyone screaming!" Carver said. "You — you're cops —"

"Sorry, there goes my dog," Mark said.

The dog raced through the kitchen, and Mark hurried after him, followed by Ragnar and Carver with Carver threatening them with lawsuits with every step.

The door to the basement was closed.

"I told you. I heard someone screaming," Ragnar said. "There's more screaming!"

"No one is screaming!" Carver protested.

"The dog hears it. He's going crazy," Mark agreed.

"You people! This is illegal! This is my residence —"

"Taken under a pseudonym. Reasonable cause for entry, then again, you did let me in. And now? Someone is screaming. We can hear it!" Ragnar said.

"You do not hear screaming!" Carver protested. "And a pseudonym! What the

16

hell? I will have my day in court!"

"Oh, yes, you will," Mark agreed. He stared at the man. "What? You don't think we hear screams? Is your victim dead already?"

Carver backed away, staring at him.

The basement door was locked. Ragnar and Mark looked at one another and thudded their shoulders against the door simultaneously. Mark barely regained his balance; steps led down to the basement below and a fall could have been serious — even deadly.

Red barked furiously again, weaving through their legs and tearing down the steps.

Carver realized he'd been made; he turned to take off running, grabbing a Smith & Wesson pistol off the table as he did.

Mark didn't know for sure if Carver was the man who was now the scourge of a dozen police agencies and the FBI.

"The Embracer" as he had been termed in the press.

But Carver had been holding Sally Smithson. Red was never wrong.

"Drop it!" Mark thundered, drawing his own weapon from beneath his jacket.

Carver fired wildly. Mark fired a warning shot.

"Drop it!"

Carver started running.

"I've got him," Ragnar said to Mark. "And the 911."

Mark nodded and followed the dog down the stairs. And there, on a cot, lay the woman they had been seeking. Sally Smithson. Her eyes were closed; she was pale as ash. A bucket for a toilet lay at the foot of the cot.

The basement also held some lumber and some tools. No built boxes or coffins, just the usual supplies that a basement might contain. Nothing there proved that the man was *the* Embracer.

He could already hear sirens. The local police chief had not minded the FBI intervention. Sally had been taken from her home in Maryland, and they were now in Virginia. Mark had been confident about the Krewe and the certainty they would find Sally, and the police chief acknowledged that what few clues they had led to Virginia, so he had been happy to agree to their handling of the case.

Mark hurried to the young woman, feeling for a pulse. It was there — weak, but steady.

"Sally," he said softly.

Red whined and gave her a sloppy lick.

Sally opened her eyes, screaming hysterically and edging up against the wall.

The girl had just turned twenty-four. She had large brown eyes, a tangled mane of dark hair, and a pretty face filled with fear and despair.

"Sally, Sally, it's all right," Mark assured her. "I'm FBI. You're safe," he said softly.

She stared at him at first, afraid to believe she might have been rescued. Her eyes switched from terror to mistrust. Then she started to cry. Red set his paws on the cot and whined as if also telling her it was okay. The girl threw herself against the dog, sobbing.

The local police and emergency crews had been put on alert, and they must have been near when Ragnar had put through his 911 call.

A paramedic hurried down the basement steps, followed by a county deputy.

"Sally —" Mark began.

But she threw her arms into the air and started shaking and crying and speaking in disjointed sentences that made no sense.

"Let me get her to the hospital," the paramedic said. "Give her time. You can talk to the doctor later. They'll get her checked out, hydrated, and sedated, and by tomorrow morning, she'll probably make more sense."

"Thanks," Mark said, and turned to the deputy. "Carver ran. I'm going after him — my partner is already on him."

The deputy nodded and Mark hurried back up the steps, Red on his heels.

"Which way, boy?" Mark asked.

Red ran to the left; Mark followed.

They were in a quiet suburban neighborhood an hour out from DC, a bedroom community for many who worked in the city. The houses were large here, with nice yards — probably costing about the same as a small apartment close in. That was the way it was. Mark was glad; neighbors were at work or in their houses. It was too early for kids to be playing outside.

Carver didn't seem to know how to shoot very well, and the last thing they wanted was a civilian casualty.

Red suddenly veered to the right, heading into an adjacent yard. Mark took off after him. As he raced around the side of the house, he heard a shot. Then Ragnar's voice.

"Drop it, Carver. You have nowhere to go. It's over."

"I'll kill the kid or the damned stupid dog!" Carver raged.

Mark slowed his gait, sliding against the

20

side wall of the house, edging against it until he could see exactly what was going on.

Red certainly wasn't a stupid dog. He had stopped against the side of the house as well.

Carver was about two feet in front of the back door, his gun against the head of a boy who was sobbing and appeared to be about ten.

Mark quickly weighed his options.

Shoot the man in the head from the rear?

That would free the kid.

But he calculated his distance, Ragnar's position, and Red's. And he decided he had a better option.

"Okay, Red, low!" he commanded softly.

The dog whined and started out. As Mark had reasoned, Carver moved the gun from the kid's head to aim at the dog.

Mark sprinted out of his position, throwing himself at Carver.

The kid screamed and fell. Carver howled.

Carver's gun went flying, and Ragnar scooped it up in a matter of seconds. Red sprang up and ran at Carver, standing over him, growling. Mark found his feet and helped the kid to his, thrusting the boy behind him lest Carver have another weapon.

Ragnar started to inform Carver he was under arrest, but he didn't get far; officers from the county had followed Mark down the street. The cops were quickly in the yard, taking over with Carver. A young officer went to the sobbing boy, sliding his arm around the boy's shoulders and asking him how to reach his parents.

Lieutenant Kenworth of the county police came around the house then.

"I — uh — thank you. I told my officers to handle it from here. But . . . do you want —"

"No, thanks," Mark said. "I trust your officers to process the scene." He hesitated. "We know he kidnapped Sally. But we don't yet have any evidence to prove he's The Embracer."

"How did you get on to this guy anyway? I mean, Special Agent Crow informed me the house had been rented under a pseudonym. The guy has been Mr. Nice to the neighbors and in the community."

"Anonymous tip," Mark said. "And Carver wound up on our suspect list after we learned about the first victim. He disappeared as 'Carver' about a year or so ago. He had been wanted for aggravated assault in Fairfax."

"Then he is The Embracer?"

"We just don't know for sure," Mark said.

"Well, thank you. We may never have

known. The man assisted at our kids' baseball games! Who would have thought —" Kenworth began.

"He may threaten to sue for unlawful entry or try to get the case thrown out," Mark warned.

"But he was cocky. He told me to come in and wait when he heard the commotion at the back — Mark and Red," Ragnar said.

"And I was just catching my dog," Mark said. "And then we heard all that screaming."

"If there's any trouble, we have a legal team to fight him," Ragnar assured him.

"Our forensic team will be working with yours," Mark added. "And we will want to question him."

"Of course. You've done us a tremendous service here. That young lady — the paramedic — said she's going to be okay. She's dehydrated and half-starved, but the med tech said her vital signs are good. The bastard, the way he held her . . . Carver must be The Embracer," Kenworth muttered, shaking his head.

Kenworth was a heavyset man with broad shoulders and a stern face, and from what Mark and Ragnar had gathered on him, he was a good officer. He'd had no problem with others helping out, especially when the man being sought might be heading in the direction of serial murderer.

Killing in his community.

"Again. We don't know. He kidnapped a woman and was holding her, so it is a possibility. Let him stew in a cell tonight. Tomorrow you'll have arraigned him, and we'll work on federal charges. We understand Sally is terrified right now and in need of medical attention before she can tell us much. For tonight, we're heading back," Mark told him.

Kenworth nodded. "Of course."

"We'll see you in the morning," Ragnar assured him.

"Can I drop you two — and Red — off anywhere?" Kenworth asked.

"Our car is just down the street," Ragnar told him. "And we will be here bright and early tomorrow morning. Just make sure you don't lose our guy tonight!"

"We won't lose him," Kenworth said. "These guys are something. Like Carver, I mean. So tough when they attack the vulnerable and the innocent. Not so tough when they're caught. And we've got him now."

Mark, Ragnar, and Red left the local police and medics to finish dealing with the arrest and the traumatized boy. They headed down the street to their vehicle.

"You want to drive or make the call?" Ragnar asked Mark.

"Whichever," Mark said.

They had found Sally alive. That made it a damned good day. He smiled.

"You drive, and I'll let Jackson know we got him," Mark said.

"Or we could say, Red got him," Ragnar said as he pat the dog's head.

Red gave him an approving woof.

"We get to congratulate ourselves today. We made a hell of a team," Mark said.

He hit the number for Jackson Crow on his speed dial as they reached the car. Red leapt into the back as Mark took his seat in the front.

As Ragnar revved the engine, Mark put the phone on speaker.

Jackson came on quickly.

"Mark and Ragnar here, Jackson. We've got you on speaker. We got Carver and Sally," Mark said.

"Alive?" Jackson asked.

Mark could hear the tension in Jackson's voice. No matter how long any of them had been at this, they'd always be concerned for the outcome of a chase like this one.

"Yes. We were lucky. Sally was smart, I think. We haven't been able to talk to her yet; she was frantic, and the ERs suggested I talk to the doctors later, noting she'd probably make sense by morning. But I believe she hid her cell phone at first. Carver eventually found it and ditched it. But the trace led us to the right area, and Angela got the address and the pseudonym info. Red took it from there," Mark told their field director. "Lieutenant Kenworth has taken Carver into custody. We'll head back here in the morning, hitting the hospital first to talk to Sally, and we'll visit Carver before the state arraignment. We also told Kenworth about our 'anonymous' tip about Carver, but didn't get into details."

It was true they'd received a tip. He just hadn't told Kenworth it had come from a dead man.

"Ragnar needs to see Carver tonight," Jackson said.

Mark was surprised. "Jackson, you're the one who usually wants us to let them stew a bit —"

"Not this time. And Ragnar needs to hit Carver on his own. I'm going to need you — and Red — now."

"Jackson," Mark said, frowning, "I know we don't know if Carver is The Embracer, but I'm not sure that —"

"We don't know enough at this moment,

26

and we need everything and anything we can get. We don't know if Carver is clever, has other names, or if he has another stash house," Jackson said. "Regardless of whether he's been working on his own, I need you and Red now, before another young woman dies. Carver may be the one and only Embracer. Or he's a copycat. Or there is a copycat still out there."

"What makes you say that?" Ragnar asked, frowning quickly at Mark as he drove.

"There's been another kidnapping," Jackson told them. "Dierdre Ayers. She didn't come home last night, and we can't waste any time. Now that Carver has been taken in, we need to find Dierdre Ayers fast. If we don't, she could starve or dehydrate or worse. Or, more than one person has been carrying out these kidnappings and murders. An accomplice or a copycat might get spooked; Carver's arrest could speed up their timeline."

"Do we have anything to go on at this point? A phone trace? Anything?" Mark asked.

"We have Red," Jackson said. "And we have a new agent. Ragnar will start on Carver right away. Meanwhile, I'm going to be pairing Mark up with one of our newest Krewe members."

"Jackson —" Mark began.

But Jackson was gone.

He shook his head, glancing at Ragnar. They worked well together; they had been partners for a year, and time had given them a level of communication — a sometimes silent one — that allowed them to make the right moves to cover one another.

Red and Ragnar worked well together too. Red was Mark's dog and his loyalty went to Mark, but Ragnar was his next most beloved human.

Ragnar shrugged. "Hey. We're a good team. Or trio, I should say. But we are talking life-and-death. And whatever this new person can bring to the table, well, Jackson said it was a life-and-death situation. Seems strange to throw a rookie in on this, but I trust Jackson. And it doesn't sound like we have so much as an anonymous tip."

The tip that had led them to Carver — who'd already been a person of interest — had come from Sergeant Alfie Parker, who'd been dead since 2018, but he was still patrolling his old route — and was adept at hitchhiking to the offices of their special unit — the "Krewe of Hunters" unit. Parker had seen Carver drag a woman back into the house after she had come flying out the front door, frantic. He had known immediately that the woman was in trouble, and had made his way to Krewe headquarters as fast as he could.

A serious problem with being dead, Sergeant Parker had told them, was transportation. He didn't have his own car anymore.

They had trusted him, of course. Mark wished he had known the man in life. He had been tall and solidly built, light-eyed, with just a few strands of gray starting to show in his dark hair. He could be solemn and thorough, but he could smile and joke as well.

He'd been killed on the job, shot down during a task-force takedown at a crack house.

Now, the information he provided had been invaluable. But from what Jackson had said, it didn't sound as if they'd received any tips from anyone — living or dead — on this new kidnapping. They just had another missing woman.

"Okay. Carver had Sally; she was held down in the basement. He was abusing her, torturing her, and he would have killed her. And we got in there without having to jump through legal loops for a search warrant in time to find her alive because we know how to play it as a team," Mark said aloud, wondering why Jackson would pull him now to show a newcomer the ropes. "It doesn't make sense, him wanting me to work with a rookie, especially now. I understand him sending us in different directions. Red and I can take on the physical search and you can handle Carver. But —"

"Hey. We were all rookies once," Ragnar reminded him. "And I know you usually take lead on questioning because you're damned good at it, but I'll be all right." It was evident Ragnar was puzzled too, but he was doing his best to make the situation seem more normal and okay.

"Yeah," Mark agreed. "It just feels strange. I know you talking to him might be our best bet on finding out if he is working alone, working with someone else, or if there is a copycat out there." Mark winced and glanced at his partner. "I seriously considered shooting Carver in the head when he had that boy."

"But you didn't shoot him in the head, because you always follow the law. We'd all like to tear up The Embracer," Ragnar reminded him, "but as federal agents, we've sworn oaths. For as long as I've known you, you've been damned good at following the law."

"We might have bent it a little today," Mark said dryly.

"Hey, I heard screams," Ragnar said. "And if you remember — though I guess none of us forgets these things — you and Red found the last victim. I know how that makes you feel. Think of it this way: if you're not the one to question Carver, you won't be tempted to jump across the table and rip his eyes out."

"True."

"We found Sally Smithson alive," Ragnar reminded him.

"Yes, and I'm grateful."

"And maybe you and Red can find the next victim alive as well," Ragnar said. His eyes were on the road. "While I'm trying not to leap across the table and rip Carver's eyes out."

Mark thought about the victim he and Red had found too late.

"Maybe you have a point," he said quietly. He glanced at his watch. The afternoon was waning away. It was nearly three, which meant nothing. Krewe members didn't keep anything resembling normal working hours, so the coming night didn't matter to him. Still, if he and Red were going on a search, a bit of daylight would be nice.

"I'll have you to your car in less than forty-five minutes," Ragnar promised.

"Yep. Good. Thanks. I'm going to call

back into headquarters. I need to learn everything they have on this latest kidnapping, especially if Red and I are going to be working with a rookie."

"Colleen?"

Colleen stood at the back door of the Ayerses' house, silent and still, listening.

But no sounds — other than the chirping of birds and the slight sound of Jackson Crow's soft breathing — came to her.

She looked at Jackson and shook her head sadly. "I'm sorry, Jackson. I don't hear anything at all."

"That's all right," he assured her.

She knew he was frustrated.

Jackson had come to her small office at Krewe headquarters that morning to ask her to accompany him out to the Ayerses' house.

A frantic call from Rory Ayers, a DC contractor, had been put through to him. His daughter had only been gone overnight, Ayers acknowledged — and there were all kinds of reasons young people disappeared — but too many other young women had disappeared recently.

And two had been found dead.

Jackson Crow had gotten every other agency in the area working on the disappearance — even if a missing persons report was usually filled out after a greater length of time.

Agencies were sharing every little tidbit of information they acquired, but the Krewe was lead agency on the investigation. Colleen knew Krewe members had been sent to a small town in northeastern Virginia in search of another young woman.

Which was troublesome now, with another kidnapping apparently in progress.

And usually law enforcement could be skeptical about the urgency when a person had only been missing a short time. People had fights. Young women went off on adventures and were often afraid to tell their parents, especially if alcohol or drugs were involved.

But Rory Ayers was certain.

He knew his daughter.

Dierdre hadn't come home. No, she wasn't a disgruntled teenager defying her family. She was a solid young woman who intended to finish her college degree when classes resumed in the fall.

She didn't have a boyfriend they didn't like or trust. Indeed, they liked Gary Boynton a lot. He was courteous and respectful; he understood family. Dierdre had been with him, but they'd had their own cars that night, and she'd headed home and . . .

She'd never made it.

Just an hour ago — while Colleen and Jackson had been on their way to the Ayerses' house — Dierdre's car had been found in a ditch. The tech department had traced the location through her cell phone. Of course, first responders had feared the worst.

But Dierdre Ayers had not been in the car. The search party scoured the area for miles and found no sign of her.

Her car was now with the Krewe forensic team.

"There's a man in custody now," Jackson said as they stood at the back door. "He had another young woman in his basement. But he could have taken Dierdre last night and . . ."

His words trailed off, and he turned to look at her before continuing. "She was on her way here, but you're not getting anything at all. So, I imagine she is nowhere near the house, and you're not getting any echoes of her having been here and taken from here?"

Colleen shook her head. "She never made it home. And whoever took her, they made sure they got to her before she was close to the house."

He nodded. "I'll go in and tell her parents we're going to go through the traffic cams again, and we will figure out what happened. I'll meet you in the car. I've made arrangements to set you up with someone else who is excellent at finding people."

"Oh?" she asked.

So far, she'd only been on assignment with Jackson, learning the ropes. Learning how to be Krewe.

Obviously, one could not tell most people that ghosts often helped lead them in the right direction, or even sometimes explained what had happened in a boggling case. Not that it usually worked out quite so easily, but the dead could be extremely helpful.

"Go back to the SUV. My physical notes on the victims are in a folder on the back seat. Have a look at everything we know, which is not much different than what's in the media," Jackson said.

She nodded and went around the backyard to where Jackson's black SUV was parked. She retrieved the folder, took a seat in the front, and looked through the information.

Two women were dead.

Emily Watkins, twenty-three and a dance instructor, had disappeared on her way home from the studio. She didn't drive into downtown Richmond but took public transportation instead. They had checked all kinds of cameras, and the police had asked the media for help by putting her picture out there.

She had been found in a forest at the base of the Blue Ridge Mountains, in a pine box. At the time, it had seemed an isolated case. Friends, clients, everyone had been questioned. But during that investigation, the first letter had arrived at the newspaper.

It had been created with block letters, handwritten, no return, posted from Maryland.

And it had read: "She's with me now. Embraced by love."

A week later, Lainie Nowak had disappeared from a suburb of Richmond. Police investigated, moving more quickly. But no leads were found.

Another letter arrived with the same exact message.

The Krewe had been called in, and ever since, they'd been working tightly with local law enforcement.

A Krewe member who owned a highly skilled search and rescue dog had found Lainie.

She had also been buried in a pine box, twenty miles from the first victim, in a deeply wooded section of forest.

A man named Carver had appeared on a list of people wanted for sexual harassment charges. She knew he'd just been one of many on the list before Jackson and the Krewe had been visited by a friend.

That wasn't in the report.

The friend wasn't living.

The friend had seen Carver drag a woman back into his house.

They had an area.

So, agents had gone out.

And thanks to Sergeant Parker, a girl had been found. Alive.

Colleen winced suddenly. Jackson was going to put her with Mark Gallagher and his dog, Red.

Great.

She sincerely doubted she'd simply be accepted by a seasoned agent who would surely resent her and possibly be skeptical about her "hearing."

But it would be what it would be. She had desperately wanted to work with Jackson Crow and his special unit. They were supposed to be experts on cults and strange rites and crimes that were being committed by those who believed or pretended to believe in strange practices.

Because of course, if you saw the dead

and admitted it, most people would lock you up rather than make use of the ability.

Colleen leaned back for a minute, closing her eyes. She had known forever that she wanted to be in the FBI. And since she had first heard the rumors about the elite Krewe of Hunters unit — also called the ghost busters unit by some — she knew she wanted to be in the Krewe and work for Jackson Crow. There was nothing else to do with a talent like hers other than embrace it, and hopefully, use it to save lives.

Her eyes were still closed when something suddenly slammed against the car door. Training and instinct kicked in, and Colleen drew her weapon.

She saw the giant head of a dog in the window and a man behind the canine.

The man opened the car door; she still held her Glock.

He didn't appear to be pleased. He was tall with rugged shoulders, a man with a squared jaw and eyes so dark blue they almost appeared black.

He was quick to snap at her.

"Whatever the hell you do, Special Agent Law, do not shoot my dog!"

So, this was him. Special Agent Mark Gallagher. And Red.

The dog was wagging his tail. Colleen slid

her Glock back in her holster as she stepped out of Jackson's vehicle and lowered herself to pet the dog.

She forced a sweet smile, scratching the dog's ears and saying softly, "Well, Red, at least I believe you and I will get along."

Gallagher ignored that.

"Are you up to speed on this thing?" he asked.

"I am. And you?"

"Indeed I am. My partner and I just . . . Never mind. You're caught up. It's been a hell of a long day. And it's only going to get longer." He looked her up and down for a moment, frowning. "You're ready for this kind of thing?"

"I graduated head of my class," she informed him.

"Good for you. But that's the academy. This is real life — and death."

"Then maybe we should move since we'd like this to end in life for Dierdre Ayers," she said sweetly.

He turned away from her. "I'm going to let Jackson know we're on our way out."

"But we don't know where —"

"Yeah, we do. We have Red and . . . your ears. And hundreds of square miles to cover as quickly as possible. Let's move."

She followed him, gritting her teeth.

At least the dog was going to be a bearable partner.

CHAPTER TWO

The Blue Ridge Mountains and the valleys surrounding them were beautiful. Mark and Colleen traveled through an area where trees rustled in a gentle breeze; the forest floor was soft and redolent and rich with wild brush and earth. Birds always chirped, and not too far away, hikers enjoyed the natural beauty of the forest.

They had started off mostly in silence as they drove. While Mark believed the killer would pick a different place to bury the body of a new victim, he had initially tried the areas where the first two young women had been found. But Red hadn't reacted. He started in the southwest and stopped the car every five miles. They would leave the car and walk for a few minutes, and then try again.

On the one hand, it was awkward.

His new partner didn't talk a lot.

On the other hand, it was a blessing. He

was lost in his own thoughts. At headquarters, and on the streets, other Krewe agents were searching down anything that had resembled a lead. They were talking with Dierdre's boyfriend, school friends, friends and associates of her parents — anyone who might have seen or heard anything that would suggest she had been followed previously, who might tell them about anyone with whom she might have had a run-in.

Jackson and Angela had gone to the hospital in hopes they might be able to speak with Sally Smithson, and Ragnar had gone to interrogate Carver.

Mark glanced at his new partner as he carefully drove over rough roads that were off the beaten path. She might have been twenty-five, five-five in height, and a hundred and ten pounds. She was a green-eyed redhead with her hair tied back in a severe braid, almost as if she feared she might not be taken seriously if it were free around her face.

She studied the road as they traveled, pausing now and then to stroke Red.

The dog liked her. And Mark usually considered Red to be a good judge of character. He realized he was jaded on this case.

But he had been the one to dig up the last

victim, with Red's help, of course. And now . . .

He wanted it stopped; he wanted the woman to be found alive, and he wanted the killer — or killers — locked away for life.

He wanted to find Dierdre Ayers as they had so thankfully found Sally Smithson.

Quickly.

Still alive.

Colleen Law was raw. A beginner. And he didn't feel this was a case in which he should be teaching a rookie the ropes.

They were almost due west of Richmond, and he was barely traveling at three miles an hour when she suddenly said, "Stop!"

He glanced at her, frowning. She set a hand on his arm and repeated her command.

"Stop!"

He braked the car and looked at her. He'd been glad she hadn't been a chatterbox, but a little more than one word repeated was sometimes good too.

The road here was paved but poorly kept. Few people traveled this way as the road led to nothing but forest trails used by bird-watchers and nature lovers.

There was a little clearing to one side of the road, overgrown — a lightly used access entrance to the forest.

"I've stopped," Mark said.

Colleen looked at him. "I heard her," she said seriously.

The dog hadn't reacted.

"If you want to look here, we can look here," he said. "But Red —"

He'd barely said the dog's name before the animal started to bark.

Mark opened his door and got out of the car. Red hopped out after him, barking and staring into the dense growth of brush and trees.

Colleen Law was already out, looking southward from the clearing.

Red took off in that direction.

"Follow him!" Mark said, reaching into the back seat of his car for the shovel he'd been keeping there.

Colleen took off.

She could move, he thought. At least she was agile and swift.

He hurried after the dog and Colleen. Red had paused about twenty feet in. Tangled vines covered a lot of the floor. Colleen, he was glad to see, had no trouble weaving her way over them.

"Hurry! I can hear her!" she called back to him.

He hurried. He thought they would burst

into a clearing and maybe see where the earth had been disturbed.

But Red and Colleen stopped in the middle of a narrow trail strewn with pebbles and debris.

He stopped too.

Twilight was upon them, the sky torn apart by streaks of deep mauve and navy with the yellow of the sunlight fading quickly.

It was still a beautiful place, perhaps more so in the eerie light.

Red barked, standing in the path, whining then pawing at the earth.

After drawing out his phone and hitting the powerful flashlight beam on the path, Mark could see the earth had been disturbed. Vines and leaves and broken branches had been pulled back over it.

He set his phone on the ground with the beam expanding to light the area where Red pawed at the earth. He carefully dug with the shovel. And he wondered if a young woman would be in a pine box beneath the earth, and if so, was there enough air left in that box to allow the possibility that she might be alive?

As if she had read his mind, Colleen said with certainty, "She is alive!"

He didn't glance her way. He was beginning to doubt anyone could be alive beneath the earth here. The boxes the killer had used had been crude; pine barely nailed together. No one could live long if the wood had broken, if dirt had rushed in, if their airways had been filled with earth.

Mark hit something with the shovel.

He dropped the shovel and fell to the ground, clawing at the dirt and leaves, aware his new young partner was doing the same.

They saw a broken piece of wood first, jutting out of the earth.

"Colleen —"

"Already calling it in," she said.

She'd been prepared, her phone ready, even while she'd continued digging with one bare hand.

He had to admit he had been skeptical. For weeks now, he had sought out victims in densely wooded sections of the Blue Ridge Mountains and the surrounding valleys.

That morning, he and Ragnar had been lucky. They'd found Sally Smithson alive. But out here, in the forest, when the killer had finished with his victim and left her in the earth to die . . .

Dierdre had just been taken last night.

So, this was different.

The killer usually played with his victims

for several days before killing them.

Out here . . . both previous victims found buried had been dead.

"There's no chance," he said softly. "The structure of the box is compromised."

"No, get her out!" Colleen insisted, heedless of the dirt and bracken on the forest floor as she dug desperately to free the woman from her shallow grave.

The top of the box had been severely damaged. Mark reached a point where he could drag the young woman out and he did so. He laid her flat and hunkered down to the ground beside her to first roll her over his knee and thump on her back to clear her mouth and nose of dirt and debris. He then stretched her out to begin artificial respiration, and prayed that for once they might be successful.

He hesitated for a second to take a long deep breath while fighting a feeling of hopelessness. He could feel no pulse. He wasn't a doctor, but she'd been in the earth breathing dirt for too long.

"Don't quit!" Colleen snapped. "Or else move and I'll —"

He ignored her tone of voice and went back to his actions, not taking the time to inform her he couldn't give anyone air if he didn't have it himself.

Colleen fell to her knees on the other side of the woman, nodding to him. He nodded briefly in return. She counted, and working as a team, they kept up the resuscitation efforts.

He prayed help would come soon; he believed it would. First responders across the area had been put on alert.

As she counted and he breathed again, he finally heard a siren coming closer. He knew it hadn't been long at all, given their location in the forest. It had just seemed like forever.

Paramedics arrived along with police cars and a black SUV Mark knew to be Jackson Crow's. Jackson had parked down the trail. The roads here were tight, and Mark knew he wanted to leave plenty of room for the forensic team that would arrive.

Mark stood and watched as the paramedics rushed in and began working on the woman. His new partner next to him allowed the paramedics plenty of room.

The first paramedic on the scene had immediately taken Mark's role. Her partner, a slim, wiry man in his early forties, took Colleen's place, and he was the one to say, "Let's get her in the ambulance."

"There's hope?" Mark asked.

"Yeah, she has a faint pulse, and yeah,

she's breathing, but . . . yeah," the first paramedic said.

Other paramedics were rushing in with a stretcher.

"We need to get her on a respirator stat," the woman continued.

Mark watched the paramedics work; they were competent and fast.

"You two did well," the woman called over her shoulder. Dierdre Ayers was already on the stretcher with the paramedics working over her. One was on the phone, speaking with the doctor at the closest hospital, who was waiting to take over.

Colleen remained silent next to him.

Red was sitting by her feet.

Jackson had been right, he thought grudgingly. Maybe Red would have found the exact place anyway. But . . .

Colleen had found the place to dig. She had "heard" the voice in the forest.

But he still wasn't sure about her. He'd learned she was just out of the academy. And her manner, in his mind, bordered on rude. Though he considered perhaps she was quiet because she was listening to something he couldn't hear himself.

Did it matter? Dierdre Ayers might live!

Jackson Crow came along the winding trail, looking around the area.

"Forensics are on the way," he said. "And I have the McFadden brothers tag teaming to make sure she's guarded through the night at the hospital."

He was silent for a minute.

"Two for two," he said, looking at Mark. Then he turned to Colleen. "You heard her?" he asked.

"I heard her," Colleen said softly. "But Red found the place. Mark got her out quickly. The lid on the box had crashed in and . . . I hope she makes it. She wasn't breathing when we got her out."

"She is breathing now," Jackson said. "Good work, you two — sorry, Red. Good work, you three."

Red barked an acknowledgment.

Mark turned to Jackson. "Were you able to get anything from Sally Smithson? Was she alone in the basement last night? Could Carver have done this — taken and buried Dierdre immediately? That's not the way he's been working. The women are missing, and when we find them, the medical examiners suggest they were kept for at least a day or even days before being buried."

"The doctors only let me speak with Sally for a few minutes; they have her sedated because she's still in a lot of pain. She remembers she was at a stop sign, and someone came to her window, crying for help. She opened the car door and a hood went over her head. She told me Carver wore a mask when he came down to the basement. She wouldn't recognize him if she saw him. I have Angela at the hospital still. She'll stay overnight in Sally's room and be there when she wakes up."

Angela Hawkins Crow was Jackson's wife — and his second-in-command. She was among the first six investigators Adam Harrison had pulled together to form the Krewe of Hunters.

Angela was a beautiful blonde woman who could be as fierce as a tiger. If she was with Sally and the McFadden brothers were watching over the hallways, Sally was safe.

"We know Dierdre was taken last night. Her car was found in a ditch. And she was buried here," Mark said. "We got Carver sometime right after noon, so . . . could Carver have done this? The timing may be possible — I'm not even sure how long someone could breathe in that kind of a coffin — but . . . why? Doesn't fit the way the killer has been working," he added, shaking his head. "Did Ragnar get anything out of Carver? Or did Carver lawyer up?"

"Not yet — on both. Ragnar said Carver is playing with the questioning. Enjoying it.

But he's letting it go on, and he hasn't called his lawyer. Eventually, Ragnar will hit the right button. Carver will give up something," Jackson said. "You two should head back in." He looked at Colleen and then Mark. "And maybe shower. Mark, give Red the biggest steak bone out there." He turned to Colleen. "Special Agent Law, you are an amazing addition to our Krewe. Get some sleep tonight." He turned back to Mark. "Get some rest. You had one hell of a day. In this business, a damned good day."

"If Dierdre comes to —" Mark began.

"I'll be there," Jackson assured Mark. "Angela is with Sally. I'll take the night shift with Dierdre. Get some sleep. There's nothing else anyone can do right now."

"I want to speak with Carver," Mark said.

Jackson nodded. "Tomorrow morning. You and Colleen can go in."

"Ragnar —"

"We'll keep the three of you on this. There are still too many questions for us to let go," Jackson said. "For now, go home. Start fresh in the morning with Sally and then Carver. Go — I'll meet up with the forensic team."

Mark looked at Colleen Law.

"Good night, sir," she said, turning to walk past Jackson through the trail toward the car.

Dusk had become darkness. But while the ambulance was gone, Jackson's car lights were on — as were those of the forensic team that was arriving.

They made it back to the car. Mark lifted a hand to acknowledge the members of the Krewe forensic team who were hurrying out of their vehicles and toward him.

"Just down the trail," he said.

No one stopped to talk.

Red raced ahead of him, as if he had listened to every word Jackson had said and was ready for his steak bone and a good night's sleep.

Colleen entered the passenger's side of the car after opening the rear door for Red.

Mark slid into the driver's seat.

Colleen didn't speak. She looked ahead. But Red pushed his nose between the bucket seats and she turned to scratch his head.

"You are an amazing dog!" she told him.

Mark wasn't sure if a dog could smile, but if one could, Red was smiling.

After a minute, she said softly, "She's alive."

"Maybe she'll stay that way. Maybe she won't suffer any brain damage," he said.

Colleen glanced at him. "She's alive," she said. "And you and your partner rescued another woman today. You should be pleased."

"I should be."

"But you're not."

He inhaled and released a breath. "No. I am pleased. Relieved."

"But you don't think it's over."

He shrugged. "This started almost a month ago. Of course, we weren't called in at first. But when there was a second victim —"

"You found her."

"Red found her. We questioned dozens of people, checked every possible traffic cam. But the kidnapper-slash-killer seems to know he can be caught that way." He shook his head. "Take Sally. The last video showed her car leaving the highway and heading toward her house. They couldn't tell if she had still been driving it at that point. And all Sally could tell Jackson was someone had used the ploy they needed help. And —"

"The letters. The letters to the paper. No one received one of those letters on Dierdre, right?"

"No. That's one of the reasons I'm afraid we're dealing with more than one person. The pine box was the same, but the killer usually kept his victims. The timing is improbable, but it's not impossible. Dierdre was taken and then almost immediately put in the box. And there was no letter — not that we know about, at any rate."

"How could there be? The Postal Service is great, but no regular letter could have been written last night and arrived already."

" 'She's with me now. Embraced by love,' " Mark quoted.

"Right," Colleen said. "I know serial killers tend to receive monikers, but this one seems cruel — to the family and to those left behind. We're living in the age of social media. And once something starts . . .'"

Mark knew even the media were trying to make sure the killer was referred to as "The Embracer."

But they often slipped and referred to him as "The Lover."

"This is four," Mark said. "We have Carver, but . . ."

"If Carver isn't The Embracer," Colleen started, "and there is someone else out here, and if he sticks to his present schedule, he'll kidnap another woman within a few days."

"So, we're staying on it," Mark said.

"You and Ragnar work great together. I'm sorry you're being saddled with a rookie agent," she said, shaking her head.

"You have your special talent."

"But then all Krewe agents have a special

talent," she said.

"True, but Jackson told me you have special hearing. With your mind?"

She shrugged. "I don't know. Of course, my parents had my ears checked out; they sent me to therapy. There's nothing different about my hearing."

"But you can hear the living and the dead?"

"Yeah."

"And you can tell the difference?"

She winced. "Most of the time. I mean, we both know that sometimes, the soul or the 'ghost' remains for one reason or another after death. Sometimes, maybe, there are echoes that remain? But yes, I usually know if we're going to find someone living — or dead."

"That is unique," Mark acknowledged. "Of course, the problem here is whoever is doing this, there are acres upon acres of places to bury a body. Whoever is orchestrating this —"

"You think it's orchestrated?" she asked curiously. "Carver could have done this. As we've established, the timing isn't the same, but he *could* have done it. The pine box was the same, right? I didn't see any mention of the boxes in the file. Were they the same?"

"Yes and no. We found wood in Carver's

basement, but nothing assembled — just a pile that might have been for anything. Pine is available at any lumberyard. Nails are available at any hardware store. I don't know yet if the construction will prove to be different. Forensics will tell us more."

"No fingerprints on anything. The kidnapper-slash-killer always wore gloves."

"Right."

They had reached the Beltway, and Mark turned off to drive toward their headquarters, where he assumed their new agent had her car.

But she told him, "Sorry. I didn't drive in today. But I am just a few blocks from our offices. I mean, you could still drop me at work, and I can walk, but —"

"Just give me your address."

She did.

"Don't drive in tomorrow. And be ready at seven," Mark told her.

"Yes, sir!" She turned to study him. "Look, I'm sorry you don't like me —"

"I don't like or dislike you. I don't know you."

"You're a bad liar for an agent," she said. "It's okay. I don't like you either. You're an arrogant ass. But at least I like Red. And whether you're okay with it or not, Jackson has said I'm on this. With you. So, please quit treating me as if I'm an errant school-kid."

"I am not treating you like a schoolkid. I'm telling you that you need to be ready. I want to be out at the hospital and then the jail where they're holding Carver by eight. All right?"

They'd reached her address. He pulled to the side of the road. She lived in new apartments that had been designed to resemble the old row houses in Alexandria.

"I will be standing on the sidewalk right here at 7:00 a.m. sharp!" she assured him.

They were both silent then.

Red whined.

Colleen turned to the dog. "I'm sorry, Red! You're such a sweetheart. I'm sorry."

"You're sorry I'm an arrogant ass, I take it?" Mark muttered.

"Well, you are."

He lowered his head, surprised he was smiling. He shook his head.

"I'm sorry."

"What?" she asked, frowning and startled. "You're sorry you're an arrogant ass?"

He smiled grimly. "Yes. I'm sorry if I've been an ass," he said. "I found the second victim, dead in a pine box. And when we got Carver today. Well, I thought we had the bastard who's been torturing and killing young women so cruelly. And now . . ."

"I . . . Yeah. I get it. Okay. I'm sorry too."

He laughed. "So, you are sorry I'm an ass?" he asked dryly.

"No, sorry for calling you one to your face," she told him. But she smiled. "Look, I know I'm a rookie, and you've been with the Krewe a few years, and before that —"

"US Marshals Service," he said.

She pointed to herself. "Orlando Police. Does that help any?"

"And first in your class at the academy."

She nodded, stroking Red's ears. "Yeah. I've known since I was a kid I . . . I wanted to make being weird pay off."

"That's the way it was with many of us."

"You knew since you were a kid too?" she asked him.

He nodded. "What happened when you were young?"

She hesitated and then shrugged. "First, I was just in the park across from my house, and I heard a woman screaming for help. She was all trussed up and stuffed in a guy's trunk. Turned out our friendly neighbor was planning on disposing of his girlfriend. But she lived, and everyone wanted to know how I knew. They said I couldn't have heard her, because she was unconscious. I was a kid and I felt like a freak. My parents were great though, and it wasn't long before I discovered my siblings also had unique talents. They told me whatever it was, I'd saved her life, and doing that had been the best thing ever. Then . . ."

"Then?"

She looked at him.

"I was at a bus bench by the cemetery, and Mrs. Glenn — who had died the month before — asked me if I could hear the dead as well as the living. She wanted me to tell her son she'd left him a stack of bonds, but no one had found them because she'd hidden them in her mattress. Luckily, her son hadn't emptied the house yet to sell it. It was easier for me that time. I said his mom had told me about not trusting banks, and she'd put little treasures in her mattress." She took a deep breath. "So, I went to college and majored in criminology, worked for the Orlando Police for three years, then applied to the FBI and went to the academy. Like I said, I'm sorry I'm new and raw, and you're stuck with me."

"We all start somewhere," Mark murmured.

Okay, he *felt* like an ass now.

It was just at first . . .

He'd found the woman in the pine box, he and Ragnar had found Sally Smithson, and while they weren't supposed to let their feelings interfere . . .

Jackson had told them all they were no good if they lost their humanity.

And he was aggravated because they just didn't know if Carver had been guilty of all the kidnappings and burials, or . . .

If someone was still out there.

As if she'd read his mind, she said, "Maybe it was Carver. And maybe it is over."

"I wish I had that feeling," he said.

"Gut instinct can be amazing. It's not just a Krewe thing — gut instinct is shared by many law enforcement officers, not just the weird ones," she said lightly, then added, "Tomorrow, I'll just observe and be a good and silent rookie."

He shook his head. "Gut instinct, huh? Is something else going on?" He frowned. "Do you read minds?"

She laughed. "I should say yes to that. But no — I just hear people when they're crying out."

"The living and the dead."

"The living and the dead."

"Well, rookie, you don't have to stay silent. But it might be good if you were to observe. Or . . ." he trailed off as a thought struck him.

"Or?"

"Or maybe I'll have you go in with him."

"Oh, no, seriously, I wouldn't presume —"

Mark shook his head again. "No. I'm wondering how he would react to a woman." He studied her. Of course, he'd first noted she was attractive, and like many young female agents, she seemed determined to play down her looks. But with her eyes, the perfect oval of her face, and a waving fall of red hair . . .

She'd be a beautiful victim in Carver's mind.

And that could be helpful.

"Wear something a bit feminine and wear your hair down," he told her.

She stared at him with surprise for a minute and then realized his intention. She didn't balk. "That could be interesting," she said. "I'll even put on makeup."

"I'll talk to Ragnar tonight. We'll send you in first."

"Got it. I'll be out here at seven. Red!" She turned to pet the dog good-night. "You're a wonderful partner," she told him.

Red woofed his agreement.

She got out of the car. Mark leaned to speak to her out the passenger-side window.

"Hey!" he called.

"Yeah?"

"I'm glad you had supportive parents and siblings."

She smiled back at him. "Thanks." She started to walk back to the car. "How did you first know you wanted to be in law enforcement?"

He winced inwardly.

"That's a story for another time. I'll see you in the morning," he told her.

He revved the car as she walked up the path to her town-house-style apartment.

It was a story he seldom shared.

A shower!

Colleen felt the spray of steaming water rush over her, and it felt delicious. She hadn't realized just how much dirt she had been wearing until she watched it slide down the drain.

She hadn't realized, either, that her hair had been studded with leaves.

Mark Gallagher hadn't mentioned that.

But he probably hadn't noticed. He had apparently — no, obviously — thought of her as little more than an annoyance at first, something like a gnat buzzing around his head.

But he'd been almost decent toward the end.

She hadn't known Mark before, as she had

yet to meet many of the agents. They tended to be all over the country, and sometimes, they were even asked to help on bizarre cases in Europe and beyond.

But she'd heard about Mark.

She'd walked into Angela Hawkins Crow's office one day when the Krewe's second-in-command had been on the phone with him. He had just solved a case out in Denver, brought it in without further casualties and left solid evidence for the prosecutors.

"That was Mark," Angela had explained quickly. "We're lucky to have him. The man was scouted by the pros when he was playing college football. He could be making a fortune now, but instead he's with us."

She didn't remember what else she had done that day. She'd spent a week in the tech department and then the forensic department.

And then today . . .

She was grateful, but she was also nervous. She was on a major case, and most of all, she was grateful her "hearing" had allowed them to save a life.

But now . . .

Once out of the shower, scrubbed and clean, she slid into a nightgown, curled up on her bed, and turned on the television.

Carver was, in her mind, barely a human

being. But he was a sick one beyond any doubt. And she was going to be sent in to lure him into talking.

Scary.

Jensen, her scruffy-looking rescue cat, hopped up on the bed.

"You smell that dog on me, huh? Hmm, maybe on the clothing I just took off, since I'm squeaky-clean after that shower!" she said to the cat. "The dog's cool — super-cool. I think you would like him. And I'll bet he'd like you, even though you're a cat!"

Jensen had always gotten along with dogs; both Colleen's sister and her brother were dog people. Jensen got along with Megan's shepherd and Patrick's wolfhound. But then, Jensen was a huge cat, mostly Maine coon, and very above it all when it came to causing trouble.

"Jensen, I'm a little scared," she told the cat.

He purred as if he understood and curled against her.

Animals, she thought, made the best companions.

Red was better than Mark Gallagher. Red just wagged his tail and sought out her attention.

Mark, on the other hand . . .

He was a tall man, broad-shouldered, with

a fine, strong jaw, deep blue eyes, and dark hair. She could see that he wanted to question Carver himself. She was sure he had a way of looking at a suspect that played on a man's nerves.

He'd managed to look at her in a way that did a number on her nerves.

Yet she was curious why he had possibly given up a career that could have left him set for life. He obviously cared about the work.

About people.

As she fell asleep, she found herself wondering just what had happened with him, how he had discovered he could see the dead when most of the world couldn't.

She fell asleep wondering about the man's story.

And her dreams were bizarre. She saw him without his typical dark suit. She'd had a glimpse — just a glimpse, but still a glimpse — of his ability to smile.

She realized as much as she had disliked his attitude, there was something about him that drew her and made her want more.

No.

Work the case with him. That's what they did at the Krewe. They worked unusual cases.

She needed to stay the hell away from

him. Let him cast his attitude on another poor soul. At least the dog was great.

She woke to her phone ringing, her memory touched by strange dreams.

It was his voice that came to her over her cell.

"It's six. Just making sure you're going to be ready."

"I will be ready," she told him. "Outside, on the sidewalk, at precisely seven." She gritted her teeth and added lightly, "And ready and able to accept the command of my senior officer."

She hung up before he could reply.

Chapter Three

Mark had asked Colleen to appear feminine and attractive.

She had certainly managed that.

Nothing overboard. But her hair was in a sweep around her face and shoulders with a shimmer like a sunset. She'd chosen a skirt suit with a white blouse that offered a slight fringe around the neckline — one that dipped a little, but wasn't overly provocative. Her heels added to the athletic shape of her calves while still being moderate. She had managed everything he had envisioned; she was extremely attractive while still giving the appearance of a professional at work.

Red woofed a greeting and his tail wagged so hard it was almost a lethal weapon.

Naturally, she greeted the dog first.

Then she looked at Mark with a little frown.

"Is this outfit all right?" she asked him, indicating her clothing with a sweep of her hand as she slid into the passenger's seat.

"It's . . . perfect," he said honestly.

"Oh. Good," she said, looking ahead. She glanced his way. "Any instructions for me while I'm speaking with him?"

"I'd wanted to go to the hospital first, but they've asked us to come a bit later. I don't want to waste any of the morning." He paused for a minute, knowing the woman's health came first, but wishing they could talk to Sally before seeing Carver.

She just might be able to give them something that could help.

"Mark?" Colleen asked.

"Right. Sorry. Don't accuse him of being The Embracer at first. All we have on him right now is that he kidnapped a woman and was holding her prisoner in his basement. Talk to him about Sally. Why did he take her? What was his intent? Gradually ask him about other women in his life."

They reached the jail where Carver was being held. Ragnar was waiting for them at the entry, and he nodded as Mark introduced him to Colleen.

She offered Ragnar a hand. "Pleased to meet you, Special Agent Johansen."

"Ragnar. Please, we're informal when it's just us. Just call me Ragnar. Yeah, I know — interesting name. Norwegian parents," Ragnar said.

"I think it's a cool name," she told him, smiling.

Ragnar smiled back and then looked at Mark.

"I take it we're sending her in first?"

"You agree?"

"Oh, yeah. I tried talking to him last night. He ignored me and acted as if he was the injured party. We have about an hour, then he goes to arraignment."

"Let's do it then," Mark said.

Red followed them in.

Red had the right credentials to get in anywhere.

Their weapons were checked, and they were brought to an observation room. Carver had already been brought in. Mark was glad to see his cuffs were chained through metal loops at the table where he had been seated.

"Any last notes?" Colleen asked, looking from Ragnar to Mark.

Ragnar glanced at Mark.

"I told her to talk about his kidnap victim and women in general," Mark said.

Ragnar nodded.

"He may decide he needs more attention and confess," Ragnar said, smiling grimly at Colleen. "But that's doubtful. Still, you might just throw him off his game."

The deputy at the door opened it for Colleen; she thanked him and walked in.

Mark watched Carver's eyes light up as he saw Colleen enter. He straightened in his chair.

"My, my!" Carver said. "Who do we have here?"

"Special Agent Colleen Law, Mr. Carver. FBI. How are you doing? Have they been treating you fairly?"

Carver's brows shot up. He lifted his hands. "I have been more comfortable."

"I'm sorry. I'm actually a guest here. I have no control over the cuffs," she told him.

"Well, at least you are comfort for the eyes!" he told her.

"Thank you. Well, of course, I'm here to talk about Sally Smithson."

"Ah! You're a friend of hers?"

"No. I've never met her."

"Then what is there to talk about?" Carver asked, a grin on his face, as if he were especially clever. Then he leaned forward. "She asked me to take her, you know."

"She asked you? You were friends?"

He shrugged. "Women like Sally . . . so pretty, so sweet. And always with the wrong guys. She was a kinky one. Wanted all kinds of rough play!"

71

"She did?"

"Oh, you bet! Hey, more women than you would imagine like it rough. Here's the difference: I really care about them. I'm going to get out of here, and then . . . well, you'll see. Sally will want to run right back to me."

"That's not what she's said," Colleen said, grimacing.

"What? She's still al— I mean, she's talking to you? Lies, all lies," Carver said.

"Well, it's good to hear your side."

"She dated a real jerk. He left her. I picked her up. She wanted a man who would love her!" Carver spoke and then inched closer to Colleen. "I love them, and I embrace them!"

"Them?" Colleen asked.

He started laughing. "You want to know if I'm The Embracer?" he asked.

"Are you?"

"I just love women. Really love them."

"But she was found in very bad shape — suffering!" Colleen said.

He waved a hand in the air. "I told you. She wanted it rough."

"Again, that's not what she says," Colleen told him, a certain sadness in her voice.

"It will be her word against mine," Carver said. "Sad! She's embarrassed. She doesn't want to tell the truth. You know how many women are bra-burning liberal bitches, screaming about men being awful creatures? She doesn't want any of that type coming after her! I helped her! I gave her the love she wanted!"

"Ah. You're a godsend to women who want it rough but don't want others to know."

"Exactly."

"How many women?"

"Oh, trust me, honey, there have been a few."

"And you embrace them all? But I'll bet there are others out there like you." Colleen asked the question in a teasing mode. She was almost coquettish.

"No one out there is just like me."

"Ah! So, you're saying you are The Embracer? The true one and only?"

"I'm not saying that. I'm saying there is no one quite like me. You should find out."

In the observation room, Mark turned to Ragnar.

"Maybe we should get her out now," he suggested.

"Soon — let's see her handle this," Ragnar said.

Mark knew Ragnar was right; she was a full-fledged agent. She could handle herself.

And she did.

73

"Oh, not me. I'm not . . . well, just not into that kind of thing. But I'd love to hear about the other women you've known."

He leaned back, smiling. "I don't kiss and tell."

"I see." Colleen stood up. "Well, thank you for speaking with me."

"You're leaving? Already?"

"Yes. We need to speak to another young woman. We found her in a pine box last night. She may have wanted it rough, but I don't think she liked the coffin at all. Hard to breathe, you know."

"What?" Carver demanded.

He was seriously ruffled.

And watching the man's reaction, Mark thought he had been taken off guard.

He hadn't known.

He wasn't the person who'd put Dierdre Ayers in the coffin.

"Yes, I guess you have a disciple," Colleen said. "Again, thank you for speaking with me."

She moved toward the door; the guard opened it for her.

And Carver screamed after her. "You're lying! There is no other! There's me, me, me! I give them love. I — Hey, come back! Come back!"

She turned to face him. "So, you are The

74

Embracer?" she asked softly.

"What? No! I told you — I give women what they really want."

Colleen simply shrugged and walked out.

"Wait!" Carver shrieked.

It was gratifying to watch the man strain against his cuffs.

And turn a mottled shade of angry red.

Too late. Colleen was already out of the interrogation room.

She met Mark and Ragnar just outside and looked through the one-way glass to observe him.

"Where do we go from here?" she asked them.

"We leave him to stew," Mark told her.

"I'm not sure I —"

"You did excellently," Ragnar said.

She looked at Mark.

"You really did," he agreed. He hoped his tone wasn't a grudging one.

She had done exactly what he'd asked of her.

"You're going in now, right?" Ragnar asked.

Mark debated what action to take. They could leave, and he could feel he was right. Carver was The Embracer.

The man had been angry someone else out there was putting women in boxes. He had almost confessed.

Maybe he could clinch it.

Mark nodded and left Ragnar, Colleen, and Red behind the glass, thanking the guard who opened the door for him.

"What the hell?" Carver said.

"Yeah, what the hell?" Mark echoed.

"Send the broad back in. Or the dog. The dog is probably smarter than any of you."

Mark shook his head. "I can't let Red in. He'd try to chew your face off. He knows you threatened to kill him."

"Right. A dog."

"You said he was smart."

"Smarter than you guys. That's not saying much."

"Smarter than you, since I'm just sitting in a chair, and you're cuffed to a table."

Carver shook his head. "I'll be out of here. Illegal entry."

"Probable cause," Mark said, smiling. "But, hey, you'll have your day in court. And I'm afraid the victim we found in your basement is not in love with you in any way. You will go down on a kidnapping charge."

"She wanted me."

"In your dreams. So, how many women have you killed?"

Carver leaned back. "You don't understand. I love them. Take the beauty who was just in here."

"My partner," Mark said.

"And you treat her like garbage. You think you're superior. I treat women like they're queens. I give them what they want. And I'd sure like to see her again."

"Wouldn't you, now? But that could be a problem. She's not a victim. She's not weak. She's not easily fooled."

"They can all be fooled," Carver said softly.

"What? Did you pull the 'I'm injured! I need help!' bit on them?" Mark asked.

"Trust me, they can all be fooled."

"I'll ask you again. How many did you kill?"

"Numbers . . . and I didn't kill any of them. I just loved them." He paused and smiled. "I embraced them with my love!"

"You're a hell of a liar."

"Am I? You haven't got anything on me. You found a woman in my basement. It's her word against mine."

Mark smiled and shrugged. "I think her word is going to ring true to a jury. And the pictures taken at the hospital will speak volumes. You need to make up your mind. You're either The Embracer, or a pathetic wannabe."

"I'm not a pathetic anything. Ask your

girlie out there!"

"I don't think she has much of an opinion of you."

"You didn't see her face up close and personal."

"She'd kick your ass, Carver. And you couldn't take that, could you? Being beaten silly by a woman."

Carver sat back. "No bitch kicks my ass!"

"So, you're just a wannabe."

"I didn't say that."

Mark shrugged. He started to rise, but Carver was speaking again, and it was strange because it seemed he was speaking aloud to himself, almost as if he had forgotten Mark was there.

"No one, no one, not the toughest guy in the world, is invulnerable. No one. And when it comes to a woman . . ." He stopped speaking, as though jolted by an invisible force. He looked at Mark and smiled. "You have no evidence against me," he said.

"Don't we?" Mark asked quietly.

Then he did rise to leave. And again, Carver was agitated, struggling against his restraints.

"A dog dies when it's shot!" he shouted.

Mark ignored him and kept heading for the door.

"You think you're something? FBI, all tall,

strong, and noble. Well, you can die too, and that jerk you were with can die and that woman, well . . . no one is invulnerable!"

Mark exited the room, thanking the guard again.

He looked at Ragnar and Colleen, who had witnessed the whole thing.

"Well, I do believe he is The Embracer," Mark said. "And that now he has at least one fan trying to follow in his footsteps."

Colleen was silent.

"What do you think?" he asked her.

"I don't know," she said. "He was certainly angry enough when we suggested he wasn't The Embracer, but I don't know . . . I guess I veer toward him being the killer. The original killer, at any rate."

"Maybe Sally and Dierdre can tell us something," Mark said grimly. "We can hope."

"Maybe," Ragnar agreed. "I've spoken to Jackson; he said we're clear to go in now. He stopped by and spoke with the doctors. It's fine if we question them, just so long as we are gentle and quick."

"Let's do it," Mark said.

As they thanked the guard again and turned to leave, Red — who usually stayed right at Mark's heels — pulled back. He looked at the door to the interrogation room and growled.

"Red," Mark said softly.

The dog let out one more growl, a sound that was something like a dog's way of voicing disgust, and then followed Mark obediently.

They retrieved their weapons and signed out.

"Meet you at the hospital," Ragnar said, waving as they headed to the parking lot.

"See you there," Mark agreed.

Colleen and Red followed silently as they walked to his car. Red hopped into the back. Colleen slid into the passenger's seat. There was a strange look on her face.

"What?" he asked.

"Thank you."

"For?"

She glanced at him. Her expression was rueful.

"Telling him I could kick his ass."

Mark grinned. "You probably could." He sobered. "He did say one thing that was true. A bullet can bring down a dog, a woman, or a man. We're all vulnerable."

She was quiet just a second. "Trust me to have your back," she said softly. "I may be new, but I can still have your back."

He nodded. "Right. I believe you."

"More," she said. "Don't just believe me.

Trust me."

He smiled. "Yeah. Yeah, I believe you and trust you. So, we're solid. And we have Red."

"I'll have his back too," she promised solemnly.

Red barked as if he understood every word.

They'd reached the hospital. As they exited the car, Mark was surprised to realize he'd told her the truth.

She was new, she was raw.

And they'd only worked together for a night and a morning.

But he found himself thinking she was the real deal. And he had to admit, her talent was an exceptional one. He also had to admit he was glad she was working with them.

"Let's see what else we can find out," he said, and they walked toward the lobby.

Ragnar was okay, the dog was great, and Colleen was even beginning to find Mark bearable. She liked that he didn't rush in to say nothing would happen to her with him around. He had given her credit for being able to take care of herself.

Of course, Carver had been right.

No one was invulnerable.

"Divide and conquer?" Ragnar asked.

"Sure, divide and switch — going gently, of course," Mark said.

"Is Red allowed in the hospital?" Colleen asked.

"Red is a service dog. He can't go into surgery, but he's allowed to be with me," Mark said. He smiled at her. It was a good smile.

Okay, to his credit — he loved his dog.

"This hospital works with service dogs, especially in the kids' cancer ward," he told her. "When I can, I bring Red there. It's amazing how much a dog can do for a sick kid."

"That's great," she said. "So, what's the plan?"

"We'll talk to Dierdre and you take Sally," Mark said, looking at Ragnar.

Ragnar nodded.

Sally Smithson and Dierdre Ayers were both on the same floor of the hospital. The woman working security at the desk apparently knew Red. She greeted him happily, but then looked at the three of them. "Of course, you're not taking my favorite pooch anywhere he's not supposed to be, right?" she asked.

"Gloria, you know me better than that," Mark said.

"I do. I still have to ask," she said. She was wearing a uniform and had a friendly but no-nonsense look about her. "And you know I have to snap your pics for your name badges —"

"Yes, we know that too," Mark assured her.

They all handed over ID and stood to have their pictures taken for name badges.

Even Red got one for his collar.

"And, Gloria, the local police —" Ragnar began.

"They've had a man on duty all day, watching both rooms. Sally Smithson is in 407 and Dierdre Ayers is in 420."

"Thanks," Mark told her.

They headed for the elevator.

"You guys come here a lot?" she asked.

"Sadly," Ragnar said.

"Well, not so sadly," Mark said. He looked at Colleen and grimaced. "Better here than the morgue."

She nodded. "Right."

"I'm off to 407," Ragnar said.

Mark indicated room 420 to Colleen. He tipped his head to the uniformed officer who stood between the two rooms.

Evidently the cop knew Mark.

"You work closely with the police often?" she asked him.

He nodded. "I tend to work Northern Virginia, Delaware, and Southern Maryland. That's a lot of different police forces, but we wind up at various departments for task forces."

"Ah," Colleen murmured. She realized he had her curiosity. She didn't know where he'd come from originally. Or what had drawn him to the FBI and the Krewe of Hunters.

But now wasn't the time to be asking him questions.

A nurse came out of Dierdre's room as they approached it.

She smiled a little grimly.

"FBI?" she asked, and then frowned, looking down at Red.

"Yes," Mark said.

The nurse was confused. "The dog is FBI?"

"Yes, he is," Mark said. "Red has hospital clearance for regular rooms."

"Red saved the young woman's life," Colleen said.

"Oh! He finds people," she said. "Well, the doctors just warned Dierdre isn't to be worn out. You may speak with her, but please —"

"Oh, we won't upset her, I promise, and we'll be brief," Colleen said.

The nurse nodded. "Okay, then." She paused. "That is a beautiful dog!"

Red made a sound and wagged his tail. It was almost as if he was far too polite to bark loudly in a quiet hospital.

Colleen felt Mark's hand on her shoulder, indicating she should go in first.

She did so.

Dierdre Ayers was the only patient in the one-bed room. She was young, in her early twenties. Her dark hair had been washed and fell softly against her face.

Colleen wouldn't have recognized her as the woman they had rescued from a pine box the night before. She had only seen her covered in dirt.

She remained pale and ashen, and an oxygen tube was attached to her nostrils. But she managed a weak smile as Mark and Colleen entered. She lifted a hand before it fell back to the bed.

"Hi. This is Colleen Law, and I'm Mark Gallagher," Mark said. "We don't want to cause you stress, but we need to see you."

"You're the ones who saved me!" she said. "Thank you," she added in a whisper.

"We're thankful you're alive," Colleen said softly.

"But I wouldn't have been without you," she said. She frowned and then saw Red was by her side, wagging his tail but keeping his distance.

"I thought — I thought there had been a dog!" she said. "I thought maybe I'd been dreaming. I remember . . . darkness. And I couldn't breathe. I was choking."

"Colleen and Red found you," Mark said, his manner easy as he walked around the bed. "And we are so grateful you're alive. But we need your help. We're hoping you remember something, but we don't want to upset you. Do you remember much? How did you get into the box? I know people have already spoken with you, but I'd like you to close your eyes and try to remember."

Colleen glanced at Mark and continued, "We need to know everything, where you were and who you were with before this all started. We need you to think about anything you saw, heard, or even anything you smelled."

Red whined softly.

Dierdre seemed to know he was Mark's dog. She looked at him. "May I?" she asked.

"Red would be delighted," Mark assured her.

She sat up, reaching out for Red. The dog stood on his paws, and Dierdre wrapped her arms around his neck, heedless of the paws on her sheets. She closed her eyes as she did.

"I remember you," she whispered.

"And he remembers you," Mark assured her.

"We were out, Gary and I, as we often are. Not late; we'd just had dinner. I'm still living at home. And my parents worry. They love Gary because he is very respectful."

"What happened then?" Colleen asked. "Didn't Gary see you to the door?"

She shook her head. "We took two different cars."

"And then?" Colleen asked softly.

Dierdre shook her head. "The strangest thing is, I don't remember. I was driving home. It felt like I hit something and there was a man in the street. I thought I had hit him, and I jumped out of the car, and then there was something dark . . . that's all I remember! Well, that's not true. I remember waking up in the box in the pitch-darkness and screaming and screaming and banging and . . . The darkness was overwhelming."

"Any smells, any sounds, any anything?" Mark asked.

"I'm sorry," Dierdre said. She hesitated. "I hear the doctors and nurses talking. I heard you caught a man who was holding another missing woman. The Embracer. I guess he could have come after me while he had her in his basement?"

"Possibly. But the kidnapper and killer they call 'The Embracer' has always held only one woman at a time. This guy had a woman in his basement when you were kidnapped," Mark said.

"Well, still . . ."

"We just don't know," Colleen said gently. "We were hoping you could help. Any tiny thing helps. Even that you didn't see a man's face helps us know this person hides his identity when he's on the prowl. Your main job now is to get better."

"Thank you." Dierdre hesitated and looked from Colleen to Mark. "They haven't let my parents see me yet, and I haven't even been able to talk to Gary. Please . . ."

"I'm sure by tomorrow it will be fine," Mark said. "We'll assure them you're on your way to doing much better."

"Thank you. And thank you again for saving me," Dierdre added in a tremulous whisper. "They told me I would have been dead in just another few minutes. You were my miracle."

"We thank you," Mark said. "You were strong and resilient."

"And we're grateful! We love being your miracle," Colleen told her.

Red woofed.

"But it is important that if you remember anything, anything at all, you call us," Mark said, producing a card and putting it on her hospital tray.

Colleen set one of her cards next to Mark's.

"I would do anything to help you!" Dierdre said.

"You never know what you might eventually remember," Colleen said. "Not to worry — but something might just come to you."

"We'll bring Red back to see you," Mark promised. "Oh, and we're working as a bit of a team on this. We have several task force teams across the area, but Red, Colleen, and I are also working with my partner, Ragnar Johansen. He'll stop by in a minute to see you too. I hope that's all right."

Dierdre grinned and Colleen thought she was a pretty girl with a great smile when she let it through. It was tragic this had happened to her.

But she was alive.

"Ragnar?" Dierdre said. "Cool Viking name. Send him on in."

"Will do."

Mark turned toward the door. Red gave a final whine, nudged his head against Dierdre's hand, and quickly followed his master.

When they stepped into the hall, Ragnar was just coming out of the other room.

He and Mark had clearly worked together for a while; it seemed they could communicate silently because, as they met in the hallway, Mark said, "We didn't get much of anything either. Except we know how he got her. He set something on the road and made her think she might have hit him with her car."

"Same with Sally," Ragnar said. "We'll switch off."

"When we leave here, we'll let the hospital know they have our okay to let Gary and the parents in for Dierdre," Mark said.

"Right," Ragnar agreed. With a nod, he headed for Dierdre's room, as Mark, Colleen, and Red moved on to speak with Sally Smithson.

Sally was sitting up in bed. Despite what she had suffered, she appeared to have good color as if just one night of freedom had restored her.

She brightened seeing Mark and Red.

"Ragnar told me you'd stop by," she said. She reached for Red, who obligingly hurried over for a hug. Sally gave Colleen a quick smile, but her attention was on Mark. "The two of you — I don't know how you did it. It seems everyone thought that horrible man was some pillar of the community because he was helping out with kids' sports and . . . my God, the very thought terrifies me!"

"I'm so glad to see you're doing well," Mark told her. "And, Sally, this is Special Agent Colleen Law."

"Pleased to meet you," Sally said.

"I'm sorry. We're going to ask you to go over everything again," Colleen told her apologetically.

"It's okay. Ragnar told me the man — Carver is his real name, I guess — is claiming I wanted to be with him? That I was with him because I like it rough? I swear to you, I don't think it would be possible to hate anyone more. He . . . he drugged and abused me, and he meant to kill me!" Tears suddenly stung her eyes.

"You're safe now," Colleen said gently.

She nodded, looking away.

"Sally, I'm sorry," Mark added. "But the more you tell the story, the more you might remember little details that could help."

She shook her head, a hand on Red's soft fur as she stared out the window. "I don't get it. I just don't get it. You found me in his basement. After all he did . . . ." Her words choked off and she turned to stare at Mark. "And Ragnar told me what he said.

91

He's going to get a lawyer and try to make it out like I'm a horrible person, and he's innocent, and . . . that I wanted to be with him! That you had no right to burst into his house because it was an illegal entry —"

"He may have a lawyer, but we have lawyers too. And I don't think any jury will fall for anything he's saying," Mark assured her. He hesitated. "We heard you scream. Exigent circumstances," he added.

"You heard me scream?" she asked.

"Red, especially," Mark said.

They hadn't heard her scream, Colleen thought.

But they had known she was there. And the time it takes to do things by the book might mean the difference between life and death.

"Can you talk about how it happened?" Colleen asked her.

Sally sighed. "I was on my way home. I'd met friends for dinner in DC. I . . ." She paused. "I had a bad breakup about a month ago. Guy I'd dated forever. We disagreed over a few things, had a fight, and the next thing I knew, he'd moved to New York. So, friends were trying to make me feel better."

Mark was putting notes into his phone. "His name?" he asked.

"His name is Brant Pickering, but trust me Brant had nothing to do with this. I may be angry with him, but he's a great guy. He's a historian who writes wonderful books. So far, they've been on the history of DC and surrounding areas . . . well, I guess they'll be on the history of New York now. I don't hate him. I . . ."

"You still love him," Colleen said softly.

Sally nodded. "But now, even if I decided I could leave my job and family, I don't think he'd . . . I mean, how could anyone want me again?"

"Sally! No, no, no — horrible things were done to you. You didn't do horrible things. You're still you. And yes, you're going to need therapy, and I promise we will help you find support and more, but there is nothing wrong with you at all!" Colleen assured her. "I can only try to imagine how you feel, but I do know this — you're still you. Do not let that horrible man hold on to your mind, keeping you a prisoner for the rest of your life!"

Sally smiled at that, tears shimmering in her eyes again.

"I just feel so . . ."

"I believe it will be better when he's convicted," Mark assured her.

"Do you?" Sally whispered.

"Any man who doesn't want you because you were victimized by a monster isn't worthy of you," Mark said.

That brought a real smile to her lips and she nodded slowly. "You're right."

"Sally, please, I know it's hard, but we'd love to hear your story, from the beginning," Colleen said.

"I was driving home, heading past a patch of old farmland where the houses are all kind of far apart. I stopped because there was something in the middle of the road. I thought it was an animal, hurt, maybe dying. Then I thought it was a human being, and it was! But when I went to see if he was alive, he suddenly leapt up and slammed me against the hood. I must've gone out like a light and I woke up chained to a bed in a dark room. And I couldn't scream, and I couldn't move. Then he'd come, and he'd be wearing a bizarre black cowl and mask, and he'd give me water, but there was something in the water and . . . Oh, God! I wish I knew more. I wish I could help more!"

"We know where the basement is and it's been searched, and Carver has been arrested," Mark said. "Sally, you're going to be all right."

"Not if he gets off," she whispered.

94

"He won't get off," Mark said. "Excuse me a minute."

He nodded to Colleen and left the room, looking at his phone.

She guessed that meant she was to continue.

"You never saw his face?" Colleen asked.

"No." Sally let out a breath, shaking her head. "I never saw his face. I never saw much of anything; he kept it so dark down there. And he wore a hood, eyes cut out, that kind of thing."

"I understand. More details may come back to you in the days to come —"

"I wish they wouldn't!" Sally said fervently.

"I know, and again, I am so, so sorry. But remembering helps. Think about things you heard, things you felt, you smelled. It may help us determine who we're after now, and just how many victims Carver might have had. I know it's hard. We're grateful for anything at all."

Mark walked back into the room. "Sally, this is up to you, but there is someone here who would like to see you. I spoke with your nurse, and she thinks it might be good. But it's your decision."

"Who — Brant?" she whispered, amazed.

Mark nodded.

95

"I — I . . ."

She was going to burst into tears again. Colleen looked at Mark, who shrugged. She saw something in his eyes, though.

He was hoping Sally would say yes.

He wanted to see the two of them together.

Before Sally could answer, there was a commotion in the hall.

Colleen heard a man's distressed voice.

"I have to see her. I have to see her, please!"

Mark strode to the door. Colleen knew he would have blocked the distraught man who was trying to enter except Sally cried out then.

"Brant! Let him in!"

Mark stepped aside and a man in his late twenties with tousled dark hair and a look of desperation about him started through the door.

Red let out a warning growl.

"Down — it's good!" Mark said quickly.

The dog moved away.

Brant Pickering hesitated just a second, respectfully looking at the dog and then at Mark and Colleen, then he rushed forward, reaching for Sally, who took him into her arms as he balanced at the hospital bedside.

"You're alive, you're alive, you're alive!"

he whispered. He pulled back. "I'm not hurting you, am I? Thank God! You're alive!"

Sally started to sob softly, and he cradled her against him again.

Brant Pickering continued to hold her as he looked back at Mark and Colleen.

"We'll give you two some privacy," Mark said. "Sally, we do have a policeman in the hall if anything frightens you at any time."

Sally looked around Brant's chest and said, "Thank you, thank you!"

She was happy, Colleen thought. She was with Brant.

And Brant, well, he certainly appeared to be someone sane, grateful — and tender with Sally Smithson.

"Our cards are on your table," Mark said, setting his card down before Colleen did the same. "Red! Let's go."

Sally was barely aware they were leaving. She was staring at Brant Pickering with all her love and gratitude apparent in her tearstained eyes.

"Brant," Sally whispered.

"You're alive, Sally. You're alive," Brant said.

Colleen believed the two of them just might be all right.

CHAPTER FOUR

It had been a pretty picture, seeing the way Brant Pickering had held Sally Smithson, almost as if she were cherished porcelain, loved and fragile, and not to be broken.

But Mark wondered.

Too good? Too caring to be true?

They met up with Ragnar in the hall.

"So, the boyfriend is in!" Ragnar said.

"I thought it was . . . touching," Colleen said. "Maybe just what she needs right now."

"That's what Jackson thought," Mark said.

Colleen looked at him quizzically.

"Someone else is out there," he said. "I don't believe Carver is the same man who kidnapped Dierdre. Naturally, the boyfriends are people we need to look at."

"I'm hoping that was real," Colleen said.

"She wanted to see him?" Ragnar asked.

"Yes, and for some reason, he was in town. He had moved to New York, according to Sally," Mark said. "Jackson and Angela are on it. They'll find out if he could have been in the area when Sally or Dierdre were taken, or if there is proof that he was in New York."

"You found Sally in Carver's basement!" Colleen said. "If they were working together, then we wouldn't have a copycat out there, we'd have an accomplice."

"It's possible," Mark said. He shook his head. "But I don't think so. Hey, we've all gone through classes on spotting lies, on watching reactions, and looking for the truth that lies beneath. How answers can twist and turn, but mostly, how body language can give someone away. I don't believe Carver had any idea another woman was buried out in the woods."

"So that's not really an accomplice," Colleen stated.

"A fan," Ragnar suggested.

"Maybe," Mark said. "Or an accomplice gone rogue."

"Someone helping him who wanted a kill all his own?" Colleen suggested.

There were some things to be said for the new partner who had made Mark and Ragnar's team a threesome. She was asking good questions, comprehending his thoughts easily enough. And it didn't hurt that she was stunning — that had worked well with Carver when they'd wanted to get reactions out of him.

And maybe most important of all, Mark thought, the dog liked her.

"I hope we find proof that Brant Pickering is innocent," Colleen said. "Sally needs . . . well, I think he really loves her." She shrugged.

"It looked like the real deal to me too," Mark assured her. "But it will still be good to know what Angela and Jackson might discover."

Colleen smiled. "Social media. So many people reveal so much on there."

"Even seemingly routine posts are a big help. Time stamps with a person at a certain place or with certain people. Anyway, we've at least seen Brant Pickering. I say we now need to find out about Dierdre Ayers's parents and her boyfriend, Gary Boynton," Mark said.

"Should we leave them?" Colleen asked.

"A cop is watching the camera set discreetly in her room," Mark said. "Jackson covers his bases."

"You want parents or boyfriend?" Ragnar asked him.

"Your pick," Mark told him.

Ragnar grinned. "Parents — they might be easier to find."

"Let's hope we get somewhere," Mark said.

He and Ragnar headed for the elevators. Red walked along obediently, but Mark realized Colleen had hesitated.

She was looking back at Sally's hospital room.

She looked at him. "I'm worried about leaving them alone."

He smiled. "They're not really alone. Jackson made sure of that from the get-go. There's a good cop on this, and even if he did look away, there's a screen at the nurses' station. They can see anything that goes on. And we have another cop in the hall. We're good to go. Besides, I thought you liked what you saw in Brant Pickering?"

"I did — I do. I guess I have some of your 'suspicious of everything that walks' in me too."

He grinned. "We're good. Sally and Dierdre have eagle eyes on them." He shrugged. "Let's see your take on Gary Boynton."

"Have any idea where we're going?" she asked.

"Yes, our subject lives in Fairfax. We'll head there."

"And if he's not home?" she asked, catching up with him. Ragnar was holding the elevator door.

"Angela is checking out his work and his hangouts," Mark assured her. "But I think we'll find him home. Not even Dierdre's parents are permitted to see her yet. If he is guilty of anything, he'll be playing the victim."

"Should we call and make an appointment?" she asked.

"You could, you know," Ragnar told Mark.

Mark glanced at him and sighed and pulled out his notes. He put a call through to Gary Boynton. The man answered.

Mark knew he would.

"Special Agent Mark Gallagher, Mr. Boynton. I'd like to come by and talk to you. We're grasping at straws and hoping anything you might have seen or heard leading up to Dierdre's kidnapping might be helpful."

He didn't know if Colleen and Ragnar could hear Gary Boynton's answers.

"Yes. Sure. I'm working in my garage. Anything to keep busy, you know? They won't let us see Dierdre yet. I'm anxious, so, you know, working on projects helps. I thought you caught the guy?"

"We caught a man. But we can't yet prove he was the one to kidnap Dierdre."

"But — on the news, it sounded the same."

"We can't be sure. We need to speak with you."

"I'm here. Ready and willing to help in any way. But hurry. They've said I can see Dierdre soon, and I want to see her as soon as possible!"

"We're on our way," Mark said, and hung up.

"I got a hold of the parents just now too," Ragnar said. "They're ready for me to come by — quickly. They want to see their daughter. I guess we don't get to switch around today." He saluted. "Catch up later. Bye, Red!"

Red woofed.

"He really is an amazing dog," Colleen said.

"He is." Mark grinned at her. "In another life, I think I could have been . . . I don't know."

"With the circus?" she asked, a strange little grin on her face.

"Ha ha. Well, maybe. I always loved animals. But yes, this guy is special. Anyway, he's usually a good judge of character."

"Oh, thank God I made the cut."

"Ah, maybe he's still observing."

She grinned. "Maybe you should have been a vet?"

"Naw. Too squeamish around blood."

"You?"

"No, sadly, not really. I just knew I wanted to be FBI."

She shook her head as they got into the car and he revved the engine.

"There are dog treats in the glove compartment. He may judge you even more highly if you were to give him one," Mark told Colleen.

She grinned and did as he had suggested. Red rewarded her with a sloppy kiss on the cheek.

"I wonder if he knows how amazing he is," Colleen murmured.

"He's a dog," Mark said, looking ahead and smiling. "An amazingly cool one. But he's like most dogs attached to their owners. He's unconditional love, which, as you know, is pretty nice after some of the days we've had."

"Yep," Colleen said. Her phone rang and she glanced at the caller ID and then at him. "It's my sister. Is it okay if —"

"Of course. Talk to her," he said.

Colleen answered her phone with a smile.

"Megan! What's up?" Then: "Oh, that's great . . . Yes, of course. I don't know about timing, but if you're going to stay at my place, it's perfect. I'll get to see you. You have your own key, so just let yourself in whenever you get here . . . Yes." Colleen paused and glanced at Mark. "Yes, I'm working what they're calling 'The Embracer' case . . . Yes, I'm sorry, it's horrible. Trust me, no cop or agent created that moniker. Killers just wind up with monikers. Okay . . . Oh!" She glanced at Mark again and this time covered the speaker area of her phone with her hand. "Megan works for a press in New York. Is it all right if I ask her about Brant Pickering?"

He nodded.

"Megan, what do you know about an author, Brant Pickering?"

He could hear the rush of words that followed. They were effusive. Mark wasn't sure what she was saying, but it was clear that she admired the man.

Colleen thanked her and ended the call.

She looked at Mark with a grimace. "Well, I'm sure you heard some of that! She's not only heard of him, she's read his work and she admires him. He's highly respected among historians, readers, and other writers of historical works."

"Did she say anything about him being in New York?"

Colleen nodded. "She's excited. He's supposedly working on a book about the Five Points area of the city, what it once was and

105

how it evolved over the years."

"So, there's a reason he moved to New York."

"I guess."

"One sister?" he asked her.

"And a brother."

"Are you the oldest, youngest, in the middle?" he asked.

"Yes — we're triplets."

"Triplets! Wow. Are you identical? Oh, man, sorry, that was idiotic. I guess not — you have a brother."

Colleen laughed. "You'd be surprised how often we get that with people not realizing it isn't possible. We all have green eyes. Patrick's hair is close to black, it's so dark, and Megan is much fairer than I am. She's kind of a honey blonde. I think you'd know we were related, but besides that . . ."

"Nice. Nice to have siblings."

"Do you —" Colleen began.

He quickly cut her off. "Well, the guy is a legit historian and author. So, yes, he had reason to move to New York. Center of publishing and a historic city. I assume he does decently —"

"Megan would tell you no matter how esteemed you may be, you don't necessarily get rich when publishing in academia."

"True. But it sounds as if he makes a fair

income."

Colleen frowned and then shook her head. "I wonder why they broke up? Sally is a teacher. I wonder why she didn't want to move to New York. There are schools everywhere, and teachers are always in demand."

"A lot of people just don't want to pick up and move. I don't know. We'd have to ask them."

"I hate the personal stuff," Colleen said. "And I wonder, how do we explain what we're asking in this situation?"

"You mean asking personal questions about intimate relationships when we really have no reason — other than that they were an item — to suspect the man of anything?"

Colleen nodded. "How do we do it?"

He smiled, looking ahead. "Very carefully," he told her.

"Ah, great. Lots of help."

"We'll do it together. Though . . ."

"Though?" Colleen pressed.

"You might be better at that kind of thing than me."

"Thanks. Thanks a lot!"

He glanced at her quickly, grinning. "We do all have our special talents!"

Colleen groaned. "Whoever said that careful, tactful questioning was mine?"

"It's obvious. You're just so nice."

She looked at him, arching a brow. "I'm so good and I'm so nice, huh? Okay, why did you change the subject —"

"I didn't change the subject. We've been discussing Sally and Brant Pickering and their breakup."

"Ah, but you asked about my siblings. And you knew I was going to ask about yours."

"Did I?"

"You know you did. Please. I'm pretty much so an open book. We're working together, whether you like it or not —"

"You've proven yourself competent."

"Wow! What a compliment!"

He stared at the road ahead and shrugged.

"Well, I didn't come from a family like yours," he said.

He was quiet for a minute. She didn't press him.

He shrugged again, let out a long breath, and decided to answer her.

"When I was just a boy, my mother was working as a stripper. I loved her. I didn't really understand what she did." He turned to look at Colleen. "She had been orphaned, and she needed a way to make a living. But then . . . she was murdered. They found her body in an alley. She'd been raped and her throat slashed."

"Oh, my God, I'm so sorry!" Colleen said.

108

"I shouldn't have pushed you like that."

"It's okay," he said, his eyes on the traffic as he continued. "There had been another, similar murder a few weeks before. The FBI had been called in almost immediately. The FBI agent who had the case came to the funeral. I admired him. But it was at the funeral that I, well, saw the dead for the first time. My mom. She said she knew I was still young, but she needed me to know that while she'd never had a chance to marry my father, she had loved him very much. He'd been a soldier and was killed in combat. She was hoping to find him, but she wanted me to know I had been loved and wanted. She asked me to please remember that — whatever was to come. Anyway, she also gave me information about the man who killed her and warned me I shouldn't tell anyone how I knew; they would think that I was crazy. So, I told the FBI man about the guy — just saying my mother had been bothered by him at work. They got a search warrant and came up with evidence that linked him to not only my mom's murder, but also the one before — and three before that."

"And you were how old?" Colleen asked him.

"Seven. Anyway, I kind of shifted through

a few foster homes. When I was eleven, I was adopted by an incredible couple. I went to a good school, and they involved themselves in my activities. I'm grateful to think my football career in high school and college made them happy and proud. But they always knew I was set on law enforcement. I started with the United States Marshals Service, but never forgot the special agent who had helped me. And when I was in the academy, I learned about the Krewe of Hunters. Luckily, they had their eyes on me."

"I am so sorry about your mom," Colleen said.

He shrugged with a small, twisted smile on his lips.

"In truth, I was lucky. Not many kids get a second chance with a couple like Beth and Larry Flannigan. They were amazing."

"Were?" she asked softly.

"I don't know how they managed it, but Larry was almost seventy when they adopted me, and Beth was sixty-seven. We lost Larry five years ago, and Beth followed two years after. They saw me through school, they applauded when I became a marshal, and they got to see me join the FBI. I didn't become a football hero in the NFL, but that was okay with them. They wanted to see me achieve *my* dream, and they were . . . wonderful."

"I'm so sorry you lost them," Colleen said softly. "And so glad you had them."

He grimaced at her. "Me too," he assured her. "It's a sad story, and an oddly good one too. Anyway, we're getting close. Back to the case. Sally was taken and held for several days, abused, kept prisoner for hours on end in a basement where Carver visited at his whim or when he wasn't busy trying to look like the best man in the neighborhood. Dierdre was kidnapped and put in a pine box almost immediately. Supposedly, Gary Boynton is a pillar of society. Liked by Dierdre's parents. In a solid relationship with Dierdre. She had just seen him before she was taken."

"And what do we know about him? I'm not sure I like him already," Colleen said.

"Oh?"

"Well, at least Brant Pickering was at the hospital, anxious to see Sally, though not sure he'd be able to. Gary . . . is at home."

"Well, I don't think we can convict him on that. And when she was found, they were told absolutely no visitors until further notice."

"All right."

"People work out stress and fear in different ways," Mark reminded her.

"What do we know about him?" she asked.

"He's twenty-nine, grew up in the area, and has a degree in finance. He owns his own company — Boynton Acquisitions. His biggest clients are construction companies."

"Hmm. Construction."

"Meaning?"

"He'd know how to build a pine box — a coffin."

"I don't think it takes a degree to build a pine box."

"So, you don't think it's him?" Colleen asked.

"I didn't say that at all. I'm playing devil's advocate. And there's nothing to say Brant Pickering making a return doesn't mean he isn't a fine actor."

"Or that Jim Carver didn't have one woman in his basement when he kidnapped and buried another."

"No, that's why it's so handy that there are cameras and paper trails, and hopefully, something or someone somewhere who will get us to the truth."

"What else do we know about Gary Boynton?"

"Goes to work. Posts pics of himself and Dierdre on social media. Seems like an all-around good guy."

"And he could be."

"Yeah."

"What?"

Mark let out a sigh and shook his head.

"He could be great. He could be playing a game well. Both he and Sally's guy might be the real deal, and someone else is out there. It's all up for grabs at this moment."

He glanced at Colleen briefly as he turned the corner. She was looking out the window.

Virginia was beautiful, especially with summer on the way; the trees were rich with fresh green leaves, and the landscape was dotted with flowers as they approached the upper-middle-class neighborhood Gary Boynton called home.

Mark spoke quickly and said, "It could be someone we know nothing about, but we have to go with what we can first. The thing is this — I seriously don't believe Carver is guilty of kidnapping Dierdre. He was too stunned to hear about it. I do believe that if Carver is The Embracer, he has fans. Or acolytes. Someone out there is trying to be him or trying to impress him. Carver may or may not know who it is, but I honestly believe he had no idea another woman had been taken until you told him. And at this point, he's busy planning his defense."

"How can he defend against the fact you

113

found a woman in his basement? No jury is going to fall for that!"

"You'd be surprised what a defense lawyer can do," Mark said.

"Actually, no."

"Of course, they're going to try and say Ragnar and I entered his premise illegally. But I don't believe he'll get away with it."

"You kind of did, didn't you?"

"No," he said stubbornly. "We were just there to talk. He let Ragnar in. And there was the screaming."

"Is this car bugged?" she asked.

He looked at her again. She was grinning. "What?"

"You simply knew Sally was there," she said.

He shook his head again. "We always need to be careful. There's an excellent reason our justice system is what it is. Back in Salem, back in the days of the Massachusetts Bay Colony, they let in 'spectral' evidence. Innocent people were executed. Evidence needs to be solid. I believe that with my whole heart."

"But you knew Sally was down in the basement."

He nodded. "But we don't have dead men that only a small percentage of people can see or hear testify in court."

114

Colleen pursed her lips. "They won't let him out on bond, will they?"

"I sincerely doubt it. And I think him trying to defend himself by saying Sally was kinky and wanted him is laughable; I can't imagine a judge or jury anywhere will buy it. There's nothing in Sally's history to suggest she would be willing to go with such a man. Well, we're here, and I believe that's Gary Boynton."

They had pulled into the driveway of an impressive colonial home with Doric columns. Mark thought the neighborhood of acre estates was new. The home had been specifically designed to fit the historic image of the area. The large, modern two-car garage was a giveaway. Of course, many a carriage house or barn had been modernized into a garage, but Mark believed the house to be comparatively new in this neck of the woods, along with the entire community.

New house — new money. Gary Boynton had quickly made money with his company and his degree. He did remind Mark of the successful frat boy — good college, good grades, good company now.

He was standing by a new-model sports car with a buffer in his hands.

Girlfriend in the hospital after being

buried alive. Why not buff the car?

"True what you said," Colleen muttered. "We all deal with stress differently."

Boynton saw them and walked toward them. His expression was duly serious.

"FBI?" he asked.

Red barked a yes.

"And a dog!" Boynton said dryly. "Did he help find Dierdre?"

"He did," Colleen said.

"I'm Special Agent Mark Gallagher, and these are my partners, Special Agent Law and Red."

"Nice to meet you. And I'm grateful to all three of you." He started to offer them a hand, then realized he was holding the buffer and his hands were oily with whatever he'd used on the car. "Sorry. I'm doing anything not to go nuts. I can't concentrate on work, can't read . . . I just keep thinking about Dierdre and they won't let me see her. I have to move or I'll lose my mind. But her folks called me. I guess they're visiting with another of your colleagues, and then they're going to head to the hospital. I'm going to do the same."

"We understand completely," Colleen said commiseratively, glancing at Mark with a little twitch of a smile.

"I'm hoping they let us in when we get

there," Boynton said. He wiped a hand across his brow.

The man had soft brown hair, a little damp, with a lock that fell over his forehead. Mark couldn't help thinking of him as an animated character — one who believed in his own masculine beauty and was quick to play upon it.

He was smiling at Colleen as he brushed back that lock of hair, tall and lean, with well-toned muscles obtained from working out regularly at a gym most likely. Charming, courteous, and financially stable. What wouldn't a girl's parents love?

"I'm sure they'll let you see Dierdre very soon," Colleen said, smiling pleasantly. "What she went through, though . . . well, they're taking excellent care of her."

He nodded. "I'm sure. It's just so hard."

"We were hoping you could help us," Mark told him.

"Me?" he asked, sounding surprised.

"You two were out before this happened, right?" Colleen said.

He nodded. "I was working late. We met for dinner. Dierdre drove into DC to meet me. She's been taking classes and working, so we've both been ridiculously busy. We had dinner. I walked her to her car. I'd have given up any business to have kept this from

117

happening! If only we —"

"No one can foresee the future," Colleen added.

"What did you do after dinner?" Mark asked him.

"Ran back to the office to finish up a few things and then I came here." He shook his head. "I knew nothing about it. I fell asleep. I had no clue she didn't show up at home until . . . well, I fell asleep, so I didn't hear the phone at first when her folks kept calling. I hate myself for that too."

"None of us can help falling asleep," Colleen said.

"Did you notice anyone at dinner?" Mark asked him.

"Notice anyone? There were other diners, of course."

"Did anyone seem to be paying attention to the two of you? When you walked to your car, did anyone seem to be paying a little too much attention or perhaps follow you too closely?" Colleen asked him.

She had a way about her, Mark thought. She was anxious and caring, and Boynton had to believe she was seeking help — and not that he might be on the suspect list.

"I don't — well, there was this weird guy in the restaurant. Bright yellow suit. It kind of looked like he should be in the circus. To

118

be fair, he seemed to be eating with his kids. Weird, yes, but not, well, not dangerous weird. And . . ." Boynton paused as if in deep thought, as if he were trying to recapture the moments when he'd last been with Dierdre.

"Close your eyes. Think about the night. Sights, sounds, even smells," Colleen suggested.

He closed his eyes. "Smells . . . Well, yes, the aromas from the kitchen were wonderful; I had the porterhouse. Delicious."

"What did Dierdre have?" Colleen asked.

He wrinkled his nose. "Salmon. Fishy, but the garlic sauce on my porterhouse weighed it down."

His eyes were closed, but he was smiling. "Your server?"

"She was fine. Pretty. Maybe twenty. She knew the menu by heart. She was super; there when you needed something, but leaving you alone when you didn't."

"And around you — besides the man in the yellow suit?" Mark asked quietly.

Gary Boynton's eyes opened. "Yes, a guy in a casual black suede jacket. Open white shirt. He was eating alone at a table near us. And — oh, my God! When I asked for our check, he asked for his. Different server — he had a male waiter. We paid at the same

119

time. I saw him get up right before us, and he was on his phone when we were leaving. He was standing out on the sidewalk. He nodded politely when we went by. And I teased Dierdre. I mean he was obviously looking at her. Do you think —"

"Did you see him after that?" Colleen asked.

Boynton thought and shook his head. "But he might have seen us. She had snagged a spot right on the street. He would have seen me walk her to the car. He would have seen her get into the car alone!"

"Anyone else on the street pay attention to you?" Mark asked him.

"Not that I can recall," Boynton said. "I wish — I wish I could help more."

"You can," Colleen said sweetly. "You can come into our office and work with a sketch artist and give us a better idea of what this man looked like. Our unit has a different headquarters than the main FBI building. The address is on my card," Colleen said, handing him her card.

"What can you tell the two of us by way of description?" Mark asked.

"Um, okay, black suede jacket, white shirt. I think he was wearing jeans — good jeans. But I wouldn't have worn them to the restaurant. He was midthirties, dark hair . . .

tanned face. Yeah, he had a tan. And he was using an iPhone."

"Midthirties, dark hair," Mark said. "Long hair, short hair?"

"Kind of like mine. Not too short, but not long."

"Thank you," Colleen told him. "And thank you for saying you'll come in. We appreciate any help we can get."

Mark forced a smile. "We'll let you get back to your buffing."

"Yeah. I'm done. Time to shower and get going. The doctors told Dierdre's folks they'll be able to see her, but it's a little harder for me because we're not officially related, so Dierdre's folks will bring me in with them. Weird, that cops have talked to her, but we can't yet."

"Law enforcement can get about two minutes with a patient," Colleen explained. "Families want to stay, and it can be emotional and draining when doctors are trying to make sure a patient is okay."

"Yeah, I get it. I guess. No, I don't. Family would be reassuring, and cops are creepy — sorry. But you're not cops anyway, right? Special agents."

"Yep. Special agents."

"Well, we're grateful," Gary said. "Very grateful. We're amazed you found her alive."

"So are we," Colleen assured him. "And we don't want it to happen to anyone else, so anything you can give us is deeply appreciated."

"Of course," Gary said.

"Anyway, thank you again. And we'll look forward to seeing you at the office," Mark said.

He gave a wave as he and Colleen turned and headed back to the car.

When he was behind the driver's seat and revving the engine, he asked Colleen, "Well?"

"I don't much care for him."

Mark chuckled. "You don't really know him. Buffing the car may be the thing that is keeping him sane." He shook his head. "But you're right, I'd have been there. At the hospital. I'd have haunted people."

"And police or security might have had you removed."

He shook his head. "No, I'd have just been in a waiting room. If I loved someone . . . but it's not just that. His language was strange."

"He said, 'we're grateful.' Aligning himself with the parents," Colleen added.

He smiled and nodded. "I worked with a psychologist who worked with language as a specialty on a case a few years ago. It's amazing what you can pick out from the way someone is speaking. Most liars take care with a lie. The reason being, we all tend to forget a lie or the details of it. A lie needs to be kept simple."

"He was detailed about the restaurant."

"Everything he said about the restaurant was probably the truth."

"And it was probably the truth there was a man in the restaurant who paid his bill when they did — and was standing outside watching Dierdre?"

"Possibly. Several people might have paid their checks at the same time. And there might have been several people on the street."

"So, if he lied, it was just about going back to work?"

"Yes — simple. A lie to remember."

"Interesting. How can we prove he was lying?"

"That, I don't know. But the way someone speaks can tell us a great deal. There's the social introduction. When someone speaks or writes about someone else, if a relationship is good, they'll say 'my boyfriend, Gary,' or something like 'my brother, Patrick.' When a relationship is not so good, they'll just use one or the other. That isn't every single time — just something that often proves to be true. A young woman was lying once about an attack outside a restaurant. She said a man in a hoodie had attacked her and she barely escaped."

"A man in a hoodie," Colleen commented.

He smiled. "The thing of it is, criminals do often wear hoodies. Some know how to wear a hoodie and to keep their heads down by any surveillance cameras."

"Okay, what really happened?" Colleen asked.

"She and her boyfriend had just had a fight, but she didn't want anyone to know he'd given her a black eye. She loved him even if he was an abusive prick."

"She stayed with him?"

He nodded grimly. "And our psychologists tried to get her to bring charges against him, and she wouldn't. Instead, she was charged for filing a false report."

"I've never understood that way of . . . feeling," Colleen said. "But you're right. I was a kid with great parents, and while my siblings and I sometimes fought, we'd stand up for one another against anyone who dared taunt one of us. And we were taught personal responsibility. I'm sorry for that poor girl."

"I wonder if she's still alive," Mark said, shaking his head.

"That's tough stuff — getting people out of an abusive relationship," Colleen said, and sighed. "At least Gary Boynton doesn't appear to be abusive."

"No, but I still didn't care much for him. But who knows? Maybe he's just a privileged boy turned into a privileged man, and he's just fine. And maybe Sally's boyfriend is a wonderful writer, and they just had a spat about location, work, and his leaving — and her staying. Maybe someone else entirely is out there." He hesitated. "But I do believe this — if we don't figure it out soon, there will be another woman in a coffin, and you might not hear her, and Red might not find her."

Red whined softly, having heard his name.

Colleen nodded thoughtfully. "Right," she said. "So, where are we heading now?"

He grinned. "Lunch."

"Oh, good. It's three o'clock. I was beginning to think you never ate, and God forbid a rookie suggest food. Anyway, I know a pizza place that's up ahead —"

"Well, another time."

"Oh?"

"Cafeteria food," he told her.

"Ah. We're headed back to the hospital."

"When Jackson wants cameras up, cameras go in. And while I don't intend to announce our presence, I do want to see what goes on when Gary Boynton greets his beloved Dierdre."

"It's going to be completely loving," Colleen said.

"You're sure?"

"Positive. Say he did go and attack her himself — would he do anything now other than rush in to hold her and profess his undying love?"

"You have a point. I still wouldn't mind watching the reunion."

"Aren't there laws —"

"There are. But we're in the middle of a criminal investigation, protecting the lives of victims. You were the one who didn't want to leave Sally alone with her estranged lover!"

"Good point. Cafeteria food it is!" she said. "And then —"

"Then we'll be making another strange stop."

"Oh?"

He grinned as he looked at her.

"The cemetery."

CHAPTER FIVE

Colleen admired the way that the hospital, police, and FBI seemed to be able to work together when it came to the care of victimized patients.

Law enforcement had been given the use of a small office; screens had been set up there, allowing whatever agent or officer on duty to keep an eagle's eye on both rooms.

She and Mark took their turn together in side-by-side doctor's chairs with Red between them.

Brant Pickering was still with Sally. She was sleeping. He sat by her bed with one hand resting on hers, and his other holding his smartphone.

They watched as Dierdre's parents were allowed in to see their daughter.

The love there was real. Dierdre's mother cried as she tenderly cradled her daughter. Her father held back his love just enough to allow his wife a moment then moved in to hold her as if she were the most fragile and precious creation in the world, as would many a father, Colleen thought.

But not all, she knew. She had been lucky. Dierdre appeared to be lucky too.

They heard Gary Boynton in the hall before they saw him. He was anxious, causing problems, insisting he'd waited, and he needed to get in to see Dierdre. He knew she was going to be okay; he had to see her.

Apparently, everyone in the area heard him. On the screen, they could see Dierdre wince and look at her parents.

Her doting parents nodded, kissed her again, and went out to the hallway, allowing time and space for Gary to come in.

Mark stood as Dierdre's parents left her room; he cracked the door to the office and looked out. Colleen knew he wanted to see the meeting of the three.

"Well, it's true. They apparently love him," Mark said, shrugging as he came to reclaim the seat next to Colleen again.

"And she loves him too," Colleen said.

Gary Boynton had entered the room. Dierdre was sitting up, watching him with hope and adoration.

Whatever his feelings, he played it well. He approached the bed swiftly, extending his arms; his face was creased in a frown of concern. He enwrapped her tenderly and then eased back, worried he had hurt her, meeting her eyes with his own, moist and concerned. They were both crying, with Gary standing at the side of the bed as his arms enclosed her upper body.

"Both these guys have put on great shows," Mark said.

"And they might be real," Colleen reminded him.

He nodded, sitting back in his chair and watching the screens.

"I'll guess we'll turn surveillance back over to the police and move on," he said.

"Okay, that sounds good. Are we getting food to go from the cafeteria?" Colleen asked.

She watched him smile. He had a good smile. He needed to use it more often.

"We'll sit and eat. Ragnar will meet us."

"No problem with Red in the cafeteria?"

"Nope. That little vest shows Red has gone through many kinds of training. He can be a cadaver dog, he can find bombs, he can find drugs, and he is amazing at search and rescue. Red is really one of a kind; most dogs are trained in one or two disciplines at best. Red? He's a one-man dog army!"

"And how did you acquire Red?" she

129

asked him.

He glanced at her with a shrug. "Someone dumped him as a puppy in the middle of the street. I guess they figured he was going to be too big or rambunctious, or maybe he wasn't fully housebroken at the time. But they literally threw him in the middle of the road right by the Beltway. I stopped and picked him up. He didn't have a chip. I would have gone after the people, except it was either save the dog from a dozen cars whizzing by, or let him get hit and go after them. Anyway, a friend of mine is a trainer, and other friends are with volunteer search and rescue teams. Red was a natural."

"That's cool. And I have always loved the concept of a rescued dog becoming a *rescue* dog," Colleen said. "I have said it before and will say it again — he's amazing!"

She didn't mention the fact that maybe Mark and Red had been meant for one another. Of course, Mark's mother had loved him. She believed that, and though she certainly didn't know Mark well yet, she knew he believed it too. But in a way, both the man and the dog had been abandoned.

And they had a beautiful loyalty to one another now.

As they reached the cafeteria, Mark was

on the phone with Ragnar. But he laughed as he listened to his partner and grinned as he pocketed his phone.

"Ragnar is already in here. He said it may be a hospital cafeteria, but the fish and chips are 'to die for,' " Mark said. He grimaced. "I'm not sure that's a good analogy at a hospital, but —"

"Fish and chips sounds good to me," Colleen assured him.

As they went through the line, several of the doctors and nurses greeted Mark and Red and smiled to acknowledge Colleen.

"You guys are here often, aren't you?" Colleen commented.

"As I said before, the hospital is much better than the morgue," Mark said. "But in truth, part of it is because I do bring Red here to visit kids. When I have time. I mean, we do have days where no one has murdered anyone. Sometimes it feels like it's rare, but human beings always amaze me."

"You are one, you know."

"Yeah. But sometimes we get to see people rise to the greatest levels by giving and sacrifice, strangers helping strangers in floods, rescuing people — and animals — from fire, donating so their neighbors can eat and have a place to sleep. And then we get to see the worst of man's inhumanity.

It's a complex world. But Red loves kids. And kids love Red. Sometimes when I'm working but Red doesn't have to, my friend Lia brings him here."

"Nice," Colleen said.

She found herself wondering how good a friend Lia might be. Or what kind of a friend.

They went through the line and both decided to humor Ragnar and go with the fish and chips. They then found him sitting at a large table in the far back.

"Nothing," he said as they joined him. "I got nothing from the parents. I wasn't expecting anything, but they were just anxious to see Dierdre. And they were anxious for Gary to get to see her too. As soon as possible. Her mother was telling me Dierdre was a great daughter and always had been. She loves them, but she's young. And *in love.* They believe Gary will be asking Dierdre to marry him soon, and they're very happy. Her mother also told me about the guy she'd dated before. He had no job, went to college now and then. Well, to the folks, Gary Boynton is Prince Charming."

"We watched the reunion," Colleen said, sliding her tray over to make room for Mark's.

"And?" Ragnar asked.

"It was lovely. Prince Charming kissing his princess, making all well," Mark said.

"Is that sarcasm?" Ragnar asked.

"From me?" Mark smiled.

"We have nothing on him. Nothing at all."

"He's supposed to be coming by head-quarters to work with one of our sketch artists," Mark said. "I can only assume he's done buffing his car and will go there from here."

"He asked the hospital staff if he could stay the night, but the doctors appealed to his better senses, I guess, saying they really needed her to concentrate on sleeping and healing. He, of course, said she'd heal better with him sleeping at her side, but her main man is a Dr. Borden, who can be as stubborn as a rock. So, I guess he'll be by. Do we believe him about the man he saw watching them?"

"We can find out if we have the sketch," Mark said.

Ragnar nodded. "Your plan from here?" he asked Mark.

"Cemetery?"

Colleen was surprised when Ragnar agreed.

"Sergeant Alfie Parker," Ragnar said quietly. He smiled at Colleen. "One of the few 'remaining souls' who makes a point of visiting us at the office. He was killed on a bust. And while they rescued several women and confiscated just about every drug known to man, the head honcho got away."

"Oh no!" Colleen said.

Mark picked up the story, inclining his head toward Ragnar, as if asking his partner to step in if he had anything wrong.

"I think Alfie had become invested in the case. He'd met a young lady, a runaway, on the street. He'd gotten her to go to a home where they helped runaways like her, but then she disappeared. Her friends believed she'd been swept off the streets by traffickers, but because of her history, the police believed she'd gone off on her own accord. Anyway, Alfie believed the group was holding her. He was one hell of a detective from what I've been told. The young woman he was trying to help would be older now, of course. We don't know if she made it or not. She went by the name 'Susie,' and Alfie never knew her last name."

"Anyway," Ragnar said, "Alfie should be on payroll, except of course, he doesn't need money anymore."

"Jackson has tried to help him. He investigated the old case but couldn't find anything further about 'Susie.' The man behind the operation was only known as 'John Smith.'

If any of his crew knew his real name or where he was during the bust, they were killed in the gunfire," Mark said.

"I guess that's why Alfie hangs around?" Colleen asked.

"He is determined to be helpful, and he is," Mark said.

"When he was a detective, his area was near the house where Carver was keeping Sally," Ragnar told her. "He actually comes into our offices when he sees something suspicious. I'm sure he'll be happy to meet you. I warn you — he'll be fascinated."

"Oh?" Colleen asked.

"Your special hearing," Mark reminded her.

"Oh."

"He'll find you exceptionally gifted," Ragnar said, smiling. He looked at Mark then. "So, you're off to the cemetery hoping Alfie will be hanging out?"

Mark nodded. "As soon as we're done there, we'll head into headquarters and see if Gary Boynton shows up. Then — once we have a sketch — we can check with the restaurant manager and get him to show the picture around."

"I'll check in on our victims again and make my way to headquarters. Meet you there," Ragnar said. "Good fish and chips, huh? For a hospital cafeteria? And the price is right!"

He pat Red on the head, nodded, and headed out. Mark took a last bite of fish and looked at Colleen.

"Ready?" he asked her.

"Sure. Nothing like a trip to a cemetery," she told him dryly.

Sergeant Alfie Parker had been buried in one of the oldest cemeteries in the area.

He had been laid to rest in an area with other police officers, in a section to the far back, one that had been added in the early twentieth century.

To reach it, they drove through the oldest area, which was well maintained, but still in an area where trees were interspersed with stones that had been weathered for over two hundred years. Through the years, various groups had worked to keep up the integrity of the cemetery, and there were benches and plaques throughout. Funerary art from the nineteenth century added to the haunting beauty of the place.

"Have you been here before?" Mark asked Colleen. She had been studying the place since they'd come along the drive.

"No. I'm originally from Orlando, Florida," she told him.

"Ah, nothing old there!"

"You'd be surprised. Not to mention my field trips were often up to St. Augustine, the oldest city in the country — or the oldest continually inhabited by European settlers. Or invaders," she added with a shrug.

He grinned. "We have other Krewe members from Florida," he told her, amused.

"Where are you from originally?" she asked him.

He laughed. "About a mile from here."

"Ah, so you know this area well."

"I got to know this cemetery well once I got to know Alfie," he told her.

"He hangs out here?"

"Sometimes. Yeah, I know. Ghosts usually don't hang out where they're buried — not many good memories about being in a box. But he comes back now and then to check in with his old friends."

"Other cops?"

"Some," Mark said. "Alfie is just a good guy. He has all kinds of friends."

He parked the car along the earth-and-stone drive that bordered the section for slain police officers. Some had worked in the area, some had simply been from the area and were brought back home to lie with their fellow law enforcement officers and still be near living relatives.

Red followed as they walked to Alfie's grave.

Many of the graves were marked with flowers.

Colleen commented on that.

"Maybe we should have brought —"

"Alfie said he had been allergic. Ragnar brings a dark beer sometimes. When Alfie was off and he did drink, he liked dark beer."

"I see. And he dumps it on the grave?"

"A few sips, then he drinks the rest. Alfie also said he couldn't see the waste of a good beer."

Colleen smiled. They had walked to the grave. She knelt, moving a bit of brush that had fallen upon his marker.

Red sat, as if he knew he needed to be respectful of the dead.

"I know it could be any of us on any given day," she said. "But it's still so sad to me. Someone trying to help others — to stop horrible things from happening to people. I mean, yes, we've had a few bad eggs. But in the far greater majority, officers and agents are honorable and save lives."

"You won't get an argument on that from me," Mark said.

It was then he saw Alfie coming through the trees. He had been speaking with someone — another "remaining soul" as Alfie sometimes referred to himself and others.

He started to say something to Colleen, but she had already noted Alfie and was standing.

"Thought you might be around today," Alfie said, addressing Mark, and then turning instantly and politely to Colleen. "Sergeant Alfred Parker, Alfie to friends, and if you're with this fellow, we're friends, right?" Before Colleen could answer, he turned back to Mark. "I know she sees me. I can tell. You see it in someone's eyes when they look at you."

"Alfie, Special Agent Colleen Law," Mark said.

"I'm so pleased to meet you, Alfie," Colleen said. "Honored," she added.

Alfie had died at thirty-eight years, three months, and fourteen days, according to his headstone. He'd had dark hair, just beginning to gray at the temples, green eyes, and a tall, bronzed physique.

Cut down in the prime of life, Mark couldn't help thinking.

"It's a pleasure," Alfie said. "And, Mark, I'm proud of you and Ragnar. You got the bastard."

"Well, we have him in custody and he will be charged. You know he'll try every legal trick in the book."

"But can he get away with it, considering his victim had no history of prostitution or even a wild side?" Alfie asked.

"I hope not. I believe Sally will be a good witness against him."

"I saw her trying to escape," Alfie said. "I'd be a damned good witness. It's too bad the world can't see us. But I wouldn't change the justice system. No witch hunts should ever occur again. How can he get out of the fact he had the girl in his basement?"

"I don't see how, but he will try to say Ragnar and I entered illegally. If you want to get really technical —" Mark began.

"I don't. Anyway, you got your guy. To what do I owe the pleasure of this visit?" Alfie asked.

"I need to know if you saw him leave after he brought Sally into his house," Mark said.

Alfie was quiet. Mark didn't push him. Alfie's expression was pained.

"What is it?" Colleen asked softly.

Alfie shook his head. "I don't know. When I saw what I saw, knowing what has been happening, I went to Krewe headquarters as quickly as I could. It was late, but you know Jackson keeps someone in the office twenty-four-seven, so I was able to report what I'd seen . . ."

"Well, another young woman was kid-napped."

"No!" Alfie said.

"We found her. Rather, I should say Colleen and Red found her," Mark said.

Alfie looked at Colleen.

"She has a unique hearing gift," Mark said.

"How intriguing! You found the young woman. In time?" Alfie asked anxiously.

"We found her in time. But that's the problem. We don't know if Carver held one woman in the basement and went out after another — or if he has a copycat or someone working with him."

"I see," Alfie said thoughtfully. He winced. "I was so anxious for someone to get to the girl I knew was being held that I . . . Well, I can find out if perhaps anyone was around. At least, I can try."

"Thanks, Alfie. All your help is more deeply appreciated than we could ever say," Mark told him.

Alfie nodded.

"Where are you heading now? What are your leads?" he asked.

"Well, two boyfriends — we're trying to find out if either could be involved. And someone suspicious was seen at a restaurant with one of the victims. We're heading back to headquarters now to see if the one boyfriend shows up to give one of our sketch artists a decent sketch. Then we'll go to the restaurant and find out if anyone remembers seeing the man in the sketch," Mark told him.

Alfie nodded gravely again.

"I'll do what I can. Send my best to Ragnar. Sure wish I could pet the dog!" Alfie said.

Red woofed, as if he understood.

"Now, that is man's best friend!" Alfie said.

"He is pretty damned cool," Mark agreed.

"Okay, then. I'm off," Alfie said.

"Want a ride?"

"No, going off toward the pub over there. I'll see if any friends are hanging around," Alfie said.

He grinned, waved, and was gone.

"Wow," Colleen said.

"I know you've spoken with the dead before," Mark said.

"He's just . . . so intriguing. And helpful. And . . . I wish we could help him."

"Maybe we will. Eventually. Anyway, let's find out if Gary Boynton showed up to work with one of our sketch artists."

They headed out of the cemetery.

As they neared the car, Colleen paused and looked back.

"What is it?" he asked.

"I guess . . . I was thinking about Alfie again. And how incredible it is that he helps. And how you and Ragnar pulled off getting into Carver's residence and saving Sally. And then I was wondering . . . why? Why would anyone want to enclose a woman in a coffin and . . ."

She let her words trail off, shaking her head.

Then she looked at him and said, "And what's scarier is, more than one person might be involved. Sure, Carver could have just held Sally in that basement and gone back out . . ."

"But I don't think he did."

She winced. "I don't either," she admitted. "I don't either."

Gary Boynton talked a good talk.

Colleen wasn't sure if he just came off as rich, petulant, and totally self-absorbed, or if there might be more to him than met the eye.

Mark didn't like him. He wasn't obvious — he was professional.

She didn't care much for Gary either, but that didn't make him guilty of being a sick

143

and perverted murderer.

They'd arrived at Krewe headquarters, reported to Jackson and then to Angela, and then gone on into one of the conference rooms to go through what security cam footage they had managed to obtain. Ragnar called Mark. When Mark ended the call, he told Colleen they'd be dealing with Gary Boynton and the sketch artist alone. Ragnar was going to keep his eyes on Brant Pickering and the hospital — and watch for Gary Boynton's comings and goings.

"Boynton is on his way now, or so Ragnar believes. Let's review the traffic cam footage until we start with the sketch."

One traffic camera had caught Dierdre Ayers leaving the area of the restaurant.

She had been driving; she had been alone.

After that . . . nothing.

It was the same with what they had pulled on Sally Smithson. She'd been driving alone.

And then there was nothing. She had disappeared — into Carver's car, they knew — and her car had been driven into a ditch, something not seen on camera.

Angela entered the conference room while they were finishing the footage. "I don't have anything on Brant Pickering. His credit card was used in the New York area, but it was a swipe that didn't require a signature." She grimaced. "He's a writer. He took an apartment on the north side of Central Park, but I haven't found any cameras that show him coming or going. I'm still looking."

Mark thanked her and then quickly asked, "And there've been no arrest warrants of any kind on either man?"

"Not a thing," she said. "But that doesn't mean anything. Unfortunately history shows us many a brutal criminal has been able to lay low to carry out the most unimaginable acts. But there may still be something. I'm working with tech. We're going back to the day each of them opened social media accounts. We'll find what is out there to be found."

She left them but was gone only a minute before she poked her head back in. "Gary Boynton has arrived. Want him and the sketch artist in here?"

"That's the plan," Mark said.

"We'll get the video down. We don't want him thinking that he's a suspect," Colleen said.

"No, of course not," Angela agreed.

She left them. Mark quickly closed the screen and covered their equipment. A knock on the door brought in Maisie Nicholson, one of Jackson's favorite sketch artists, and Gary Boynton.

"Thank you, Mr. Boynton," Mark said, greeting him. "I take it you've met Maisie?"

"Please, call me Gary. And yes, I have met the lovely Maisie."

Maisie *was* lovely. She was African American, dark-skinned with large eyes and great cheekbones. She was also incredibly talented.

Red knew Maisie — he greeted her with enthusiasm and that enthusiasm was returned.

"Yes, Gary and I have met," Maisie said. "And I've promised him I can make someone come to life from memory. So . . ."

"Do you need Mark and me to leave?" Colleen asked. "We don't want to hinder you in any way."

"You won't hinder me," Maisie said. "But, Gary?"

"Not in the least."

"Why don't you two take the end of the table?" Mark suggested, drawing out the chair he'd been using for Maisie.

"Thank you, Mark. I like this. I can see Gary while he's talking and get my pencil moving at the same time."

"Of course, and thank you," Mark said, glancing over at Gary Boynton. He added,

146

"Maisie really is amazingly talented. It's as if she can read your mind and can see what you're seeing."

"Great," Boynton said.

Mark glanced at Colleen who was standing quietly by the table, her hand resting on Red's head. She glanced back at him with a shrug.

Neither of them could tell if Boynton had been unnerved by his statement.

But he took a seat by Maisie and she asked easy questions to get him started. What color was the man's hair? Was it long hair or short? And his face — squarish, or oblong? Were his brows thick? Maisie was thorough as she questioned him, her pencil moving all the while. She could keep it light — asking if the man had appeared more like a classic Greek sculpture or a Neanderthal.

It wasn't long before she had a realistic sketch going.

If he was real, he was in his mid to late thirties, dark-haired, with a bit of a look Mark would have called that of a "French artiste." The sketch showed a good-looking man with wavy dark hair and handsomely manicured facial hair — mustache and goatee. The face Maisie portrayed was of a man who could easily appeal to young women.

When Maisie had finished, Boynton sat back and said, "Wow."

"Wow?" Colleen asked.

"That could be a picture, it's so close!" Boynton said. Then he frowned. "Hey, you're not going to put that on the news or anything, are you? I mean, what if this guy is dangerous? I don't want him coming for me or finding a way to get back at Dierdre!"

"We'll be discreet for the time being," Mark assured him.

"For the time being —" Boynton began.

"If we find any evidence against this man, we'll make sure his picture goes out, suggesting we got the sketch another way. Not to worry," Mark assured him.

"Okay, thanks. I want to help in any way, I just don't want to become a target — or I mean, have Dierdre wind up as a target again," Boynton said.

Maisie took her sketch and kept working for a minute, adding pencil strokes that gave her rendering even greater life.

She held up the sketch for them all to see.

"That's him. That's him to a T," Boynton said.

"And we will be discreet," Colleen promised him. "We certainly don't want Dierdre to be targeted again — or you!"

She gave him her sweetest smile.

"Well, I'm done here, right? They've allowed me to be in the hospital with Dierdre. Those hospital chairs are ridiculous, but, right now, I'd sleep on a bed of nails to be near her."

"You're free to go with our most sincere thanks," Mark told him.

Boynton nodded, thanked the three of them, and left the conference room.

"That's amazing, Maisie," Colleen said.

"Thanks. I draw what I hear. I hope it's accurate," Maisie said.

"Did anything about him suggest he was making up a person?" Mark asked her.

"No. In fact, he sounded as if he was trying to see back with his mind's eye, so I do believe you will find this guy exists."

"Thanks so much," Mark told her. "Hang on a minute. I'm going to snap a picture and then I'll have you get it into our system. Just ours, for now. We don't know if this guy is guilty of anything, and we'll look into it first."

"Sure thing."

Maisie waited while Mark took a picture and then scooped up her artwork to enter into the Krewe files.

She headed out, saying, "Have a nice night, you guys."

"Thank you! Same to you," Colleen told her.

Maisie left, but then came back in. "I know you," she told Mark. "Do you want to leave Red with me for a bit while you try to find this guy? I'm staying on with the late shift, and I sure do love his company . . ."

Mark grinned. "Sure, thanks, Maisie. Red can certainly hang with you for a while."

"Cool! Red, come along!" Maisie said.

The dog looked at Mark. "Yep, it's okay, Red. I'll be back for you."

Maisie and Red left together. Mark turned to Colleen.

"It's been a long day. I'll get you home if you want. Your sister is coming, right?"

"She has a key. I'm a partner on this — not a nine-to-fiver," Colleen said.

"Well, we can get dinner out of it anyway. But I'll just be asking about the man in the sketch, so if you'd rather —"

"My sister is great. She'll make herself at home and be fine. She's competent and knows how to find something in my fridge or order herself some dinner."

"Okay, then. Next stop — what was the name of the restaurant?"

Colleen glanced at the notes in her phone.

"Petunia Pete's. It's a strange name. It's supposed to be on the high end of eateries, and I believe it's well rated."

"Gary Boynton would take his love to no less a place — especially if he was planning on putting her in a pine box later."

Colleen smiled. "You really don't like him, do you?"

He shrugged. "There's just something about him. That stuff with his car . . ."

"I get the same feeling, though honestly, buffing his car wasn't that terrible a thing to be doing," Colleen said. "I know my dad was sick once, and I was really scared because it was his heart. He was in the hospital and we couldn't see him. All I wanted to do was play a game on my phone. It got me through."

Mark grimaced and nodded.

"Okay, I'll give him the car buffing. Because you're right. During the pandemic, I had a friend who couldn't be in the hospital with her husband. She went crazy on phone gambling."

"I probably would have gambled if I'd been old enough," Colleen told him. "In times of stress, well, I guess we do whatever we need to do."

They arrived at the restaurant. There was no parking in front.

"I'll drop you off if you want to go ahead and get a seat."

"I actually walk quite well. I'm fine. Let's find a parking space."

He nodded and drove around and found a municipal garage. Once parked, they walked the few blocks to Petunia Pete's.

"Oh! Is Ragnar joining us?" Colleen asked.

Mark shook his head. "He's focused on the hospital." He hesitated. "I'm sure you know. Criminals who are intent on making sure a witness or someone else is dead — someone who survived a first murder attempt — sometimes find their way to the hospital. Ragnar is going to make sure both of our rescued young women remain rescued."

"Good call. But the police are there watching."

"And the police are good. It's like everything else. Most officers are excellent, doing their civic duty. But Ragnar's always afraid of a roo—"

He broke off.

Colleen grinned. "Rookie?"

He shrugged. "Someone who really doesn't expect any danger. Other Krewe members will spell him later. We're bad in a way. At the Krewe, we have come to primarily rely on one another, when honestly, there are incredible officers and agents elsewhere. But the way we work . . ."

He trailed off.

They asked the hostess for a table. Mark also pulled out his phone, explaining he was FBI, and they were looking for anyone who was working a few nights ago, and who might have seen a certain customer — a man who could be a witness in an ongoing investigation.

The hostess was flustered and worried, but she looked at the picture and assured Mark he could also speak with the manager and the waitstaff.

But as she was talking, Colleen was looking around the room.

She gave Mark a quick jab on the arm.

"Mark."

He turned to her, frowning. But then he saw what she saw.

The man captured in Maisie's sketch was seated at a window table, eyes on his phone while he took bites of meat from the plate to his side.

CHAPTER SIX

The man in the sketch was dark-haired with light eyes, probably early thirties, and dressed nicely in a casual jacket and open-neck tailored shirt.

He didn't see Mark and Colleen at first as they stood by his table. When he looked up, he was surprised, but didn't appear to be dismayed.

"Uh — hi. Can I help you?" he asked.

"You can," Mark said, producing his badge.

That did startle the man.

Mark quickly added, "We just need to ask you a few questions."

"Um, sure. I — I'm sorry. I can't see what the FBI might want with me. I don't even watch porn on the internet. Oh, sorry!" he said again quickly, glancing at Colleen.

"Not to worry," she said, sliding into the booth across from him, close to the window so Mark could join her in the booth.

The man appeared completely bewildered.

"We just need some help with something you might have seen," Colleen said quietly.

He reacted well to her words, nodding — while still looking confused.

"You eat here frequently?" Mark asked.

The man smiled. "Almost every night. I'm an accountant. My office is in the building over there." He pointed across the street.

"And your name?" Colleen asked.

"Murray. Murray Calhoun."

"Thank you, Mr. Calhoun. I'm Special Agent Mark Gallagher and this is my partner, Special Agent Colleen Law."

Murray Calhoun nodded, still anxious and confused.

"We heard you were here the night before last, and you paid your bill at the same time as another couple, also leaving the restaurant when they did. The young woman was attractive, and you noticed her?"

Calhoun frowned and then appeared to remember. "I — yes. They were obviously a couple, but yes, I saw them when I was leaving. The guy walked her to her car. She got in and drove away."

"Did you see her after?" Mark asked.

"What? No! I said they were a couple. She was certainly attractive — I'm not blind. But why would I have seen her again?"

"We're just trying to put together puzzle pieces, Mr. Calhoun," Colleen said. She gave him a smile that seemed to relax him a bit.

"Hey, I looked at her. People look at attractive people. Her guy was looking at a few people after she left too."

"You saw where he went?" Mark asked.

He pointed down the street. "I don't know where he was going, but I saw him pass by a couple of girls and he said something and grinned and they laughed back. He . . ." Calhoun paused for a minute. "It seemed he was in a hurry."

"Where did you go after?" Mark asked.

"Back to work. We handle some major businesses. Taxes are a year-round thing when businesses are trying to pay as little as possible. Thank God there's no flat tax. Accountants would be out of business."

Mark wasn't sure what their expressions might have been, but Calhoun must have seen or sensed something.

"Hey, I worked until nearly midnight. My secretary was there too. And a few other workers. You're welcome to check on me." He shook his head. "What's this all about?"

"The young lady was abducted. Thankfully, she's been found," Colleen said.

There was no sense hiding it; the media

had the information. Mark hadn't had much time for the news, but he knew there were public records that could be accessed. Angela had been handling the reporters. They always had to be careful about just what information went out, but since women had been killed . . .

The public knew all about The Embracer.

"No! Oh, my God! That sick fuck who's been killing women had her?" Calhoun asked. "Oh! Sorry," he added.

"Not a problem," Colleen said.

Calhoun's horror at the thought seemed very real.

"We don't know. But she was found," Mark said.

"Thank God!"

"Well, we'll let you get back to your dinner," Mark said. "And thank you. You won't mind if we verify with your office?"

"I'd think you were lax if you didn't," Calhoun said. "The name of the firm is Accurate Accounts. Stop by during normal hours and you can speak with whomever you want. There were several people working that night."

"Thanks. We appreciate that," Mark said, sliding out of the booth. Colleen followed him, adding her thanks too.

"Did you want to eat? We are in a restaurant. Or would you like to get back home and see your sister?" Mark asked her. "I need to get Red. And call —"

"I'll call his office," Colleen said. "And I guess I should get back. Though this place looks good."

"Then we'll get a table and eat quickly," Mark told her.

They returned to the hostess stand and were seated. Calhoun was paying his bill as they sat. He nodded to them gravely as he left the restaurant.

They ordered, and as soon as they had done so, Colleen got on the phone. She managed to get someone to pick up the line, even though it was after hours and she'd initially hit an answering machine.

"I just spoke to an office manager, a nice, talkative fellow," she said, after she'd ended the call. "Apparently, a lot of their people put in a great deal of overtime, which allows them to take personal days or vacations when they need them. I'm assuming someone should go there. One of us?"

"We may ask Ragnar to go," Mark said.

"Okay, so what next?"

"We'll see what Angela has discovered about boyfriend number two, the author. If he wasn't in New York at the time Dierdre was kidnapped . . . ."

"And if he was?"

"Then he's off the hook."

"And you're still certain Carver didn't slip out of the house and kidnap Dierdre?"

Mark shook his head. "I just don't think so. I could be proven wrong, but . . ."

Their salads arrived. Mark glanced at his watch.

"Worried about Red?" she asked.

He grinned. "No. Red has stayed in the offices all night a few times. He has a bed there and dog food, and someone is always there, twenty-four-seven. Red is fine. I'm more worried about you."

She laughed softly. "I told you. Megan is a big girl."

"But you want to see her, right?"

"I do. I love my siblings. Trust me, we were normal siblings. When we were kids, we would fight over the usual silly things, but we'd stand against the world if one of us was under attack. We're close as adults even though we've all followed our passions to different states. Yes, I want to see her and I will see her. She's staying with me for a few days. But we respect what we all do, so . . ."

"And Megan hasn't met Brant Pickering, the author?"

"No, I told you. She'd love to."

"Maybe we should arrange for that."

Their food arrived.

They'd both opted for tuna steaks.

Mark thanked their server and waited until they were alone again before asking, "Will Megan mind if we ask her to meet him and talk to him?"

"Mind? She'll be thrilled."

"Except she'll know her hero is under suspicion."

"Megan will be fine. We're investigating — she understands that." Colleen hesitated. "My family is all . . . weird. She's amazing at what she does because she knows what people really mean when they're trying to write something down. Or when they're speaking, but not finding the right words." She hesitated. "And well, you know. She speaks to the dead. That's thrilled her beyond measure too. Some of her favorite authors have . . . remained."

Mark smiled. "She sounds great."

"She is," Colleen assured him, smiling.

"I'm going to try to arrange something for tomorrow morning. Will that work?"

"I'll ask her. She's here for work, but I don't know when her meetings are. She just said she was coming, and I said she should use her key."

"Let me know. I'll need to get to Pickering too, but I'm assuming he'll be hanging at the hospital as long as they let him. Then again . . ."

"If he's a guilty man, he'll be out on the prowl," Colleen murmured. "What did you think of our sketch man?"

"I think he's just a guy who saw a pretty girl, noted her, and went about his business. What do you think?"

She grimaced. "I think you're right."

"How's the tuna?"

"Obviously pretty good since I have none left."

"Yeah. The eating here part of tonight has been all right. Let's get going. I'll drop you off and go get Red."

He paid the check and they headed out.

"Red is great. I'd love to have a dog. But I haven't thought it would be fair to be working or studying all the time and have a dog. I do have a cat. A really scruffy-looking rescue. Jensen. But he's very independent. Okay, so I do leave the TV on for him — Animal Planet."

Mark laughed. "It's true. Cats are just more independent. Dogs do need a lot more attention. Luckily Red is usually with me; and even at the office, he's loved."

"Maybe one day," she said.

"Well, Red thinks the world of you, so for

now . . ."

They'd reached the car. She managed to get into the passenger's seat before he could come around to open the door.

She smiled at him. "No need to be chivalrous. We're partners."

"Sorry, I was just raised to be polite."

"And that's a great quality," she said. "And I may be a little too . . ."

"Too?"

She laughed. "Insecure about being a third — or fourth — wheel, with you, Ragnar, and Red."

"There's no need. You possess a talent Ragnar and I are lacking, and your 'hearing' is even superior to Red's." He hesitated. "You saved Dierdre. I might not have stopped where you insisted we stop. I might have backtracked. And it might have been too late."

"Thanks," she said quietly.

At her building, he left her off on the street. "Eight a.m. tomorrow?"

"I'll be outside. Ready."

"And talk to Megan."

"Of course. I'll get right back to you."

She was true to her word. Mark's phone rang before he reached the Krewe offices.

"Hey, Megan doesn't have anything until tomorrow evening. She's thrilled to meet with Brant Pickering. And she understood immediately he was a suspect; she's happy to prove we're wrong about him."

"He's just a person of interest."

"I said that. She said 'suspect.' "

He smiled. Megan Law sounded like Colleen's sister, all right.

"Great. I'll set up a time with Pickering —"

"Okay. Megan will be downstairs with me at eight."

"The meeting may be later —"

"We might as well have her with us for whenever. And she loves dogs. She'll be fine."

Mark decided to let it go. He wasn't sure if he wanted a civilian with them more than was necessary. But maybe it would work out.

He wanted to get back to see Carver again.

And he wanted to go in and search Carver's house.

A search warrant had been issued.

Forensic crews had been in.

But he knew there was something there . . .

He just didn't know what.

"Okay. Eight a.m.," he said.

"We'll be there."

It was wonderful to see Megan. Not that

they didn't get together when they could, but now, with the three of them working in different states, it wasn't family dinner every Sunday night.

Megan was seated on the old sofa in the living room when Colleen came in. She started to rise, but Jensen, asleep on her lap, made a protesting sound.

They both laughed.

"I'll come to you," Colleen said, and she did so, heading to the sofa, leaning over the cat, and hugging her sister before falling into the seat next to her.

"Long day, huh? I hope they give you a dinner break!"

"Actually, I had a really great dinner."

"Oh?"

"We were looking for someone from a sketch, or someone who could tell us who he might be. And it happened to be at a great restaurant."

"Ah, the perks!"

Megan grew serious then. "But they have you working on those awful Embracer murders, right?"

"Hey. I wanted to be FBI. And we saved a girl, Megan."

"I get it. I do."

"We need your help."

"My help?"

Colleen explained they were just trying to get alibis for Brant Pickering and Gary Boynton.

Megan, of course, hadn't fallen for it.

"I can't believe he's a suspect — that incredible writer is a suspect!"

"Person of interest."

"So, basically a suspect! But I'm happy to prove the man innocent," Megan said.

Megan studied her.

"You're crazy, you know."

"I am?"

"Wanting to do this for a living. It has to be so hard, dealing with . . . the terrible things people do to other people."

"But we get good things too," Colleen said.

Megan nodded. "I said I thought you were crazy. I didn't say it isn't great. I just don't feel I have what you have."

"I can listen to someone ramble for an hour and have no idea what they really mean, and you can practically read minds."

Megan shrugged. "I don't think I'm a complete yellow-bellied coward, but I don't have your fighting spirit either. You're a quiet fighter. You sit there and listen. No bravado. When it comes to it, you just act!"

"We're lucky. We have great parents."

"The poor things, having to put up with

us. In all honesty, learning about the Krewe of Hunters has made me feel a lot more normal. I guess any of us with our strange abilities spend a lot of time trying not to appear crazy to those around us. And I'm pretty good at it — mainly because I've had a few playful spirits try to make me respond on a busy street or in a store or when others are around."

"Cell phones and earbuds — they're magic. Half the world walks around, appearing to talk to themselves," Colleen said. "Anyway, tell me about this Brant Pickering."

"I can show you!" Megan told her.

She winced, looking at the cat sleeping on her lap. Colleen scooped up Jensen — who remained a floppy pile of fur in her arms — allowing Megan to get up. Megan went to her overnight bag, opened it quickly, and produced a large coffee table–style book. The front cover was a striking photo of Arlington House and the cemetery that stretched behind it.

It was titled, *The Deep, Dark — But Sometimes Light — History of Washington, DC.*

Megan handed it to Colleen, and Colleen eased the cat onto the sofa to open the book on her lap.

"He writes about everything — everything!

We have a tendency to think that we're living in political division now, but people have had some harsh opinions through the years. Of course, social media has made it easier for people to remain divided. But they used to have duels. Most schoolkids know that Aaron Burr and Alexander Hamilton dueled, and that Hamilton was killed. Thanks to the play and movie, of course, more people have become interested in that stage of history. But Pickering goes further with everything. He explains the culture and the mix of people during each era — I think he's just amazing. This book follows history from the determination of the area that would become DC to the present, covering a lot of dark days we got through."

"Dark days, huh?" Colleen murmured.

"He points out America has weathered many storms. Yes, he covers the dark — but in an optimistic way."

"That's almost an oxymoron."

Megan laughed. "Glad you know the word!"

"Hey!" Colleen protested.

It was late; she meant to be on the sidewalk in front of the townhome at eight sharp in the morning, with Megan by her side.

"I have to get some sleep. And you do too.

I'm not sure about the schedule tomorrow, but I said that you —"

"I heard you. Oh, wow, and come to think of it — how's your partner?"

"I have three of them," Colleen said.

Her sister grinned. "You have three — but one main partner?"

"He's polite."

"Ah! Let's see. He really rubbed you the wrong way at first. But there is something about him you respect. Is he tall, dark, and gorgeous, tough as nails, gruff, or older than the hills?"

"I really like the dog," Colleen said. Her sister's abilities could be annoying sometimes.

"The dog?"

"Red. Mark Gallagher and Ragnar Johansen were partners with Red. Red is fantastic — a dog for any occasion. He can find people. And I'm willing to bet he's a good judge of character too."

"Ragnar Johansen? You're working with a Viking?"

Colleen shrugged. "Well, his heritage is Norwegian. And yes, Ragnar looks the part. Very tall, broad shoulders, blond. Mark is . . . very tall."

Megan started to laugh. "There is so much in what you're not saying!"

Colleen groaned. "Yes, I disliked him at first. Hard not to dislike someone when they were so totally opposed to working with you. But . . . he's been okay."

"And he is good-looking?"

"Contrary to television, not all agents are good-looking."

Megan laughed. "But he is!"

Colleen groaned. "I'm not even partnered up with him permanently. It's this case. And I don't actively dislike him anymore. He's gotten decent. And that's it. But I must get some sleep and so must you. Pickup is at eight in the morning."

"I'm going to work with you, huh?"

"I figured it would be easier than having you wait around to see when Brant Pickering might agree to meet you."

"You're telling him he'll be doing a favor for you, meeting with me?"

"Yeah," Colleen admitted.

"Well, I'm hoping you would have set it up as a favor to me anyway. So — fine. But eight? What's the matter with a nine o'clock pickup?"

"Please. Eight is better than seven, and that happens too."

"Okay. Well then, good night!"

"Don't you want to know more about the meeting with Brant tomorrow?"

Megan grinned. "I'm pretty sure I'll get briefed by one of your partners. And I know the drill. Chat. Be friendly. Be bookish — and find out where he was the night Dierdre Ayers disappeared."

"Yes, but —"

"The fact she was kidnapped and found has been all over the media. Along with the question — did law enforcement catch The Embracer or is he still out there? I will talk books, books, books — and find out where he was the day and night when they rescued Sally Smithson and you helped rescue Dierdre Ayers!"

With a little lift of her chin, Megan turned and headed into the guest bedroom.

Colleen watched her sister go and smiled.

Megan was going to be just fine.

Red sat by Mark's feet, probably wondering why they hadn't gone home yet.

But while he looked up at Mark imploringly now and then, he was, as ever, a well-mannered dog. He was Red.

To think someone had tossed him onto the road as a puppy.

That shouldn't surprise Mark, he knew. He saw enough of what man was willing to do to his fellow man.

But the carelessness of one individual for

the life of a puppy had been a lucky thing for Mark. Red was truly one of a kind, he thought affectionately. He scratched the dog's head absently while staring at the computer screen.

He couldn't find anything that suggested Brant Pickering might be hiding a secret life as a serial killer.

Then again, it wouldn't be a secret life if anyone knew about it.

Pickering had made the move to New York City about a month ago.

Before that, he had been with Sally Smithson for several years. Since he was considered an academic writer, he wasn't on every billboard, but he still had a legion of readers. Mark had been through every bit of his social media.

He wrote frequently about cool pieces of history that warranted a book.

And he wrote about his personal life as well. His social pages had dozens of pictures of him and Sally — at amusement parks, at a comic con, exploring museums, and more. When he had moved, however, his social posts had stopped. He never mentioned he'd had a breakup. He just didn't mention his personal life at all.

Mark sat back. He could do this at home, of course, and he really needed to go home to get started early in the morning.

At some point, he wanted to talk to Carver.

The man might give up a clue to something eventually.

But he wanted to start at the hospital with both men. He could be wrong, of course. But in every situation, even in eliminating suspects, it was important to start with those closest to the victims.

That probably meant going back to the girls who hadn't been so lucky.

He was starting to pull out the files when Red woofed and wagged his tail.

Looking up, Mark saw Ragnar standing at the entrance to the office they shared.

"Burning the midnight oil, eh?" Ragnar asked him.

"It's one of those cases. Doesn't let you go, you know?"

Ragnar walked around and sank into the chair behind his own desk. Mark had called and briefed him earlier — telling him about Boynton and the sketch artist and how they had easily found the man depicted in the sketch.

"You're burning midnight oil too," Mark commented.

"It's one of those cases," Ragnar agreed sheepishly.

"But you left the hospital."

"Because Bruce McFadden arrived."

"He'll do until morning?"

Ragnar nodded. "Then Axel Tiger is taking over."

"Great."

"I had to tell myself the other officers and agents are vigilant. I don't want anything to happen to our victims while they're in the hospital."

"I know."

"And now?" Ragnar asked. "The guy in the sketch seems legit."

"I think he was just a guy in a restaurant who happened to finish eating at the same time as Gary Boynton and Dierdre, and he just looked at a pretty girl."

"Your instincts are good, but —"

"We checked him out. Unless a whole lot of people are liars, I believe he's telling the truth."

"And you still don't like Boynton."

"I don't."

"What about the writer?"

"What about him? You watched him all day."

Ragnar shook his head. "I don't know what to think yet. He didn't kidnap anyone today — that's for sure. He was at the hospital. The police are working with us. He has a tail. He's staying at a hotel near the hospital. Under surveillance."

"And he probably knows he's being watched. Which brings me to a plan."

Mark explained to Ragnar about Colleen's sister, Megan.

"A civilian?" Ragnar said.

"But she's a fan; she's in love with the man's work. That will be honest. She may be able to find out things we can't."

He nodded. "And Megan — does she hear?"

Mark frowned. "Does she have what Colleen has? No. Something different, but it's there. And yes, she sees the dead. She makes an excellent editor because, according to Colleen, she knows what people mean when they're speaking or writing. We all talk in circles sometimes. I guess she's something of a —"

"Psychic?"

"No. More like a mental interpreter. There's something jaded in me. I keep thinking one of these guys is involved. Of course, we can go back and investigate the cases of the girls who — who weren't so lucky. But I could swear Carver was guilty in both those cases."

"Emily Watkins and Lainie Nowak," Ragnar said. "Yeah. But I think we need to talk to Carver again. See if he has details only he would know."

"So, tomorrow, I'll pick up Colleen and her sister at eight. We'll meet at the hospital. Try to set Megan up with Brant Pickering. And then we'll take another run at Carver."

Ragnar nodded. He stood. "I'm really going to go home," he said. "I suggest you do the same."

To prove he agreed, Mark stood up. Red barked and leapt to his feet too.

"Even the dog knows you need to get some sleep," Ragnar said, giving Red a good-night pat. "Then again, I never suggested either of us was smarter than the dog."

Mark grimaced and nodded.

"All right. Tomorrow, then."

They left the building together, Red trailing after them to their cars in the parking garage.

When he reached home, Mark noted it was eleven.

He usually slept in quiet.

That night, he turned on the television.

One thing about the news — it was dedicated and didn't let any situation go.

Maybe that was a good thing.

The anchors on the show were discussing The Embracer case.

And just like him, they were wondering if the man arrested with a kidnapped woman in his basement was the one and only "Embracer," or if there were others out there.

He turned the television off.

He had his own mind to keep up steady arguments and suppositions.

And yet he found himself wondering about their new partner.

She was the real deal. And he had to question himself, wondering why he had assumed someone young and new wouldn't be exceptionally talented and right for the case.

Exceptional. In many ways.

Tomorrow might well bring more. If Colleen believed in her sister . . .

Well, she was probably exceptional too.

He found himself doubting anyone could be quite as exceptional as Colleen.

Then he was angry with himself.

Because he realized while he'd always recognized she was an *exceptionally* attractive woman, he hadn't thought her appearance meant anything to him.

And maybe it hadn't.

But now he realized he was coming to appreciate the way she smiled, the sound of her voice, and the way she moved. And there was no denying the fact he admired her integrity — and the desire she had to work for the innocent, to possibly save lives, and find justice.

Okay, okay . . . he liked her.

He turned the news back on.

Better than his own thoughts.

But even then, his thoughts wouldn't turn off.

They were careful to live real lives. Many Krewe members had families now. They went to kids' birthday parties and worried about home and schoolwork and what to eat for dinner.

It was important, Jackson always stressed, that they have lives.

And so, his thoughts switched between the case, and wondering what it would be like not to be seeking a horrific killer with Colleen, to maybe instead be having dinner. Outside, near the ocean, on a sandy shore, with a soft breeze blowing . . .

He groaned with such aggravation Red jumped up from his dog bed in the hall and raced into the room, ready to do battle for him.

He groaned again, but softly.

"Sorry, boy. It won't happen again," he vowed.

He turned the TV off again, then punched

his pillow and willed himself to sleep.

But still . . .

It was probably another hour before he slept.

CHAPTER SEVEN

"That's him now, I imagine," Megan said, pointing down the street as Mark's navy SUV moved along, signaling a stop.

"That's him," Colleen agreed.

"Wow," Megan said.

"Wow — beautiful dog?" Colleen asked. Red was seated in the front seat at the moment. Once Mark pulled over, Colleen knew the dog would jump in the back.

Megan laughed. "Well, yes, wow. Beautiful dog. But your new partner . . . perfect for the job. Square jaw, great face . . . those eyes. He's perfect. Not the guy you want to be interrogating you. The guy you want with you in a fight."

She grinned at Colleen.

"Not that I want you in a fight!" she said.

"Honestly, Megan. A lot of the job is sitting in the office poring through information, looking for clues on social media, or sometimes, just watching people. Like sitting in a car all day."

Mark's car had pulled up to the curb. He leaned over to open the passenger-side door.

He gave Megan a very nice smile.

"Hi, Megan. I'm Mark. I'm sure your sister has told you what we're doing."

Megan started for the back door. Colleen urged her into the front passenger's seat instead.

"There might be a little dog hair," Mark said.

"I love dogs," Megan told him. "And he's beautiful. Red, right?" she said, twisting around to address the dog.

Red let out a woof and Megan turned to stroke him. She looked at Mark, and he returned her glance right before pulling back onto the road.

"I'm a dog person," Megan told him. "I have a German shepherd mix. Her name is Lily. I'm probably wearing a little German shepherd hair as it is."

"Was Lily a rescue?" he asked, driving.

"Yep. But she wasn't horribly abandoned. Her owner passed away and the woman's son was overseas in the military. I went to school with him, and he knows how much I love pups, so . . . anyway, Lily is great. Nothing like Red, I imagine, but she does love people. She keeps me exercising."

Megan seemed to get along easily with Mark.

And Mark kept smiling at Megan.

Colleen wondered if even Red noted how much easier his master took to Megan than he had to Colleen.

Granted they had been thrown together to find a woman buried in the earth before she suffocated.

Megan grew serious.

"Special Agent Gallagher —"

"Mark, please."

"Of course, Mark. I just don't see how this man who is so incredible with descriptions and words, who has such a handle on the customs and mores of people during different times in history, could be a horrible monster."

"You'd be surprised," Mark said quietly.

"So, I'm just supposed to find out if he left New York the night that Dierdre Ayers was taken?"

"Megan," Colleen said, "obviously, you can't just ask him if he was in New York City."

"Duh!" Megan said, glancing back at her, frowning. "My question is — that's the main thing you want me to find out? And it's all right if I tell him how fabulous his work is?"

"Fawn all over him," Mark said.

"Oh, I don't really fawn. I mean, I have professional integrity, you know. And sadly, he's never worked with my publishing house. Of course, maybe my adoration would make him want to in the future!"

"If he's innocent, you're welcome to the writer," Mark assured her.

Megan asked about Red as they drove. Mark described how he happened to have a friend who was a dog trainer — one of the best in the country — and Red had just proved himself to be exceptional at many disciplines.

The two engaged in conversation all the way to the hospital.

Ragnar was already there. He was standing in the hall on the fourth floor when they arrived. Mark was a bit ahead of the two of them.

Megan caught Colleen's arm lightly. "My Lord! And that's the partner? Well, I'm a little relieved. Patrick would be relieved. It looks like you have a pair of giant bastions to guard you. Not to mention the dog."

"Definitely the easiest partner to get along with," Colleen assured her.

"Put pigtails on that guy, and you could walk him into a Viking movie," Megan said.

"I admit I thought the same thing."

"And that's —"

"Ragnar Johansen."

They were only a few steps behind, and Mark quickly performed the introductions. Ragnar was distant but polite. And Colleen knew why, of course. He wasn't happy about a civilian being involved.

But he couldn't help but hope for results.

"Axel just left," Ragnar said, escorting them into the office where police and agents — someone at all times — kept watch over the rooms. "Gary Boynton left last night; he slept at his house. Brant Pickering never left the hospital. He slept in the recliner chair in Sally's room. Apparently, Dierdre is going to be released this afternoon." He hesitated, glancing at Megan. "Dierdre was taken and stuffed into a box. She wasn't . . . held for long. Sally, on the other hand, spent days being abused in the basement. She'll be under observation another twenty-four hours. Then, she'll be released too."

"Well, Dierdre may be madly in love with the most courteous jerk in the world," Mark said. "But I'm willing to bet she'll go home to her parents' house when she's discharged."

"I think she'll want to go to Gary Boynton's house," Colleen said. "But I imagine her parents will be persistent. And because she does love them and she may still feel a little shaky, I think she'll oblige."

"We'll have observation on both residences," Ragnar said. "Anyway, you want to be the one to talk to Brant Pickering and ask him if he'd speak with your sister?" he asked Colleen.

"I think I'll be most convincing if it's a favor the man is doing for me," Colleen said.

She noted Mark and Ragnar looked at one another briefly, and she had to admit the two men had a great partnership. All it seemed to take was a glance for the two to know if they were in agreement or not.

And they were.

"Just tap on Sally's door. He's in there, as is Sally," Ragnar said. "We'll stay in the office to watch on the screens."

"Red, stay," Mark told the dog.

Red, apparently, had thought he was going too.

"Of course." Colleen could see the room on the screen in the office. Sally was in the bed. Brant Pickering was at her side in a chair, holding her hand.

The IV was in her arm on the other side.

Colleen headed out of the office then across and down the hall to tap on the door and peek her head in.

"Hello," Sally murmured.

Brant Pickering stood. "Special Agent . . ."

She smiled. "Law. Colleen Law. I'm sorry. I don't mean to disturb you."

"I don't mind being disturbed in the least," Sally said. "I'm alive. Disturb me. Though I'm afraid I won't be of much help. If I could remember anything at all, though . . ."

Colleen nodded as she walked up to the bed. "I am disturbing you for a different reason," she said quietly. She winced. "Sally, with his agreement, would it be possible to steal Brant for about ten or fifteen minutes?"

"I — Yes, of course," Sally said. But, puzzled, she looked at Brant.

Brant looked back at Colleen.

And Colleen spoke quickly.

"I'm a triplet," she explained with a rueful smile. "And —"

"Wow. Cool. I think you're the first triplet I've met," Sally said. "Are you identical?"

Colleen smiled and shook her head. "We're fraternal triplets. I have one brother and one sister, and no, not identical at all."

"Ah," Sally said.

Brant was still staring at her.

"The thing is," Colleen continued, "my sister's an editor, and she's read everything Brant has ever written."

Brant smiled then. "She has? I didn't think anyone had done that!"

"She thinks you're one of the finest historical authors out there. And she'd love to meet you."

"Oh, cool," Brant said.

"I hoped maybe you wouldn't mind giving her a few minutes in the waiting room."

"Brant, of course — you have to meet a fan, especially one who knows all your books!" Sally said.

Brant smiled. Then he laughed. "I thought maybe you guys wanted to interrogate me! I mean, I am the boyfriend — was the boyfriend." He stumbled over the words and then looked at Sally. "With any luck," he said softly, "I am the boyfriend again?"

Sally looked at him adoringly.

The look he bestowed on her was impressive too. For a brief moment, Colleen might not have been there at all. They were together, and that was it.

Then Brant looked at Colleen. He cleared his throat.

"It's rather sad how it takes almost losing someone forever before we realize how precious they are. The people we love matter more than anything in the world."

Colleen nodded. "I'm so grateful Sally was found, and you two are . . . together."

"I hate leaving Sally. Even for a minute."

"I'll stay in here. I'll just give Megan a call and tell her you don't mind meeting with her. And I am so sorry to bother you with a personal favor like this."

"Are you kidding? I appreciate those who enjoy my work!" Brant said. "We on the academic side of publishing don't often have adoring fans."

"Well, my sister is adoring. She says you have an uncanny way with understanding people and the times they lived in," Colleen said.

That was true.

She knew they were being watched, but she made a point of calling Megan's cell. She wasn't sure if, in the small room, Megan's voice might carry.

"Brant Pickering will meet you in the waiting room."

"Cool," Megan said.

"Oh, and not to worry. We'll get you home after that."

She pretended to listen to an answer, aware Megan was already moving toward the waiting room.

She ended the call and looked at Brant.

"I don't need a babysitter in here every second," Sally said. "I mean, I'm happy to

have you in here, Special Agent Law, but
—"

She broke off as Brant frowned.

"Not a problem," Colleen said. "I'm
delighted to stay! I'll take the chair by the
bed, if I may. What were you two watching
before I came in?"

Sally laughed softly. "What do you think?
We're watching the History Channel!"

Colleen laughed, then took the chair by
Sally's side as Brant left the room.

Colleen and Megan weren't identical, as
Colleen had told him, but it was evident
they were related.

Megan might have been an inch shorter
than her sister, and where Colleen's hair
was a deep, dark, burning red, Megan was a
honey blonde. Like her sister, though, she
had large, expressive green eyes.

Her hair fell around her shoulders in
gentle waves. She was wearing a skirt suit
— prepared for whatever meetings had
brought her to the DC area — but the
blouse she was wearing was a soft white
with a sash that fell in a feminine flow from
her neckline to her waist.

Mark was objective, he thought, as he and
Ragnar watched her.

And objectively, he noted she, like her

sister, was a beautiful young woman. She was also capable of being composed and determined.

She had hurried to the waiting room to sit and wait.

Luckily, there was only one other person in the room, a man who had nodded a hello to Megan when she'd entered, and quickly turned his attention back to his phone.

Megan was good with people. She stood and shook Brant's hand, not throwing herself at him in any way, but clearly greeting him warmly.

As they sat together, they chatted about books in general.

Then she commented on one of his titles, and why she had enjoyed it so much.

"The bloodstains on the Capitol stairway — I loved the way you explained them. And then the way you covered the controversy and arguing between William Taulbee and the journalist, Charles Kincaid. That Kincaid *wrote* the article about Taulbee's adultery that ended his political career — and turned him into a lobbyist. You wrote the facts — that after one of their arguments, Kincaid went and got a gun and shot Taulbee in the head. And Stewart, the architect, said in 1966, the stains were where it happened. He never said they were

189

the stains, but they could have been from the shooting. I guess politics have always been . . . messed up to say the least. You write about the witnesses who had seen Taulbee threaten Kincaid earlier in the day — and how Kincaid quickly surrendered, how the trial was delayed, and how he was eventually declared not guilty, by self-defense. Of course, he was guilty, but had Taulbee's aggressive behavior against a smaller man swayed the jury? The thing is, you have a way of finding and printing facts, but not being slanted one way or another. You let people make up their own minds regarding what may or may not be! I read so much that *is* slanted — I have just so enjoyed your work! I wind up becoming so fascinated by the subjects you write about too, and then end up reading more and more about them."

Megan Law knew what she was talking about.

And it was apparent her admiration was real.

It was equally apparent Brant Pickering appreciated everything he was hearing.

Then Megan sat back, shaking her head.

"I'm so amazed at the many incredible tales you know about Washington, DC. And I must tell you, I'm excited about what you're going to discover in New York City. Of course, NYC is full of amazing stories throughout history too. Is that why you chose to leave this area and head to New York?"

Pickering sighed at that. "I wanted New York, yes. For exactly the reasons you're saying. From the beginning of European colonization of the New World — and possibly before that — New York with what are now all the boroughs has been an intriguing place. New Netherland, New Amsterdam, and even New Orange, once. Stuyvesant ceded the area to British warships in 1664, but the Dutch recaptured it in 1673, so it was briefly New Orange. They exchanged it for control of Suriname. Native Americans, land sales, Five Points, crooked politicians — the city has had them all. Civil War riots — 'Irish need not apply' — and so much more. Yes, I'm fascinated by the city. Now . . ."

"But you've decided to move back here?" Megan smiled. "I have to admit, that meeting you, I was hoping I'd be invited to a launch party. Sure, different publishing houses, but I have tons of friends working at different houses. We bid against each other in auctions. But we're friends — we all love books!"

"I just . . . well, I never could have imagined what happened to Sally," he said quietly. "She's going to need lots of therapy, but more than that, she's going to need love. We never stopped loving one another. There was a stage where I grew frustrated, and I believed if I made the move, she would follow. Sally couldn't understand my determination or need for something else to delve into. We went so far as to argue children. If we had children, we couldn't just up and move every time I wanted fresh history. And she didn't want kids with a dad who came and went continually, and . . . arguments escalate." He winced, looking truly pained. "I love Sally."

"I can see that," Megan said quietly.

"So, now, I'm not sure."

"On the bright side, New York isn't really all that far from DC," Megan reminded him. "And there's always the train. I love trains. I book myself one of those mini — really mini — compartments, but it's all mine and I work the whole time I'm riding."

He grimaced. "Driving, the distance is about two hundred and fifty miles," he said. "Four or five hours — in light traffic. Which never happens in DC or New York! But I will agree with you that the train has its benefits. As you said — you get a compartment and just lock yourself away. And if you're being smart, you turn your cell phone off!"

"You must have had to do the trip up and back a few times since you've moved . . ."

"Oh, yeah, I've had to come back and forth a few times. Sally and I were together, basically living together, but I'd had my own apartment. I had to close it out and . . . well, anyway. If Sally wants to stay here now, we'll stay here."

"I'm glad to hear that. My sister has told me Sally seems to be a truly lovely person, and we're all sorry she was taken and hurt and traumatized like that. And of course, we are all so glad she's alive."

"Sally sees it that way — at least she says so. But she woke up choking and screaming last night, and I was so grateful they let me stay with her, and I was able to hold her."

"Yes, that's wonderful for her," Megan said. She offered him another smile. "I want to thank you again for meeting me. I am in awe of your mind."

"Thank you! Sadly, Tom Cruise won't be doing any of my books as a movie."

"You never know. People love streaming, and a historical tome can make for a great documentary, or become fictionalized for its entertainment value. Half of my love for history came from reading fiction." She laughed softly. "Maybe you'll get Liam Hemsworth — or Zac Efron! Not that it matters — I mean, what's wrong with a book being amazing on its own?"

"You truly are kind," Pickering told her. "Maybe we'll work together one day."

"That would be great."

"Hey, it could happen," Pickering said. He glanced at his watch.

He didn't need to excuse himself. Megan spoke quickly.

"Please, thank you for meeting me. And I know how concerned you are. You go ahead and get back to Sally."

He pursed his lips into a grimace and nodded, then left the waiting room. Megan waited a minute and returned to the office.

"Was that what you needed?" she asked Mark and Ragnar anxiously.

"Perfect," Mark assured her.

Ragnar studied Megan — he was already calling Angela to ask for the tech department to get started on researching train schedules from New York to Washington.

"Did you learn anything? I still think he's wonderful."

"Megan, come on. You've been around your sister long enough, I imagine. And although she's new with the Krewe, she's not new to law enforcement. Liking or not liking someone doesn't make them innocent or guilty," Mark warned gently.

"Which," Colleen said, coming into the office, "means we can't assume Gary Boynton might be guilty."

"I'm not assuming he's guilty," Mark said. "But I don't like him," he admitted.

Colleen grinned. "As Dierdre's parents see it — employed, courteous, and caring."

"Yep. That's what they see. I see opportunist, smarmy, and yes, careful of his image," Mark said. "Though it doesn't make him guilty. But I do think we still need to talk to Dierdre and perhaps her parents about the ex-boyfriend they didn't like. And I want to talk to Carver again. Or I should say, I want Colleen to talk to Carver again." He hesitated, glancing at Megan. He wanted to go through the crime scene photos on the victims they hadn't gotten to in time.

He wanted to know if Carver had killed them both while working alone. Or with an accomplice. But he knew there would be details only someone involved would know.

Megan glanced at her watch.

"Guys, don't worry about me. I'm going to hitch an Uber back to Colleen's place, then take her car to my meeting. If it ends in time, I'm going to the Smithsonian. I'm good, really," Megan said.

Colleen reached into her bag and handed Megan a key chain.

"You don't need an Uber. We'll get you back," Mark said. He glanced at Ragnar.

Ragnar arched a brow.

"I've some detail work I want to go over with Colleen," Mark said.

Ragnar understood. "Work here until I get back. I'll get on Dierdre and her parents for anything else we might glean. All right, I'll get Megan to Colleen's place."

"We won't leave until you return."

"Hey, I'm okay!" Megan said.

Ragnar was already out of the room.

The sisters said their goodbyes and Megan followed after Ragnar.

When they were gone, Colleen looked at Mark. "Did Megan really help?"

"I think she did. In the best way, she pointed out the distance between DC wasn't that far, and the train made it an easy trip."

"Train schedules, tickets —"

"Angela is on it. Sally?"

"Well, she hasn't dated anyone except for Brant Pickering in years. Friends have been trying to fix her up with someone new, but she's not ready yet. She told me she isn't the type for one-night stands and now . . .

she thinks they do love each other, and they've discussed the future. I believe he isn't here now for just the aftermath, just to get her through; he's here because he realized he almost lost her permanently."

He was quiet.

"I know," Colleen said quietly. "The fact that we *do* like him doesn't make him innocent."

Mark smiled. "We're going back to Carver when Ragnar returns."

"So I gathered. And this time?"

"I'm going to pull up the crime scene photos on the two victims who didn't make it. We'll study them and find details, and I think you'll be able to get Carver talking. And with that, we'll find out if he did kill the first two women, and possibly, whether he did so alone."

It wasn't pleasant to bring up the photos from the first two murders. The women had suffocated in their pine boxes.

Both had been young and attractive in life.

Emily Watkins had been a ballroom dance instructor. Tall, lean, and lithe, with brown eyes and blond hair. In the first photos, of course, her blond hair was a fact that couldn't be seen — dirt had turned everything on her dark. But he continued with the photos, taken as she had been dug out and placed on the coroner's table. And little by little, the pictures revealed more.

"The red barrette," Colleen said.

"Good. Anything else?"

"She's wearing a little pendant. I think it's a shamrock."

Mark studied the picture himself.

"Yes, it is a shamrock."

"She's wearing a light blue bodysuit with jeans over it. Her shoes are gone."

"They were never found."

Colleen nodded, wincing slightly. "I think I have a good idea about Emily," she said.

"Lainie Nowak," he said, changing the range of the photos.

"You and Red found her, right?" she asked.

"Yeah, we found her."

"Before I look at the photos, any details you remember?"

"Earth and dirt. And knowing quickly we were way too late. And while at that point, it was two such murders with the same pine boxes and notes, we knew we were going to be tracking a serial killer."

They studied the crime scene pictures.

The body as it was found, as it was cleaned, as it appeared on the morgue table.

"Little jade earrings," Colleen noted. "And a mole at the side of her cheek. Clothing, navy blue business suit, white ruffled blouse. No stockings or shoes."

No. The Embracer had redressed her. Shoes were not important.

"Yeah. Details," Mark said. He glanced over at the screens showing the two hospital rooms.

Brant Pickering was sitting next to Sally Smithson, tenderly holding her hand.

Gary Boynton was seated by Dierdre. He held her hand and rested his cheek on it where it lay on the bed.

Perfect boyfriends.

And maybe they were.

But he was still convinced Carver had been startled when he'd learned another girl had been kidnapped.

And that meant someone else was out there.

Ragnar returned as they continued to study the screens.

He looked somewhat disgruntled.

"Everything all right?" Mark asked.

"Yeah, sure, of course." Ragnar glanced at Colleen. "Um, your sister is a little stubborn."

"Probably," Colleen agreed. She shrugged. "My brother is stubborn too. Maybe because we're triplets . . . but, hey —" she paused and gave him a crooked smile

"— we're great at sharing. It was a simple necessity with our folks going crazy with three kids the same age at the same time."

"Must have been nice," Mark said.

She looked at him and said softly, "Yeah, I'm sorry. I forgot —"

"You don't need to be sorry but thank you. I was a lucky kid. I loved my mother; she gave me a strange gift by reappearing when she was gone, and I was adopted by the kindest couple in the world." He laughed. "And they made me share too."

"Yes, of course," Colleen said.

"You two should get going," Ragnar urged.

"One more thing: let's pull up the articles in the paper. We need to see what likenesses of Lainie and Emily were shown to the public."

"I'll pull them up on the computer," Ragnar offered.

Two pictures of Emily Watkins had surfaced in different papers. In one, she was beautifully decked out in a shimmering ballroom gown. The necklace she wore was made of rhinestones. Her hair was swept back in a braided updo.

In the other, she was in a T-shirt and jeans, wearing no jewelry, her hair tumbling around her shoulders.

They pulled up Lainie Nowak. She was shown in an elegant black dress, spike heels, and no jewelry.

The second was a natural look as well. She was in tailored pants and a short-sleeved blouse, a broad sash at her waist.

"I'm good," Colleen said. "We'll get going."

"Is Red going with you or staying with me?" Ragnar asked.

"We'll take him," Colleen said, adding quickly, "If that's all right."

Mark and Ragnar both nodded.

As they left, Mark noted Ragnar was already watching the screens.

He'd seldom met anyone who could endure surveillance the way Ragnar did. Ragnar's eye for detail had him seeing things sometimes that others had missed.

Still, he felt bad about how boring it was for Ragnar, constantly watching for them.

No, he supposed it was for Colleen.

He didn't like it. Not one bit. Sure, he was coming to admire her. And he would admit too easily he, Ragnar, and Red had been given a stunning young woman as an addition to their team.

Carver was a detestable monster.

It would be hard to send her in with him, harder than before. And yet, she was an agent. Dedicated, determined . . . and very aware of her own strange talents and those of others. Today, though, she wasn't calling on any special talent.

Just her ability as an interrogator.

And he would look at it through the eyes of a trained special agent.

It was okay that doing so would not be an easy thing to do.

It was going to be a long afternoon.

CHAPTER EIGHT

Colleen waited in the interview room, aware Mark was watching with Red.

Aware that whatever they said could be heard.

Mark was tense and grim. Even Red had seemed to sense it. He'd made a strange sound before she'd left them to enter the room, something between a whine and growl, as if the room itself promised something evil.

She was barely seated before the guards brought in Carver.

The man beamed with pleasure as if a long-awaited relative had returned.

"Colleen! Special Agent Colleen Law. I'm delighted to see you. But to what do I owe the pleasure?" he asked. As he spoke, two guards seated him, attaching the manacles on his wrists to a hook on the table.

No one trusted the man.

"Well, I guess I'm curious, Mr. Carver."

"Jim, please. And I'm calling you Colleen. That is what they call you, right? Or Collie, maybe? Too doggish, perhaps? Col? Hmm. Any darling little nicknames?"

"No. Just Colleen."

"Oh, never 'just' Colleen."

"Am I your type?" she asked flatly.

"Yes, absolutely. Does that scare you?"

"No."

"Really? I'd thought you were so bright. Then again, maybe I'm your type — someone you would just *die* to sleep with."

She gave him a hard smile. "I sleep with my gun, Mr. Carver."

"I guess a gun will do — when you've got nothing else. Then again, a girl like you, well, you haven't been alone that often, have you?"

"Mr. Carver, we're here to talk about you."

"I'm getting out of here. We can talk then."

"I don't think you're getting out."

"I have a really good lawyer. And the agents who came to my house, well, they played fast and loose with the law. I didn't let the blond mammoth in or the dark-haired monster either. The one claimed to be a salesman, and the other was chasing after his dog. Sure. A police dog."

"Red isn't a police dog."

"Oh, right. He's an agent! Worse."

"Mr. Carver, you were holding a young woman against her will."

"She's a liar."

"You said you were The Embracer. The only Embracer."

"I've just been playing with you assholes. Sorry — you are a good-looking asshole. Wow, I think I've got it. You sleep with your gun. Which one? The blond gun? Or the dark-haired one?" He started to laugh. "Not the dog, I hope!"

"I don't think I'm your type at all, Mr. Carver. I sleep with a Glock under my pillow. I wake at the fall of a feather. I've taken just about every type of self-defense class known to man, and I'm not weak or vulnerable in the least."

"That's what you think?" he demanded. "Being kind is being weak and vulnerable?"

"Kind, hmm. I see. You chose the women you selected because they were kind and saw a man who needed help, and they stopped to help."

"I didn't select anyone. I just had sex with a girl who wanted it really kinky but didn't want anyone to know. That was it. Hard sex. Because she wanted it. You never heard of bondage, huh?"

"You are a most confusing man, Mr.

Carver. You were so proud of yourself. And so very angry when you heard another woman had been taken."

"I wasn't angry!" he snapped. "That had to have been your man. Again, all I had was sex — sex with a crazy woman who couldn't find the kind of man she wanted to give it to her the hard way. She's a liar — of course, she has to be a liar. That dude left her — the guy she'd been seeing. Writing! New places, new experiences. Bull. She was too much for him. Of course, they're both going to lie. Oh wait — oh, I love it! My lawyer will drag in Mr. Academia and put him on the stand and ask him all about his sordid little sex life. And my lawyer will make sure everyone knows the nerd can't get it up — not up enough for that wildcat. You see — it will be one person's word against another's."

"Right," Colleen said sweetly. "Sally Smithson and Brant Pickering have no arrest records whatsoever, and you were living under an assumed name. Oh, yes! You look honest — they don't."

"A jury must be obedient to the law. And you can't prove Sally didn't just come with me willingly."

"And yet you know about Brant Pickering. How long were you spying on her before you decided she was the one you wanted?"

"I — I . . ."

For a moment — a brief moment — he was flustered.

Then he recovered.

"Sally told me all about the breakup. And how he sucked in bed. No balls!" he said, and laughed at what he saw as a great pun.

"You can try all you like with a jury, Mr. Carver, but I don't believe a word you say. You were playing with us when you were furious someone else took a woman — and used a pine coffin as a tool to kill her, just like you. You said you were the one and only."

He sighed. "Because you're gullible idiots."

She leaned closer to him, smiling.

"Emily Watkins. What a beautiful girl. And she used public transportation. That might have made it easier for you. I mean, she had to walk some dark and empty streets now and then, getting to and from work. She was so . . ."

"Beautiful, athletic," he said.

"Wait! I thought you didn't do it?" Colleen said.

"I saw pictures."

"Oh? Well, yes, I guess they were in the

paper. She had such beautiful hair, all held back with that darling little red barrette."

"Soft hair," he said quietly, his eyes in the past.

"And I believe she was Jewish."

"Irish," he said.

"Irish?"

"Irish Catholic," he said. "She wore a shamrock — in the picture they had in the paper."

"Maybe it was Lainie Nowak who was Jewish," Colleen said thoughtfully.

"Could be. Beautiful and businesslike — with a feminine flair. The woman was stunning. But could she find some losers. According to what I read in the paper."

"Different from Emily, though. She didn't like jewelry," Colleen said.

"She liked it just fine," he said frowning. "Delicate earrings. Like I said, businesslike and feminine. Stunning, simply stunning."

Colleen sat back. "Interesting what you recall — from the papers."

"Of course," he said, grinning broadly. "Everything I told you was a come-on. Because you're all assholes. Even the dog. Hang around with assholes, you become an asshole."

She leaned forward, smiling sweetly. "I know. It's just terrible when such assholes are after you, isn't it? And when they record your conversations."

He lifted his arms toward the one-way mirror, knowing fully well, of course, that he was being watched.

"Record away! I'm telling you I'm innocent, and Sally Smithson is a sad slut who can't get it without begging, especially the way she wants it!"

"Well," Colleen said softly. "I believe you were The Embracer —"

"You're an ass. A damned beautiful ass!" He laughed again. "I'll bet it is a beautiful ass."

"But you're not *the one and only* Embracer. There is someone else out there. Oh, and as to Emily and Lainie, yes, you're a murderer. A very sick, psycho murderer, I'm afraid. You see, the pictures of the dead women that appeared in the papers were not pictures of them as they were the night you killed them. You described them as they were discovered — murdered. And we assholes have this conversation on tape, Mr. Carver, and it will be played in the courtroom when you go up for murder."

She stood.

He tried to stand as well, furious.

"No, no. Harassment! You tried to lead me. You tried to get me to say things.

Entrapment! I'm telling you, I didn't murder anyone. And I took pity on a girl who couldn't get what she wanted from another guy. You don't believe such women are out there? Oh, yeah, you poor wretch, you're just like them. You sleep with your gun. Or your damned dog or —"

The door flew open. Mark was there, Red at his side.

Red let out a warning growl.

It wasn't quite as intimidating as the look on Mark's face.

"I think we're done — we got what we came for," he said, staring at Carver.

The man was furious, slamming his chains against the table.

Two of the guards rushed in, but they had done their duty well. Carver couldn't budge from the table.

Mark led her out of the room.

"Are you all right?" he asked, his brows furrowed, his tone dark. She could see he was barely containing his anger.

And she could see he'd like to throw a punch at Carver's smug face.

But he was in control.

"Yes, I'm fine, thank you," she assured him. "The man is truly a monster, but in this case — trust me, please — his words mean nothing. I really do know how to manage against an ass. I can take it. Especially if we got what we needed."

He nodded, eyes closed for a second, a long breath escaping him.

"Monster. To call him a pig would be an insult to swine."

She smiled. "I agree. Mark, he was The Embracer. This time around with Dierdre, there was no letter to the press. And I do believe that's because his accomplice — or copycat — had maybe expected Carver to be proud of him and write the letter. But you, Ragnar, and Red had taken Carver and rescued Sally, so this new would-be killer couldn't go to Carver and tell him what he had done to get his approval. So, maybe that's the reason there was no letter? The copycat-slash-accomplice meant to go to Carver but couldn't. And worse for whomever it is — we discovered Dierdre in time to save her life."

He nodded.

"Let's get out of here," he said.

They retrieved their weapons and thanked the guards and staff. When they reached the car, Red obediently hopped into the back seat.

"Where are we heading?" Colleen asked as she buckled in.

He glanced at her. "First, I'm going to

give Ragnar a call."

"Do you think either of the men have left the hospital?"

"If they leave, they'll be followed," Mark said. He was quiet a minute. "As for a way to follow up, well, there's a ton of paperwork to go through again. And while I don't believe we need to follow up on family members or disgruntled lovers of Emily and Lainie, it would be interesting to find out if anyone in the families had a connection to Carver — or to Gary Boynton or Brant Pickering."

"Right," Colleen murmured.

"We can relieve Ragnar at the hospital, let him get some dinner. We can get dinner, or better yet, I can get you home and you can spend time with Megan."

"I don't need to worry about Megan tonight. She's meeting with one of her authors."

"Nice. I never knew editors came to their clients."

"From what I understand, they do for a few reasons. Sometimes, to wine and dine an author to lure them to the house, but that's rare. Or it could be because the author is a special case. She came down to see Justin Millhouse — an author she works with and loves — because he uses a wheelchair and getting out is difficult for him. She's going to work with him on a few videos for special venue bookstores and his web page."

"That's great. So, fish and chips?"

"No! I mean, they were fine, but . . . not again. The hospital cafeteria is okay, but —"

"Ragnar is probably being spelled by other agents. But he's determined to watch this pair as long as he can handle it. And at this time . . ."

He shrugged and said no more.

"At this time? What?"

He hesitated, and then went on, "It's been a while now. Maybe two — no, almost four years ago. It happened before we were partners. Ragnar was engaged. His fiancée was a Maryland cop who had just been accepted into the academy. She had to have been an amazing woman. I never met her, but she died jumping in front of an out-of-control car while saving a toddler in a stroller. She got there just in time to shove the stunned mother aside and thrust the stroller off the road. She had to have known there would have been no time to save herself."

"How tragic. And what a person she must have been."

"Yes. Ragnar throws himself into work.

He would anyway — the Krewe is filled with agents who don't believe in hours. They manage outside lives, but being with the Krewe isn't just a job . . ."

"It's a vocation. But I see it as more. It was strange, learning how to pretend I didn't see or hear things. And with the Krewe —"

"We all get to feel normal. And useful."

"Yeah, exactly," she said softly.

She turned to watch him as he drove. And she winced inwardly. Well, he'd been a jerk — an attractive jerk — but his evident distaste for adding her to his team at first had been truly irritating!

But now . . .

She looked back at the road. It would definitely be a mistake to find her partner not just an imposing and attractive man, but . . . a man who attracted her.

"Any cravings?" he asked her.

Cravings?

Oh, Lord, she had to stop the way her mind was twisting!

Right. Cravings. Food.

"Um, no, anything is fine. Except anything too spicy. Sad palate — no jalapeños for me. I like Mexican just fine. Especially in Mexico. I just watch out for the jalapeños."

She was babbling a little ridiculously. She

didn't babble.

"No jalapeños. That's easy enough. There's an Asian restaurant on our way to your place — cooked entrées and sushi. And it's all good. We'll just check in with Ragnar."

"Works for me," she told him.

They reached the hospital. Red jumped out.

And even at this hour, the dog seemed to know everyone at the hospital.

Ragnar was where they had left him, staring at the screens.

Colleen couldn't help thinking about the tragedy that had marred his life. But she knew he wouldn't want her pity, or even her condolences at this point. Maybe one day she could talk to him and tell him how very sorry she was.

"Have you moved?" Mark asked him.

Ragnar grinned. "Yes, I've checked in with both couples. They decided to release Dierdre in the morning rather than tonight, and I think they'll release Sally the day after tomorrow. From what I gleaned from the doctor, both are doing well physically. However, he strongly suggested therapy for both women, and I concur."

"Never hurts that I know of," Mark said. He grimaced to Colleen. "Ragnar and I

215

have been through it. We need to be cleared anytime we fire a weapon."

"And you've learned how to do therapy — without making yourselves look crazier than it's suspected you might be?"

"Huh?" Ragnar and Mark said together.

She laughed softly. "You don't explain a dead man's spirit told you how to find someone, I take it?"

"No," Mark said. "Right, got it. But I think we all learn how to talk around the truth — once we've been stared at or called crazy a few times."

She glanced at the screens. Little had changed in the hours she and Mark had been gone.

Both men were seated at the hospital bed-sides.

Both were holding the hands of their loved ones.

"Have they moved at all?" Mark asked Ragnar.

"Yep. But not far. Gary gobbled some food down in the cafeteria. Brant picked up a sandwich and brought it back with him to Sally's room," Ragnar said.

"We thought you might want to run down and get something," Colleen told him.

"And I'm assuming you have someone coming in?"

"Axel Tiger."

"Great. But if you want —" Mark said.

Ragnar shook his head. "Go. Axel will be here soon. By the way — anything today?"

Mark gritted his teeth with aggravation. "Carver was . . . totally evil. He pulled all kinds of crass sexual innuendo on Colleen."

"Pig," Ragnar muttered.

"We decided that would be an insult to swine," Colleen told him. "He was obnoxious."

"But Colleen handled him," Mark said. "And," he added, "her conversation with him did prove to me, beyond a doubt, he was the one who killed Emily and Lainie. But I still don't think he was the one who kidnapped and buried Dierdre Ayers."

Ragnar nodded. "I pulled some paperwork, and I talked to Mr. and Mrs. Ayers when they were here. I got them talking about the ex-boyfriend they didn't like who managed to make Gary Boynton look like the last Boy Scout. His name is Vince Monroe. He's a musician — unemployed half the time. He is working now, though. Has a gig in a club called A Little Night Music near the Smithsonian." He swung around to the computer and brought up a social media page. "He calls himself 'The Second Piano Man,' in reference to Billy

Joel, I imagine. Anyway, I've left a message on his voice mail — a nice friendly one — telling him that we need to speak with him."

Colleen leaned around Mark to study the computer screen. Vince Monroe's profile picture showed him holding his guitar and smiling. He had a really nice headful of dirty blond hair, friendly brown eyes, and a great smile.

She realized she was leaning against Mark. And he wasn't protesting. Of course, that would be rude on his part. She also realized she liked leaning there. And she also liked the scent of his soap and himself and the fabric she leaned against.

She straightened quickly. As she did, her eyes met his. And she knew he knew that . . . she'd felt something. There was amusement in his glance.

But something else too, she thought. And she couldn't help but wonder if their initial friction was turning into something else.

"No reply yet, I take it?" Mark asked Ragnar.

Ragnar shook his head.

Mark turned to Colleen. "Change of plans for the night? Want to go clubbing?"

"Sure." She already had her phone out, looking up the club. "Hey," she told him, "it looks good. I just read a few of the reviews on the club. 'Great food and the perfect entertainment. You can sit and have a nice meal without being drowned out.' "

"So, no heavy metal concerts, huh?" Ragnar asked.

"There's nothing wrong with a heavy metal concert," Mark said, smiling. "Except when you're trying to enjoy date night or a night out to catch up with a few friends. Sounds good. Are we all going?"

Ragnar shook his head. "I'm going to hang out until reinforcements arrive. Then, I'm going to sleep. Happy you two are headed out. But hey, maybe leave Red with me. You won't look so much like a pair of cops without the dog. No offense, but the two of you scream law enforcement when you've got Red with his tags."

"True," Mark said. "But Red can be a good judge of people."

"And we should let him judge Vince Monroe. But maybe after you've had a chance to watch the guy and see what you think?"

"Okay. You get Red for the night. And Colleen and I will head out now."

"Perfect. You're such a pretty couple!" Ragnar said teasingly. "Colleen, don't be afraid to let your hair down. I know what it's like. People think I'm too pretty too."

Mark laughed. "Sure, if you like the muscle-bound, axe-wielding Viking type."

"Hey!" Ragnar protested. "Any of us can go back and find ancestors who ravaged and slaughtered, all believing in divine destiny or the power of whoever their god or gods might have been."

"Just teasing," Mark said. "You're a very pretty Viking."

Ragnar let out a weary sigh. Colleen laughed, and Ragnar said, "Well, this conversation — pathetic as it might have been — has been a high point after staring at screens."

"Neither man left the hospital?" Mark asked.

"Neither man left," Ragnar said. He glanced at his watch. "Go and have fun. At least, try to eat something decent anyway. Maybe Vince Monroe is good, so there's a little entertainment for you. Axel should be here soon. Don't call me — okay, call me if there's something major."

"Got it," Mark said. "Ready, Colleen?"

She pulled the clip and band out of her hair, shaking it around her head.

"Better?" she asked Ragnar.

"Nice!" Ragnar said.

Mark laughed. "Almost human, huh?"

She punched him in the arm.

"Ow!"

Ragnar laughed.

"Hey — she punched hard!"

"I'm well trained!" she said, grinning.

"Real strength usually lies in the ability to avoid violence," Mark said. Then he laughed. "It's okay that you punched me."

"Don't go punching each other at the club!" Ragnar warned. "You'll get kicked out."

"We'll be on our best behavior," Mark promised.

He set his hand on Colleen's back, urging her to the door. But then they both stopped, almost simultaneously.

Red was whining.

Mark stooped by the dog, patting his head. "You keep Ragnar company, okay?"

Red woofed.

Apparently, he just liked to be informed.

But Colleen paused to pet the dog too, promising they'd be together again soon. Red seemed to understand.

She found herself glancing at the screens again before they left.

Sally and Brant, Dierdre and Gary. Two devoted couples.

And yet, she thought Mark's instincts were right. Something that looked too good, usually wasn't.

"Let's go meet a piano man," Mark said.

"Ah, you guys have all the fun," Ragnar said.

Mark paused. "Ragnar, you can —"

"No! Get, go, leave me — and Red — in peace!"

They left at last and headed for the club, A Little Night Music.

The man was talented, Mark thought.

Vince Monroe had started playing just a few minutes after Mark and Colleen had been seated. He had an amazing mix of numbers at his disposal, throwing in a few classic pieces here and there as he kept up a light banter throughout his performance.

Naturally, he played a number of Billy Joel pieces. But he had piano versions of numbers by classic rock bands, country-western bands, and he even did a damned decent job with his own arrangement of a rap number.

"We are just watching a performance," Colleen said softly.

"But a good one."

"Yes," she agreed. "I wouldn't have a problem in the least coming back here on my own time — and my own dime."

"Well, my steak is also excellent."

"My chicken is . . . hmm. It's chicken!

But it's good," she told him.

He grinned. "Glad to hear it. But I told you to try the steak. They're known for their steaks. It says so — right on the menu."

"Ah, but you didn't get the little sweet potato tot things with your steak, as I did with the chicken. And they are to die for!" She winced. "I can't believe I used that expression."

"May I?" he asked. He didn't wait for an answer; he reached across the table with his fork to steal a sweet potato tot.

She laughed, so it was okay.

He winced inwardly. Here, at the club, with them teasing over food and laughing together, he could almost forget they were working.

He never forgot he was working.

And he hadn't now — not really, but he'd always admitted how attractive she could be. And tonight, her hair was down, she was smiling more often . . . They'd learned to be . . .

Partners?

Well, no, he thought dryly. He didn't feel quite the same way about Ragnar. Ragnar was the best, but he didn't have fiery red hair with constant glints of gold, or a voice that teased and slipped into the mind and conscious thought like a whisper of air that

223

circled around and around . . .

He had to stop. This wasn't right.

Or, he taunted himself, *maybe it is just right.*

"Not to worry," she told him. "Hey, partners, right? My potato tots are your potato tots."

"I will remember that," he assured her. "Being a fan of potato tots. And John Lennon," he added, nodding toward the stage.

"He's good. His stage presence would suggest an easygoing personality. Then again, that may just be stage presence. Maybe he has a temper."

"Maybe Dierdre's parents just don't consider a musician a person with a 'real' job."

"That's more than possible too," Colleen agreed. "And while I had thought a prejudice against long hair went out long ago, they may see him as a . . . belated hippie or the like." She leaned closer to him. "Do we try to talk to him tonight? Even if we pretend we're just a couple out for the night? Compliment his music or something?"

"I don't like pretense like that. Although, yes, we use it when we need to — that's how we got into Carver's house. But we're going to want to talk to this man again in a more professional setting, so I'm not sure a cover story is necessary."

She was close to him. The music was permeating the room, but she still had to come close in order to speak quietly.

He realized she had been out all day, and yet, she still smelled subtly of perfume. *Back away.*

Remember they hadn't started off so well.

His fault, of course.

"There's something I need to say," he told her.

"We're going to tell him about Dierdre and ask if he knows of anyone who would do such a thing?"

"Well, that, yes, but I meant, there's something I need to say to you."

"Oh?"

"I'm sorry."

She gave him a quizzical look, half smiled and half frowned.

"It's really okay that you take my potato tots."

He laughed softly. "No. It's just . . . I wasn't a good partner, especially not a good senior partner when we met. It was just that."

"It's okay. I know where you'd been on this case, and you and Red and Ragnar do have an incredible way of working together."

"Thank you. But you have an extraordinary talent — one I don't have. We all started out somewhere, sometime. And I should have been more supportive."

"Like I said," she told him quietly, "I know you found the last dead girl. And the same day we started together, you and Red and Ragnar had managed to find Sally alive. I honestly understand. This is a tough case. And throwing a new person in . . ."

She paused and shrugged.

He thought the silence between them that followed should have been awkward.

It wasn't.

It was oddly comfortable. Almost . . . intimate.

Then their server swept around to pick up their plates. And they noted that onstage, Vince Monroe had risen, thanking the audience for their attention and applause.

"Hey, I'll take a cruise around and see if anyone has any requests!" he said, bowing and stepping from the stage.

The restaurant tables were arranged in a semicircle around the stage in rows, each on a step up.

They were seated in the fifth row, the last row, but almost directly in front of the stage.

They watched as Vince Monroe moved easily among the tables, laughing and chatting with guests. Mark thought he'd follow the layout of the tables.

He didn't, but rather after greeting the first row, he came to the top, allowing him to wind his way back down.

"Hey, folks! Anything for me?" he asked.

"Well, hard for a solo artist, I imagine, but Queen?" Mark suggested.

"Elton John, Leonard Cohen, David Bowie," Colleen suggested.

"All right! My kind of music. Love it!"

"Maybe Tom Petty, Roy Orbison," Colleen said. "Ah! Bruno Mars."

Vince Monroe smiled, looking at her with appreciation.

"Nice to see you two here. First time?"

Mark quickly made a decision and said, "We came here specifically to see you."

"Oh? Well, great. I didn't know I had any kind of a following!"

"We're FBI agents," Mark said.

Monroe started to laugh. Then he sobered, frowning. "You're kidding, right? You really make a handsome and natural couple. Wait, I can tell. You're not kidding."

"We just need your help," Colleen said.

There was a flash of real pain on his face.

"Because of what happened to Dierdre?" he asked. "I heard about it, of course. It was all over the news. She was in a pine box? In the nick of time. Oh, wow — did you guys find her?"

"It seems you still care about her," Mark said.

"Of course. From a distance. But yes, I loved her." He angled his head ruefully to the side. "Still love her. It just wasn't to be."

"Why?" Colleen asked.

"Oh, my God! Why, yeah, well, her folks think a piano player might as well be a bum. If you don't know how to play the stock market, you're not a serious contender for their princess."

"Kind of what we thought might have been the problem," Colleen said, empathy rich in her voice. "They're not bad people, they just have . . . I guess, different priorities? They didn't want their daughter struggling. But Dierdre isn't like that, is she?"

He shook his head. "No, I just don't think she could handle them pressuring her all the time. Anyway, she's happy. She has a man they see as perfect now. And it seems she loves him." He shrugged. "If she's happy . . . She is okay, right? She's going to be okay?"

"Yes, she's going to be okay," Mark said. He didn't tell the man Dierdre would be leaving the hospital the next day.

He seemed like the laid-back easy musician they had seen onstage.

But maybe he could take stage presence with him wherever he chose.

"Ah, man," he said. "I've got to get around to the tables. It was nice seeing you — FBI agents or not!" he added.

"Would you be willing to come into the office and talk to us? Tell us anything else you can think of?" Mark asked him.

He looked surprised.

"I'm not sure how I could help, but if you think I can, sure, I'll come in. I'd hate to think about that happening to another young woman. But — I thought the news also said you caught the man who did it?"

"Yes and no. We need to be sure," Colleen said.

"Yes, of course then." He winced and made a face. "Just don't call me in when Dierdre's parents are going to be there, okay?"

"We will make sure," Mark promised. He passed him one of his cards and looked at Colleen. She did the same. "Just in case one of us doesn't answer right away, the other will. Our unit's headquarters info is also on the cards. We're all briefed on whatever everyone else is working on."

Vince Monroe nodded. "Pleasure," he said, and pocketed the cards and moved on.

They watched as he greeted the next table down the line effusively, commenting on a young woman's lovely dress, and moving on to music.

"Well?" Colleen said. "He's willing to help."

"Yeah, and killers sometimes want to insert themselves into an investigation."

"True. So, are we going with the upright citizen type who are secretly organized killers, or those who appear to be a bit of the norm?"

"Too soon to tell," he said. "Dessert?"

"I couldn't eat a full dessert."

"We could share."

She smiled. "Yeah. We could share."

They opted for a strawberry cheesecake and wound up laughing about their efforts to politely leave each other the puffs of whipped cream on the plate.

Vince Monroe returned to the stage. He was pleasant, talking about the requests he had received most, then moved into "Rocket Man," saying that if he was the "second" piano man, he really needed to give a great tribute to Elton John — and fulfill a request by a beautiful redhead up on the high tier.

"He likes you," Mark commented.

"Let's hope it gets us something."

230

They left soon after and he drove her home.

She was an agent. She had a gun. She was capable. He knew he could drive away.

Hey, everybody — including him, Ragnar, and Red — needed to have support at their backs.

He watched her walk to the door of her town house.

And he thought she paused briefly before she fit her key into the lock, then turned to wave and made a motion she was locking the door.

And still, he hesitated.

Was there something else she'd wanted to say to him? Or had it been something else? *Had she seen or sensed something?*

He needed to respect her abilities. He drove away at last.

They had to move and quickly. Because there was another killer out there, and he would strike again.

CHAPTER NINE

"Hey, you had a late night again," Megan said, greeting her as she came in.

Jensen was sleeping on her lap as before, but this time, he rose and stretched as Colleen came in, jumping down to walk to her with typical cat arrogance. He would allow her to stoop and stroke him that night.

"I thought I'd still beat you back," Colleen said. "I don't feel I've seen much of you — other than you helping us with Brant Pickering, and thank you very much by the way."

"I've always wanted to meet Brant Pickering. I think his mind is amazing. Oh, and honestly! I know you — you're thinking the worst immediately. With a mind like his, he can surely come up with all kinds of ways to be a heinous killer."

"Someone else is out there. We can't go by liking someone or not liking them," Colleen said.

"Oh, I know. Anyway, I saw my writer, we had a great evening, and I'm going to head back to the city by tomorrow evening. Make sure you wake me and we'll have breakfast together. So, where did you go?"

"To a place called A Little Night Music."

"Oh! So, you are seeing your partner! A sweet dinner in a darkened room, music, and romance?" Megan said.

"No! We were working."

"At a supper club?" Megan asked dubiously. She cast her head to the side as she grinned.

"One of our girls was dating the musician before the guy she's seeing now."

"Aha! So, you're thinking a spurned lover taking revenge?" Megan asked.

Colleen grimaced. "This is far more than that. Nothing when it comes to crime is written in stone, but these killings — and kidnappings — don't appear to be about irrational anger. They're planned and organized. I believe —"

"But you do have Carver in custody."

"Yes, but we don't believe he took Dierdre."

"I know. And I do understand. But if everything was done the same —"

"It wasn't. There was no note this time. And Carver was holding Sally when Dierdre disappeared. So . . ."

"I know. Well, I'm glad work took the two of you to a nice place! Your partner is extremely . . ."

"Yeah, I know. Good-looking."

"It's more than that. He's kind of like the Rock of Gibraltar. He gives off . . . vibes? Very . . ."

"Hard-core."

"No, that's not the word I was thinking."

"Then what?"

Megan started to laugh. "So, you're not immune! I know that attitude in your voice. You're drawn to him."

"He's one of my partners."

"Yeah, right. Whatever."

"Megan! How eloquent from a woman who spends her life working with words!"

Megan grinned. "Well, I'm glad it's him. The other one . . ."

"Red?"

"No! Ragnar. I mean, what does he think? That Vikings exist and it's their way or the highway?"

"Megan, he wanted to see you home safely."

"I'm quite capable on my own."

"That was a courtesy because you extended a courtesy to us!"

"Whatever." Megan waved a dismissive

hand in the air. "I'm just glad you're getting it on with Gallagher."

"I haven't gotten anything on with my partner!"

"Ah, but you will. And that is not a bad idea. Let's face it — neither you, Patrick, nor I will ever have a normal relationship."

"What?"

Megan shrugged and hesitated. "It's just too hard. When I'm with someone and I think it's going places . . . inevitably I will see someone who isn't living. I give myself away, I'm awkward, and then angry, or the guy thinks I'm not all there. Or I know what someone is really saying no matter how they try to hide it, and I correct them or give an answer that makes them mad or . . . I don't know. But this guy . . . well, he knows all about you. And he doesn't think you're too out there; he appreciates what you have."

"I don't think he believed it at first."

"But he does now. Hey, if you have a chance tomorrow, I'd like to meet your guy at the cemetery. Sergeant Alfie Parker? From the little I've gathered, he sounds fascinating — and a little sad."

"We can probably arrange it if Alfie is around," Colleen assured her. "We're hoping to get Vince Monroe, the musician we went to see tonight, into headquarters tomorrow. We need to talk to him more. Find out about him —"

"To see if he was after revenge?"

"Or if he knows about anyone else who might want to hurt Dierdre."

"Right. So, we'll just see. But I think I'll be on the train returning home tomorrow evening. And next, you can come up to see me!"

"Sure. I love NYC."

"Okay, it's a deal. Hey, I brewed some tea. Let's have some and then call it a night!"

"Sounds good."

They had tea along with some store-bought biscuits that were in the pantry. They talked about their parents and their brother and life in general including the ownership of cats over dogs or dogs over cats.

"You're the weirdo in our trio. Patrick and I both have our pups."

"Jensen is almost like a pup. I can't keep a dog, Megan. I'd love to. I'm just not home enough."

"Ah, you need a dog like Red! One who goes everywhere."

"One day," Colleen said.

Megan bit into a cookie and then paused for a minute.

"You know," she said, "I have the thing

with knowing what people mean, and I see the dead when they're all right with being seen, but I don't have . . ."

"What?"

"Well, a sense that someone is around. At least, not more than most people."

"Neither do I. I can hear things, but . . ."

"It was odd. When I got back tonight, I felt as if I was being watched. But no one was around."

"Strange," Colleen said. "I had the same sensation. But I paused and listened, and I didn't hear anything."

"Maybe we're both paranoid," Megan said.

"Maybe. But we're fine now. I have a great alarm system, and I sleep with a gun on the bedside table."

"I know. I have to admit, I was glad when you got home, even though I was here maybe just twenty minutes or so. Anyway, I guess we'd best get to bed. I have a lunch meeting with a few of our local crew here tomorrow. If you can set up a time for me in the afternoon, that would be great. And if not, you know I'll be back. Anyway . . ."

Megan stretched and yawned.

"Yep. Let's call it a night."

They picked up the mess they had made, said good-night, and went to their rooms.

Colleen was tired. She felt she would sleep easily.

But she lay awake awhile.

Her thoughts turned between the strange coincidence that she and Megan had both thought they were being watched . . .

To remembering the way she and Mark had clashed forks, and how sharing a piece of strawberry cheesecake had been far too seductive and intimate.

Yes, she admitted to herself. She respected her partner and liked him too.

And yes, she was sexually drawn to him.

Oddly, the self-admission allowed her to sleep.

Because maybe, just maybe, sharing cheesecake was as intimate as it had seemed.

It was nearly eleven when he reached his house.

He immediately opened his computer, searching social media pages on Vince Monroe.

Ragnar showed up about fifteen minutes later. Red bounded into the house, happy to have spent time with Ragnar, but thrilled to be home with Mark.

"I did think about just keeping Red for the night, but I had to talk to you anyway, and might as well stop by and see what you thought about our ex-boyfriend," Ragnar said.

"Thought you were going home to get some rest?"

"Yeah. Well, I left a little later than I planned. And I played on the computer too. I'm going to go home and get some sleep now."

"Anything noteworthy at the hospital?"

"Both girls are being released tomorrow. Between our people and the police, we have Dierdre's house staked out and Brant Pickering's hotel room. And Sally's home, of course, because I'm assuming Brant will probably check out and stay with her."

"And even if we tried, we'd never convince either woman her boyfriend might be a psycho killer," Mark said wearily.

Ragnar winced. "I tried speaking with Mr. Ayers. He was appalled I might think Gary was anything other than perfect for his daughter. He is convinced there was only one killer, and that killer was Jim Carver. He thinks I'm overstepping my position to begin to suspect a man as fine as Gary Boynton of having hurt his daughter in any way. He'll be her husband soon enough."

"What a wonderful life," Mark muttered dryly.

Ragnar shook his head. "To each his own,

I guess. So, what about the ex?"

"I liked the ex," Mark told him. "But I'm planning on drawing up everything I can find on him and asking Angela to continue to look into him and get our tech people on it too. I believe they started a file on him when Dierdre first went missing."

"But what impression did you get?"

Mark shrugged. "First, the guy is talented. I think he probably makes a decent living as a musician, but since Mr. Ayers is in the upper tier of moneymakers, it might not have seemed enough for him."

"Ayers said the ex was always unemployed."

"Not from what I'm seeing on the computer. He works solo and also with a band. They're studio musicians and not fond of hitting the trail. He works with a group called Decadence."

"Decadence?" Ragnar said. "I've heard of them. The guy has to make a decent living."

"On his own, he books a club for a week or two every so often. I've got Angela checking his financials."

"Yeah, but it sounds as if he's okay?"

"To me, so far. But you could make a case for the long-haired, hippie type being the bad guy, or for the rich guy living a secret life, or even the famous writer who digs into the deep, dark side of history who has a deep, dark side himself."

"Well, you'll never convince Megan of that. She told me she knows people, knows what they really mean, and it's obvious he just really loves delving into little-known stories about the past."

"She could be right."

"Yeah, but I told her we don't work that way. In the courts, you're innocent until proven guilty. When you're working this kind of case, someone is guilty — until proven innocent. I'm not so sure about Megan's abilities."

Sparks had evidently flown between Ragnar and Megan. "Hey, I didn't believe in Colleen's strange talent either until she heard something she couldn't have heard by normal means and found a location even before Red did," Mark said.

Ragnar shrugged. "Well, it's late." He grinned. "Next time, I get the supper club."

Mark laughed. "You could have come."

"It looked more natural for just the two of you to go."

"It was good. We watched his first set, and in between, he came out to talk to the audience. We told him the truth about who we were. And here's one thing — he admitted he does still love Dierdre, but Dierdre just couldn't take the pressure from her father. Now that could mean if he couldn't have her . . ."

"No one could. But you didn't get that vibe?"

Mark shook his head. "And yet, in all honesty, my feelings are no more valid than Megan's — if that valid. I didn't like Boynton from the start."

"Yep. I understand that."

"Monroe is going to come into headquarters. We'll see what he can tell us," Mark said.

"All right. I'm heading out."

But before Ragnar could open the door to leave, Mark's phone rang.

"Hey, it's me," the caller said.

The "me" was Angela Hawkins Crow from Krewe headquarters.

"What are you doing working this late? I asked you to try to get everything you could in the morning," Mark said.

"Yeah, the kids went to bed, Jackson fell asleep, and my mind wouldn't turn off," she told him.

"You found something on Vince Monroe?"

"No. No more than what you had gleaned from him already. He isn't rich, but he's doing okay. But I did find something very interesting — about Mr. Ayers and his admiration for Gary Boynton."

"This area is huge for my company," Megan told Colleen.

They'd decided to go all out making breakfast that morning, since Megan would be leaving later in the day. Omelets with cheese and lots of vegetables *and* waffles and toast and bacon. They'd woken up early enough to get going on it. When they were kids, there had been no fighting in the kitchen. All three of the Law children could cook, chop things up, and clean up as they went along. And they always had fun while cooking.

"You mean the DC area?" Colleen asked curiously.

Megan nodded. "We publish science fiction with a bit of paranormal thrown in. And our owner and publisher, a man named James Swenson, started off as a criminal attorney. He's a good guy. He told me once he loved science fiction as a kid, but when he started working, he loved it more. It was the best escape in the world. I'm assuming a lot of your Washington types feel the same way — they need an escape."

Colleen laughed. "We could all use an escape from politics!"

"Anyway, I have one last lunch meeting

with one of our marketing and promo people. Since the days of COVID-19, a number of our people have continued working from home, so it's nice to sometimes hit the road and meet in person. And, even better, I get to see you!"

"I'm glad when you come here! I'm also glad when I can get to New York. I love the city, the music venues, the comedy clubs, and, of course, the Broadway shows."

"And your sister!"

"And my sister!" Colleen agreed.

"What time is tall, dark, and hunk-ishly handsome picking you up today?" Megan asked.

"Not sure, actually. Usually around eight. I guess I should —"

"Call him and see if he'd like breakfast?" Megan announced.

Mark called Colleen as she picked up her cell to call him.

"Figured we're okay to run a little late," he began. "We have some interesting interviews today, but —"

"Good. Thanks. Megan is leaving later today but she wanted me to invite you to breakfast."

"Breakfast?"

"It's a meal normal people eat in the morning," she said lightly.

"Right. I do know that. But where —"

"Here. We've been doing a Law kitchen thing," Colleen said.

"Uh, sure. When?"

"Whenever you can get here."

"Do you need anything?"

"Nope, we're covered. Food, coffee, orange juice."

"I, well, yeah. Tell Megan thank you."

"Will do. Oh! What are our interesting interviews?"

"Believe it or not, our musician must not sleep too much. Vince has already called me and he's happy to come into headquarters. He's supposed to arrive at ten. I think he'll be on time. Because he doesn't like Dierdre's father, who's arriving at one."

"Oh? Rory Ayers? Does he know something he hasn't told us yet?"

"We'll see. Because he did fail to mention he and Gary have been working on a deal to garner a government contract together, which could mean more money than I can imagine to both of them. Buildings with special tech built right into the infrastructure."

"Oh! So, that's why he likes his prospective son-in-law so much?"

"Maybe. That's what I'm curious to find out. I also want to find out from both men if we're missing anyone in our pool of suspects. Someone Dierdre maybe even inadvertently slighted. Angela is going through the web, trying to find any kind of communications between Carver and other men who might be . . . intrigued by his sexual proclivity. Anyway, we'll worry about that when we get there. Enjoy your time with Megan. Red and I will be there shortly."

She ended the call. Megan was looking at her.

"He's going to come in?"

"Yes."

"Great! Oh, what do we have for Red?"

"I'm willing to bet he'll be allowed a few bits of bacon for a treat."

Mark arrived just as they finished cooking and started setting the table. Red followed, causing Jensen a minute's pause.

"I forgot about Red meeting Jensen!" Colleen said.

"They're suspicious of one another, but they're going to be all right," Megan said. "Hey, Jensen hasn't even hissed."

"As long as Red doesn't go near Jensen's food bowl," Colleen said. "Maybe I should just pick it up —"

"Red is never so rude as to attack another

animal's food bowl," Mark assured her, grinning.

And he wasn't. He did, however, seek out pats from Megan and Colleen. And Mark headed into the kitchen, asking what he could help with.

Megan handed him the silverware.

"Nice to see a guy who doesn't expect to be waited on hand and foot," Megan approved.

"My mother would have never allowed it," Mark said. He glanced at Colleen and grimaced. "Well, my adoptive mother."

"Oh, you were adopted?" Megan asked.

Colleen looked at her sister.

"I'm so sorry. I didn't mean to be rude," Megan said quickly.

"Yep, adopted as an older kid by a great couple. My dad actually got testy if someone thought he was incapable of doing things himself, and when dinner is being set out, well, since everyone is eating, everyone pitches in."

"Oh, they sound great!" Megan said.

"They were," Mark assured her.

"Oh, again, I'm so sorry."

"They had good lives," Mark said. "Hey, you wanted to go to the cemetery to meet Sergeant Parker, right? I'd forgotten about that."

"Me too," Colleen said.

"After lunch sometime? I'd like to get a train before it's too late," Megan said.

"Not a problem. We have a one o'clock interview but that shouldn't take too long. Unless something unexpected comes up, we should be all right to schedule anything else after."

"Yeah, that would be great. Do you ever see your adoptive folks?" Megan asked.

"No. I did see my mom. But then she went on, and I'm glad. I think she might have found my father, and a peace and happiness that didn't get to be hers in life. At least, that's the way I like to think of it."

"Me too," Megan said.

Everything was on the table; they passed dishes around.

Mark complimented the omelets.

Then Megan laid her bombshell.

"So, do you think you two will ever go on a real date — or just sleep together and get the initial awkwardness out of the way right away?"

Colleen's fork fell on her plate with a tremendous clatter.

Mark stopped halfway through chewing.

"Megan!" Colleen said. "That was . . . I mean . . . our relationship is professional. It's —"

She was stunned when Mark shrugged and interrupted her.

"I don't know, Colleen. What do you think? A real date? That would definitely be the option our parents would approve of."

"Ah, but they were a different generation," Megan said. "Hey, you must know yourself — being weird does not make relationships easy!"

"Nothing makes relationships easy," Mark said. And to Colleen's surprise, he quickly turned the tables. "Speaking of which, what is your problem with Ragnar?"

"What?" Megan said.

"Obviously, there was some spat."

"The man is . . . well, what you're not! He didn't think I was capable of getting home!"

"Well, maybe he was just being cautious and courteous."

"But I said I was fine!" Megan waved a hand in the air. "That doesn't matter — we aren't partners, professional or otherwise. Anyway, look at the time. You two had better get going," she said.

Mark glanced at his watch, then took his plate to the kitchen.

"Hey, hey," Megan protested. "I'm all for a guy helping in the kitchen, but I don't have to be anywhere for hours, and you two need to get to the office. I don't mind cleaning up. Go, please, go! Hopefully, I'll see you all later. I'll text you after my lunch, and you can let me know what's up after your one o'clock."

"Okay, great," Colleen said. "We'll just get Red and —"

She stopped speaking. She'd turned to see the dog.

To her astonishment, Red was lying near the door.

Jensen was curled up against him.

"I guess we don't have to worry about the two of them, huh?" Mark said.

"I'll get Jensen so you can get out of here," Megan suggested, reaching for the cat and taking him up into her arms.

Colleen and Mark were finally out the door. She was silent as they approached the car, still ready to throttle her sister for her bizarre — and far too personal — questions.

But Mark didn't comment other than to say, "You two really manage good omelets."

"Our mom is a good cook," Colleen said. "And our dad can cook too. He worked in the kitchen in the navy. Sometimes, I think he thinks he's still in the navy with some of the things he says and does."

"Ah, well, once a military man, always a military man," Mark said.

"What do you think Vince Monroe can tell us?" Colleen asked him.

"Anything he knows about Gary Boynton, for one."

"I doubt if they even know one another. Then again, maybe they met at some point? We will hopefully find out."

They arrived at headquarters about fifteen minutes before ten.

They headed into one of the conference rooms with Angela.

Red expected a greeting from Angela, and he got it. She gave him a pat and he sat obediently at Mark's feet.

"People going into business together doesn't really mean anything," Angela said. "Except this is . . . huge. It would be huge for both men. Rory Ayers runs a lucrative business and has for years, but apparently, Boynton is something of a tech wizard. So, if you put them together on certain projects, you're talking really big money."

Colleen shook her head. "Do you think Ayers is afraid that if his daughter isn't with Gary Boynton the deal will fall apart?"

"I'm not sure. Maybe Boynton has let him know that if he and Dierdre aren't together, there might be no deal. Or . . . I don't know. But it is interesting, and extremely curious, that neither of them mentioned the fact that

251

this business deal was going on."

"Maybe neither of them thought it pertinent to Dierdre being kidnapped," Mark said.

"I don't know. But I was thinking we should be speaking with Mrs. Ayers too," Angela said.

"Now, there's something. We've only seen her being a doting mother at the hospital. Maybe she doesn't even realize she knows something. Maybe Dierdre confided in her about other men. Men we don't know about."

Angela glanced at her watch and rose.

"Vince Monroe should be arriving. I'll escort him in," she said.

Angela disappeared, and they waited until Angela brought him back.

She was sweet and gracious. He'd apparently thought she was the receptionist, which, of course, didn't bother Angela. It was often better when those being questioned saw her as an office worker.

Monroe had his hair neatly pulled back. He wasn't in a business suit, but neither had he opted for a rock band T-shirt and jeans. He looked casual and well put-together in a tan jacket, trousers, and light blue tailored shirt, open at the neck, and no tie.

"Hello," he said, greeting them both. They'd risen when he entered, and they shook hands. He then looked down at the dog.

"Give him a pat. He'll love it," Colleen suggested.

She knew Mark was watching Red's response to Vince Monroe.

The dog wagged his tail.

She automatically had more trust in someone who seemed to like animals, or at least treated them decently.

"This was great of you to come in so quickly," Mark said, indicating a chair for the man.

He shrugged. "Well, I figure the ex is always under suspicion. But I was working the night Dierdre disappeared, and I was hanging out at the club until about two in the morning."

"You figured you were under suspicion?" Colleen asked him.

"Even with my alibi verified, you have to be sure, right?" he told them. He leaned forward suddenly. "I can only swear to you I'd never hurt Dierdre. I loved her. I love her . . . I will probably love her a little bit forever. And I would do anything to help you. I'd never want this to happen to another woman." He paused, frowning, looking concerned. "You did catch a guy, right?"

"We did," Mark said.

"And you don't think —"

"We can't be sure," Colleen told him.

He leaned back, sighing deeply. "I'm surprised her dad didn't have a computer chip inserted under her skin somewhere. The man is a tyrant. And . . ." He paused, shaking his head. "You have to understand. Dierdre is sweet and innocent. She's not the kind who makes waves. She'd never hurt anyone. She wants to give money to anyone who is down and out, especially if they have a dog or a kid or someone depending on them. I try to tell her they're going to take her money to buy alcohol or drugs, and she just tells me that sometimes they're not. She wanted to work in the church's soup kitchen, but her dad told her his daughter did not hang out with the riffraff. I don't know how she's survived him all these years."

"So, he's strict?" Mark said.

"No, it's more than that. He's an elitist."

"Okay," Colleen said, then smiled. "He's a well-to-do jerk and you don't like him. But do you think, despite him, Dierdre might have seen another man? Or seeing as how she might have been afraid of his reaction — spurned another man?"

"I think I'm the only guy she spurned," he said dryly, grimacing. He frowned. "But she did call me about a week ago."

"And?" Colleen asked.

"She wanted to know if I was doing okay, if I'd moved on. And to tell me I was a really great guy and whoever I wound up with was going to be very lucky."

"That's nice," Colleen said.

"That's all?" Mark asked him.

"I think. And yet I thought she sounded a little edgy. She said things were fine. Gary was fine, polite, cool, and all that. I guess he's hanging around now like a good puppy."

"He has been attentive," Colleen said.

Mark glanced at Colleen. She knew he was thinking about the way they'd found Gary when they had first talked to him — buffing his beloved car.

"I don't know. She didn't mention any other men. And I don't know if it's because you came to talk to me, and I'm putting things where there wasn't anything, or if I'm starting to wonder if the conversation wasn't a little . . ."

"A little?" Colleen asked gently.

"Like I said, she just sounded edgy." He hesitated again. "Afraid."

255

"Do you think she was afraid of Gary Boynton?" Mark asked.

"I'd like to say yes. But I'm not sure. She said he was great, and while I don't believe she's in love with him, I do think she has an honest affection for him."

"But she sounded as if she were afraid?" Colleen said.

"The call was so bizarre. I felt she was reaching out to me, and yet, she didn't dare."

"But if she wasn't afraid of Gary . . . what?" Mark asked.

"Maybe work? She said she liked to get home while it was still light. She drove some country roads to get home, and she didn't like the dark. But she told me that because she was hanging up. She has always been someone who will not talk on a phone, even on speaker, when she's driving. She said she hoped we'd always be friends, and hoped I'd really forgiven her."

"And what did you tell her?" Colleen asked.

"I said I'd be there for her, always, no matter what, if she needed me." His eyes were distant, as if he was remembering the phone call and the woman he had loved. "Then I heard about what had happened to her on the news. Thank God, I heard she was alive and in the hospital before I heard she'd just been taken, possibly by The Embracer. But the news came out at about the same time that a guy had been arrested, so . . ."

"You presumed the culprit had been caught," Mark said.

"I think most people believed that, yes," Monroe said. "But . . ."

"We have to be sure. There's a bit of a timeline we're working on, and every little bit of information helps."

"Have I helped you at all?" he asked hopefully.

"Yes, like I said," Mark assured him, "every little bit of information helps. For one, we didn't know she never had her phone out when she was driving. That explains why she maybe didn't call for help, I guess. And knowing how nice she is explains why she would stop to help someone in the road."

"I'm glad that helps," Monroe said, giving them a weak smile.

"It does," Mark assured him. "Trust me, you can't ask someone if they happen to be a nice and caring person or not. Well, you can ask, but . . . that's really something you need from someone who knows them."

"Oh, good then."

"What can you tell us about her current boyfriend?" Mark asked him.

"Gary Boynton? I met him a few times at the Ayerses' house before I knew I was being replaced by him. He's got some business deal with Dierdre's father. He was . . . polite. Far more courteous than Dierdre's father — he treated me like a bum from the first day I met him." He laughed. "I even heard Dierdre giving him a hard time once for being rude to me. She told him it was against everything she had ever been taught about being decent to everyone. He said he couldn't be decent to a man who was totally wrong for her." He paused again. "Boynton was . . . I guess the word I would use is *indifferent.* I was a musician. I didn't deal in Bitcoin or the stock market or e-commerce. I just wasn't interesting to him. But he was polite enough."

"Thank you. Did you ever see him interact with Dierdre?" Colleen asked.

"Again, courteous, thoughtful . . . My encounters were brief."

He waited to see if they had any more questions.

"I wish . . ." he began, and then he shook his head. "I wouldn't mind speaking with Dierdre — without her father or Gary Boynton. I'd love to know what had bothered her that day."

"Maybe we can arrange that," Mark said.

Ragnar walked in as he spoke.

Vince Monroe stood, an automatic gesture, Colleen thought. It was the polite thing to do. She and Mark stood as well.

"Hey, guys, sorry. I've been at the hospital."

"And Dierdre is all right?" Monroe asked anxiously.

"Fine. She was released. She, Mom, Dad, and Boynton have headed home."

"Ah. Well, thank God she's all right," Monroe said.

"You're the musician," Ragnar said. "Sorry. I'm Special Agent Ragnar Johansen. Thank you for coming in."

"For whatever good, though your partners have said I've given them something, so . . ."

"You will call us if you think of anything else, no matter how trivial it seems?" Colleen asked.

"I swear," he vowed.

"You're free to go with our most sincere thanks," Mark said.

Monroe nodded, paused to give Red a pat, and left the room.

When he was gone, Ragnar told them, "I was watching with Angela. We had the camera running."

"And what did you think?"

"If he's not the real deal, he deserves an Oscar," Ragnar said. He shrugged. "What do you say, Red?"

Red woofed.

"And still . . ." Mark mused.

"And still," Colleen agreed.

And yet it was true the man had given them a great deal more to think about.

"We do need to get him together with Dierdre without her father and Gary Boynton," Colleen said.

"Of course," Ragnar agreed.

"But how —" Colleen began.

"Trust me. We'll make it happen," Mark assured her.

CHAPTER TEN

Ragnar called when they were in the conference room going over everything they knew about Rory Ayers and Gary Boynton and their prospective project. The buildings they were planning would be state-of-the-art — cameras, screens, internet access, communications available at the highest level — with the highest possible security and shutdown systems that were instantaneous should any of their security ever be breached. Businesses — law enforcement and government — could trust in knowing who was where and when while knowing their secrets were safe.

Colleen watched as Mark answered his phone, putting it on speaker when Ragnar identified himself.

"We're all out of the hospital. Both young women have been released. Cops are on Brant Pickering's hotel; he and Sally both headed there. I'm watching Rory Ayers get

261

in his car now. Gary Boynton is in the house along with Mrs. Ayers and Dierdre." There was a silence. "I'm going to stay on this one myself."

"Sounds good. Ayers is supposed to be on his way here," Mark said.

"Well, he's in his car. Want him followed?"

"Anyone undercover around?"

"I can arrange it."

"Then, sure."

"You've got it. I wish I could get into the Ayerses' place."

"I could get in," Colleen assured them.

"Oh?"

"Yeah, I'm just a woman checking up on another woman, just making sure she feels okay. I can be pretty nonthreatening." She looked at Mark and shrugged.

"What do you think?" Ragnar asked.

"Ah, sure, take a run over," Mark said. "I'll talk to Ayers. I'm going to try to make it friendly."

"Okay. I will need your car," Colleen told Mark.

He nodded and produced the keys.

"I'm going. I'll just check on things. Of course, none of us can watch them all the time now, but I'll do my best to make sure she's going to be all right."

"I don't think Gary Boynton — or anyone

with half a mind — would attack Dierdre now, in her house and with her mother home," Mark said. "But it won't hurt for you to stop by and make sure they know we're still paying attention."

She nodded and said, "I'll be back. Work comes first, but if we can, we'll meet up with Megan."

Mark watched her go, his hand on his dog's head.

She was almost out the door when he called her back.

"Take Red."

"What?"

"Take Red with you. He'll keep you safe."

"I have a Glock to keep me safe. I mean, I love Red —"

"So, make me happy. Take him along."

"Sure."

Colleen went to the door, calling to Red. The dog came obediently but only after he saw Mark nod.

She wasn't sure she'd ever seen a more loyal creature of any kind.

She let Angela know what she was doing and exited the building. As she left, she saw Rory Ayers driving toward the building. Well, he was keeping his word so it seemed.

DC area traffic was DC area traffic, but she still managed to get to the Ayerses' home in a little over thirty minutes. She didn't see Ragnar's car parked anywhere, but then it was Ragnar. He wouldn't be parked where anyone might question a car in one place too long.

She had a feeling, however, he was close to the house. But she hadn't intended on stopping to talk to him anyway.

She rang the bell at the door to the impressive Georgian home. It was answered quickly by a maid in uniform, a woman who talked to her through an intercom, asking her name and her business at the house.

"Special Agent Colleen Law, FBI," she said, producing her credentials and angling them so that they could be seen through the door's peephole. "Just here to make sure Miss Ayers is doing well. And Red is with me. He helped find Miss Ayers."

The door opened. The housekeeper was a slim woman in her forties with a quick smile but a weathered face.

She wasn't alone.

Mrs. Amelia Ayers was standing behind her.

She appeared to be in her midfifties and was attractive with a short but feminine haircut in platinum blonde.

"Special Agent Law — is anything wrong?" she asked worriedly.

"Oh, no, no — I mean, nothing more than has been. I heard Dierdre had been released, and I just wanted to stop by and see how she's doing. I guess . . ." She winced. "I guess Red and I are invested in the case and with Dierdre."

"Yes, thank God you found her," Amelia said, her voice trembling. "Please, come in. We were all just in the kitchen nook. Red too, of course. Mariana makes the most delightful cookies," she continued, complimenting the woman who had opened the door.

So, maybe just her husband was a jerk. She spoke about her maid as if she were speaking about a friend. Maybe that's why Dierdre herself had turned out so giving and caring — if all Vince Monroe said about her was true.

So, how had her mother wound up with her father?

Opposites attracting?

"That would be lovely," Colleen said, turning to Mariana. "I could go for a delicious cookie!"

Mariana welcomed her in, smiling.

Gary Boynton and Dierdre were seated at the kitchen table, laughing about something. Seeing Colleen, Gary immediately rose. Dierdre started to do the same.

"Sit, sit, please. This isn't a formal visit. I just wanted to see you and make sure you are doing well," Colleen told Dierdre.

"I'm delighted to be home and grateful, of course, you care enough to come by," Dierdre said.

"Very grateful," Gary Boynton said. "And you brought the dog . . ."

"Hey, that dog helped save me!" Dierdre said.

"Right, right, of course!" Gary said. "Sorry. We just weren't . . . well, I never had a pet as a kid."

"We might change that one day now that you're a big kid!" Dierdre teased.

"Special Agent Law, please, take a seat. Oh, wait, would you like coffee, tea, water — anything?" Gary asked her.

He was evidently at home in the Ayers family kitchen.

"Coffee would be lovely," Colleen said, taking the chair Amelia Ayers indicated at the end of the six-seat table. "I was just stopping by . . . I have to get back to work, but I couldn't resist the offer of a homemade cookie!"

"Mariana is amazing," Dierdre said with affection. "So, chocolate chip, oatmeal raisin, and honey-crusted crackers — all equally delicious."

"I will go with chocolate chip. It's my usual choice; it's hard to beat a good chocolate chip cookie," Colleen said.

"No! You must have one of each!" Dierdre said. "Mariana baked them in honor of my homecoming."

"Then I shall have one of each," Colleen assured her.

She bit into one of the cookies. It was delicious — Dierdre hadn't lied.

Mariana stood waiting, but she hadn't taken a seat at the table. Maybe that would have been taking it too far for Amelia Ayers.

"Wonderful!" Colleen told Mariana.

The woman smiled happily. "And tonight — steak and lobster! We are so happy, so very happy and grateful, thanks be to God, that our Dierdre has come home!"

"And you are a sweetheart," Dierdre said. She smiled at Colleen. "The hospital's food wasn't bad, but it doesn't compare to the concoctions Mariana can put together."

"It's nice to celebrate like this," Gary Boynton said. "Tomorrow, I'll be hitting the grind again. Lots of paperwork still to be done, but today is for my girl."

The last was softly, gently spoken. He did seem to honestly care for Dierdre, but whether it was the love of the century, Colleen didn't know.

But he at least cared, or he went through all the right motions.

Colleen tried each of the cookies. Gary talked a little tech about the things he intended to do to make the kitchen even better for Mariana.

Dierdre seemed thrilled to be home and — thankfully — she had been sedated when she'd first gotten to the hospital and didn't remember how close she had been to dying. "I guess there was a point when I wasn't breathing. If you and your partner and Red hadn't come when you did — I am so lucky."

"I am so lucky too," Gary whispered.

Colleen smiled and rose. "I'm happy that everything worked out. But now I'd best get back to work. Thank you so much for the coffee and the cookies that are beyond delicious!" she assured Mariana.

"I'll walk you out," Amelia said. "You and Red."

Red woofed and wagged his tail and followed close at Colleen's heels.

They left the kitchen and passed through the dining room with its elegant table and chairs set and matching hutches and on into the handsomely appointed living room. The large mantel held many family photos and Colleen paused, smiling, and asking,

"May I?"

"Of course. Family photos. Look at that one! Ah, our wedding. And there — Dierdre as a baby. She was an early baby. Well, I guess I was already pregnant when we were married. These days, no one cares. My folks wouldn't have been so happy, so . . . Dierdre! Early baby."

"Well, she's a sweet and beautiful baby," Colleen said.

"And we probably are far too possessive and overprotective. But I had complications at her birth. I couldn't have more children. So, she is . . ." She paused and laughed. "Poor girl. She's our obsession!"

"From what I hear, she's truly lovely to everyone, so you must have been wonderful parents."

"Lucky in many ways." Amelia paused, frowning. "Oh, dear. Did you interview Vince?"

"Yes."

"Such a nice young man. Just not . . ."

Colleen shrugged. "Seems to me he does well enough. He's very talented."

Amelia sighed. "I told that to Rory." She grinned. "I told him the boy was talented, and weren't we going to feel like jerks if he made millions and millions selling records! But Rory worried so. Musicians. Druggies, womanizers, and no stable employment."

"Um, honestly, Mrs. Ayers, I know many musicians who are clean and sober and dedicated to their spouses."

"It's just . . . well, I have to admit. My life wasn't going so well when I met Rory. I had dated a guitarist. I was working my way through college. He cost me a fortune, and I discovered a lot of it was going to drugs. When I met Rory, my world turned around. I don't want my daughter falling into a trap that almost seized me. So, when Rory was so down on Vince, I have to admit . . . Anyway, now she's with Gary! And he will protect her and support her."

"Some people do like to think they can support themselves, and prefer a marriage that's more a mutual falling in love," Colleen said. She didn't want to make an enemy. And she was no one to judge Amelia Ayers. She didn't know what the woman's past had been.

Time to make a courteous exit.

"Well, I'd better get back to it," she said. "Thank you again. Thank you so much!"

"Honestly, I can't begin to tell you how grateful I am!" Amelia told her.

Impulsively, the woman hugged Colleen.

Colleen gave her a quick, firm hug in return.

Red woofed.

She headed to her car, waving. Red followed along and jumped right in the back seat.

She drove away, waving one last time.

Rory Ayers sat at the conference table, staring at Mark.

A hard stare.

He shook his head.

"You have to be kidding!" he said.

"No, I'm sorry, I'm not. You didn't tell us anything about this amazing, huge business deal you have going with your prospective son-in-law."

"It's not a done deal," Ayers said flatly. "And what the hell difference does it make? Yes, he and I are both businessmen. And yes, I admire a savvy businessman! What could this have to do with anything?"

"Well, frankly, we're wondering if this business deal colors the way you look at Gary Boynton," Mark told him.

"Colors the way I look at him?"

"Maybe he did hurt your daughter," Mark said quietly.

"Don't be ridiculous! Oh, that is just . . . Well, that is pathetic. You people can't come up with anything else? You're inept."

Mark hadn't realized Angela had come in

and was quietly standing in the doorway until she spoke.

"Inept enough to save your daughter — minutes before she would have died or been permanently brain damaged."

Mark could see Ayers's jaw clenching.

"Yes, you saved her. We're grateful. But she was the victim. We were victims, and Gary Boynton was a victim! How dare you attack us!"

"Unfortunately, in crimes such as this, we have to look at the family and those close to the family."

"Then go look at that long-haired hippie!" Ayers snapped. "Probably a jealous ass, just out to spite everyone and kill the girl who rejected him. Oh, that one! He saw himself as God's gift to women. Strumming his guitar, all that crap! Go talk to him. Why would Gary want to hurt my daughter? He's going to marry her. We're the most copacetic group you're ever going to meet. We know the power of hard work and responsibility!"

"I watched Mr. Monroe play. He's very talented," Mark said.

"Yeah, yeah, and he's going to sell a million records one day. Sure. Doubtful. He'd want my daughter to work all her life. A million records? Maybe next lifetime. He's no man for my daughter, and my wife will let you know as much!"

"Your wife felt the same way?"

Ayers waved a hand in the air. "Amelia . . . she likes everyone. And she'd give the house away, but she's grateful I'm a harder nut to crack. Her parents did well and lost everything in a crash. She wanted to go to college, and she worked liked an idiot to try and pull it off — almost fell in with a druggie crowd of musicians! She knows we're just lucky Gary fell for Dierdre the way he did. Why not? She's a beautiful young woman."

"I just wished you'd mentioned the business connection," Mark said politely.

Angela was still standing at the doorway.

"We need all the information," she said.

Ayers shook his head. "But that's not pertinent to anything!"

"What came first, Mr. Ayers?" Mark asked. "The business deal or the romance?"

"They coincided," Ayers said impatiently. "We were working on the deal. That's how the two of them met. They've been together a long time now."

"Wow. So, it's a long deal."

"It's a complicated deal. And however tech savvy you people think you are here, you can't begin to know just what the complications are! I came in. Now, I'm leaving. And you incompetent fools can get back to it. I can tell you — Gary Boynton did not attack my daughter! And that's it. Your man in custody is the sicko and you know it! Why is this any different?"

"There was no letter to the media," Angela said.

Mark leaned forward. "And there was no sexual assault before she was buried alive."

"He didn't have time, probably — he was holding another girl, right?"

"Yes, that is right."

"Well, there you go. I'm leaving. And don't bother me again! My daughter was the victim. Do you get that? The victim! Don't keep making her a victim!"

Rory Ayers stormed out of the office.

Neither Angela nor Mark made a move to stop him.

Mark swiveled his chair to look at Angela, a question in his eyes, a dry grimace on his face.

"Well?"

"Sorry. I don't like anyone who uses the term *you people* in any context."

"Did he defend Boynton because the deal means more to him than his daughter?"

"That I don't know. He did seem convinced. Any more ideas?"

"One, but I think we'll go with that tomorrow," Mark said. He glanced at his watch, and as he did, Colleen came into the office.

"Anything?" they both said.

Colleen shook her head and waited.

Both exchanged their information from the afternoon.

Mark sighed. "So. We're going to take Megan Law to meet Sergeant Parker. Maybe, just maybe, he'll have gotten something from one of his spiritual friends!"

"You know, Sergeant Parker may not be hanging around the cemetery," Colleen told her sister.

Megan waved a hand in the air. "No matter. Thank you. I've heard about this cemetery and am just happy to take in its history! I've heard it's beautiful."

Colleen glanced over at Mark. A slight smile was on his face as he drove.

Megan leaned forward as far as the constraint of the back seat seat belt would allow. "Until Colleen became involved with the Krewe, I'd no idea there were so many people who were . . . weird. I guess some might even say creepy."

"Hey! We are not creepy!" Colleen protested.

She shook her head with amusement. Megan had always felt as if they were *weird*.

Then again, Colleen had worried about herself after the incident with the woman in the trunk when she'd been a child. While her father had protected her from the outside, she had managed to keep the secret, even from her siblings at first.

She hadn't known about Megan — and then Patrick — until they'd been at the funeral of a beloved great-uncle. Colleen had seen Megan speaking with the deceased after he had given his daughter a comforting touch.

Maybe their aunt had felt that touch. She had seemed more composed.

But Colleen had seen Megan speaking with the ghost — who was then ready to move on — and she had joined them. And Megan had pretended she hadn't been talking to anyone. Then Patrick had come over and the three of them had admitted the truth.

Patrick had thought it was all really cool.

Megan had been afraid at first and then in denial.

But she had embraced her ability when she realized it could enhance her favorite pastime in the world — reading.

She had once told Colleen how much she admired her, using her ability to help others, to save lives, and bring justice to those

276

who had been cruelly taken from the world.

"I just don't have your courage," Megan had told her.

"Well, you still help people!"

"I help myself more than other people," Megan had said. "I love what I do!"

Mark interrupted Colleen's memory. "Well, we have a bit of time, and we all need a breather here and there," he said. "So, hey, a little tour of the cemetery will be good."

He parked the car along the path that curved around the section for police graves. It was adjacent to one of the oldest sections, and Megan ran out first to appreciate a towering angel over a nineteenth-century grave.

Megan then read aloud from a stone that had been carefully tended by the cemetery's maintenance crew.

"James Hanson, speaker by trade,
A difference to others he made.
As all life must fade,
And pass,
So, here in peace he is laid."

She turned back to Mark and Colleen.

"How lovely. Sounds like he was a good guy who lived a nice, long life. Born 1812, died 1899? That's not bad. I hate seeing all the graves of kids from centuries past. So many were lost so young."

"And we still tragically lose children," Mark said.

"Ah, a newcomer!" they heard.

Turning, Colleen saw that the ghost of Sergeant Parker was coming their way.

"Sorry!" he said quickly. "Do I slip away, or . . ."

Megan answered the question for him, spinning around. "Sergeant Parker! Hi, I'm Megan Law, Colleen's sister."

"Well, I see the resemblance!" Parker said, beaming. "Lovely to meet you, dear. Sergeant Alfie Parker here, at your service. Are you in law enforcement too?"

"No, sir. I edit books. Science fiction, but I'm someone who loves history. And stories in general. I understand you have a tragic tale to tell?"

"I'm fine, young lady, so don't give me your pity. I've been strangely blessed to roam the earth — even as I am — in hopes of finding answers," he told her sternly.

"Oh, I don't pity you," Megan promised him quickly. "As I said, I love history and stories."

"And you've come for the story," he said.

She nodded. "Maybe we can find out

something that will help, that will lead you to the young lady whose fate has kept you here, determined to find her?"

"Ah, then we'll talk!" Parker said. "But first! Mark, Colleen, I have checked with every one of my colleagues. Barry Turner — retired after thirty-five years with the police department — still walks the beat often enough. He was in Carver's neighborhood. He says he couldn't swear an oath Carver never left the house that night, but if he did, Barry didn't see him. And he believes he would have."

Mark looked at Colleen.

"Well, we've been convinced there is a second would-be killer out there. And, of course, there's more to the puzzle."

Colleen nodded and turned to Sergeant Parker.

"We haven't found any pine, and the boxes were all built out of pine. Carver has to have a place where he builds his coffins. I think he tortured his victims in his basement where he was holding and torturing Sally. But . . ."

"Miles and miles of land, acres and acres of forest," Parker said. "So, you think this person knows Carver, and is an apprentice or fan, and maybe he knows where the coffin building might take place?"

"Unless he has his own," Mark said.

"Carver hasn't given you anything?" Parker asked.

"Not much," Colleen began. "Except we think he's angry this person acted without him. He goes between proclaiming his innocence —"

"You found the girl in his basement!" Parker said.

"He's basing his defense on the claim Sally wanted to be there, and she wanted rough sex, and she wasn't getting what she wanted. Also, she and Brant Pickering had just broken up. Carver claims she was acting up, needing what she really wanted from a man like him," Colleen explained.

"The bastard!" Parker said angrily.

"I was hopeful we'd find his accomplice — or copycat — quickly," Mark said. "It's proving difficult. But," he added, looking at Colleen, "we've concentrated on trying to discover the man who meant to kill Dierdre Ayers — on the assumption it has to be someone close to her, someone who knows her schedule, down to the time and path she returned home from work each day. I still believe it's someone close to her. And . . . miles and miles and acres and acres. It's like looking for a needle in a haystack. But I think, maybe it's time to try to trick Carver into telling us where he took the women before he buried them, if he didn't take them to the basement in whatever place he had rented at the time. I can't help but think that he has another place."

Colleen looked at Alfie Parker and said, "He rented the house he was in under an assumed name. He might have rented another house. He might have a place in the forest. It seems most logical, since he buried his victims in the woods. And if so . . ."

"Miles and miles, acres and acres," Megan echoed.

"What about your special talent?" Parker asked Colleen. "Maybe you could hear something?"

"If no one is at his place — wherever it may be — there would be nothing to hear," Colleen said.

Parker turned to Megan.

"And are you gifted like your sister?" he asked.

"No," Megan said.

"She does have a special talent —" Colleen began.

"Of course, she does!" Parker said. "This lovely lady is speaking to me!"

Megan laughed. She and Parker had obviously hit it off.

"I know what people mean — sometimes

when they don't know what they mean themselves!"

"That's a talent, all right," Parker said. "And so —"

"I'm an editor. And I like to believe I take raw material and guide our authors into making themselves exciting and clear."

"Wonderful. But you want my story — will you write it?"

"If I'm able to help," Megan said.

"That would be lovely. As to the present circumstances . . ."

Parker looked from Mark to Colleen, letting his words fade.

"You think we should interview Carver again with Megan listening?" Mark said.

"Oh, we can't involve Megan —"

"We don't involve her," Mark said. "We never let Carver see her."

"I go in, and you watch with Megan?" Colleen asked. "But she needs to get back —"

"We go right now. I'll get Ragnar on board; he'll have the interview set up. Then we drive Megan to the train station," Mark said.

He was fumbling in his pocket. Colleen realized he was reaching for his phone.

She quickly discovered they didn't need to call Ragnar — Ragnar was calling them.

"We've missed something," Mark said, hearing Ragnar's voice. "I was about to call you. I want to take Megan Law to watch while Colleen questions Carver again."

"Now?" Ragnar asked. "It's getting late."

"Right. But we'll drive right there. I wondered if —"

"Yeah, yeah. I'll get it set up."

"Megan is going back to New York. We'll do the interview and get her to the train station. I don't know what you want to do —"

"Look for Brant Pickering."

"What?"

"I've had my eyes on the Ayerses' house. Well, I've been sneaking around the yard, looking in. Seems Gary is staying there and not slipping out anywhere. Last I looked, they were playing Monopoly."

"So, what about Brant Pickering?"

"Cops were watching the hotel and Sally's place. He and Sally got in his car and headed to a shopping district. The cops followed best they could and Sally came out and got in her car. Brant Pickering didn't."

"Did they check the store they were in?"

"Come on, Mark. Of course. They've

checked the area. They're still out looking."

"What about Sally?"

"Cops followed her home. They're watching the home again, and I've got a couple of our agents playing tag team on it now." He hesitated. "I'll meet you for the interview with Carver. Get going. I'll arrange it as I drive. But start without me if necessary. DC area rush hour traffic. Let's hope we maneuver it well."

Colleen, Megan, and Sergeant Parker were watching him; they'd gotten the gist of the conversation.

"Let's go. Sergeant Parker, as usual, thank you."

"Sir, I'll be getting back to you," Megan promised him. "I'll be working the case from a journalist's point of view as soon as I'm on the train!"

"Thank you," Parker told her. "Go!" he commanded.

The three of them hurried to the car.

Colleen worried about Megan, saying, "I think you should spend another night —"

"I really need to get back to work. There's an art meeting I need to be part of. I need to convey a different planet — a different world — to our artists. It's sad but true; a book is often judged by its cover!"

"But we won't get you to a train until

about seven and you said —"

Megan waved a hand in the air. "That's when there was no reason for me to stay. I'm heading to NYC! People, bright lights everywhere. I'll be fine. The train station is about two blocks from my apartment — two heavily traveled blocks."

"But —"

"Colleen, hey! Come on. I need to be at work tomorrow."

Red — in the back seat with Megan — set his nose affectionately on her lap. She smiled and pat the dog, talking to him, telling him he really needed to meet her girl. The dogs could be best friends.

They arrived for the interview, checked their guns, and were escorted by guards. At the security desk, they were told Carver was being transferred the next day to a federal facility.

"The DA and your people have been meeting, and they want him up on federal charges because Virginia and DC and Maryland are all involved between the different women and the way they were buried in the forest. And they're afraid of him getting off if he isn't held without bond while they're getting their ducks in a row. Of course, Special Agent Gallagher, you and your partner will need to testify. His lawyer is going to argue illegal search and seizure, and Carver's arguments continue that Sally wanted to be with him."

"All right, thanks. I'm sure our office has been informed," Mark said. "We've been in the field."

The guard nodded. "You've got to nail this guy."

"Absolutely," Mark agreed.

He slipped into the observation room along with Megan and discovered Ragnar had actually beat them there.

"Thank you," he said stiffly to Megan.

"I don't know if I can help or not," she said.

"That's a given," Ragnar said.

"Hey, let's listen," Mark said quickly.

Colleen entered the interview room where Carver already waited. He was beaming again. Apparently, he was extremely fond of getting to see Colleen.

Too fond.

But Jim Carver was in shackles; the shackles were hooked to the table.

No way he'd get at her.

"You're a liar," Colleen said to him, taking the chair in front of him.

"What?" Carver said. "Oh, sweetie, I tell you the truth."

"What truth is that? You are The Embracer? You aren't The Embracer? You see, I think you're just a desperately sick man, and you preyed upon Sally, who doesn't have your demented taste in sexual activity. But as to being someone really out there . . . nope. Some other guy is The Embracer!"

"Hey. I like passion! And Sally is the liar. She likes passion too. She is the neediest creature on earth. She cried when I left her each time. And as to someone else . . ."

"Our sessions are recorded," Colleen reminded him. "I mean, in court, you're going to have a bad time. You've basically confessed to murder."

"Tricked and coerced confessions are no good," Carver said.

She shrugged. "I think there is someone out there way better than you. I mean, someone who has a whole setup. Coffins like that don't build themselves, and they weren't store-bought. The real Embracer is still out there."

"You're an idiot. Damned gorgeous, but an idiot. How the hell did they let you in the FBI? Oh, wait — that's right. The agency is full of idiots."

"He is still out there!" she repeated.

"Do you have any idea what the forests in and around the Blue Ridge are like?" Carver asked, obviously aggravated. "I'm innocent of everything but trying to help a desperately hurt and horny woman, but come on!" He started to laugh. "Forests are full of trees!"

"I see. You find your own trees and cut the pine?" she said.

"You can never see the forest for the trees," he said, laughing.

"The lumber was store-bought. Sold in hundreds of home shops across the area," Colleen said.

"I never said I cut pine. I merely pointed out you're like a pack of dogs. Oh, yeah, there is a dog, but your pack sniffs butts and chases tails. Idiots. Which is good for me, because I'm going to walk out of court a free man."

"You think so?" Colleen asked.

"I know so."

"You're not The Embracer. Another man will get the fame."

"I will walk out a free man."

"Oh, Mr. Carver, I do not think so," Colleen assured him.

Carver leaned back, jaw tightening as he considered his reply.

Mark, Ragnar, Red, and Megan watched as Colleen confronted Carver. They had all been silent.

Then Megan spoke. "She's got him aggravated," she said softly. "Good."

"I think you're underestimating Sally and the dozens of people who can testify to her character," Colleen said.

"But desires like hers are necessarily kept secret," Carver said.

"You're going to be locked away forever, I promise you," she told him.

He leaned as close as he could to her.

"You never see what is . . . up *front*. Right in front of your oh-so-royal asses!"

"Really? Your hideout — where you prepare your coffins for the girls you kill — is right in front of us?"

"Not my hideout! But you people are so stupid. I'm sure if The Embracer has a hideout, it would bite you all right in your royal asses!"

"Prison or execution?" Colleen said cheerfully.

"You can get her out of there," Megan said.

"He hasn't said anything," Ragnar told her with a frown.

"Yes, he did," Megan said.

"I'm going in," Mark said with determination. "If you think you've got something, this can end."

He walked out of the observation room, nodded to the guard at the door to the interview room, and stepped in.

"We're needed," he said to Colleen.

"Oh, don't take her away!" Carver said. "You can go away, but don't take her away!"

"They'll be taking you away soon enough," Mark told him. He smiled.

Carver kept his own smile in place, but his eyes hardened.

"I think this is the last time you'll be seeing Special Agent Law, Mr. Carver. So sad!"

"Oh, I don't think so!" Carver said.

Mark ignored him and ushered Colleen out.

"Megan thinks she's got something," he told her.

"From that?"

They headed back to the observation room.

Colleen hurried to her sister. "Megan?"

"He was taunting you — teasing you the whole while."

"Always," Colleen agreed. "But what did he say?"

"Well, first, has he called you 'royal asses' before?"

"I believe he has called us asses and idiots many times," Colleen said.

"No, no, you're not listening to me right now," Megan said, smiling. "Has he called you *royal* asses before — and suggested that everything is right in *front* of you?" Megan asked.

"He always treats us like jerks."

"The Embracer likes to taunt people. We suspect he is The Embracer, right? That someone else is out there, but he is the man who killed the first two women who were taken?" Megan said.

"Right," Mark said.

"I've got it!" Colleen said.

Mark and Ragnar looked at her, arching their brows simultaneously.

Even Red looked at her, his head at an angle as if he was questioning her words.

But Colleen just smiled and looked at Megan.

"He does have a place where he builds his coffins — maybe where he took Emily and Lainie before he buried them alive. And where he assaulted them. That was a difference in the kidnappings too," Colleen reminded them. "There was no sexual assault with Dierdre."

"Okay, still?" Ragnar asked.

"West Virginia, Maryland, DC — and Virginia. All easily reached from Carver's latest rental. The buried coffins were all found in the woods — to the east of the Blue Ridge Mountains. Follow those trails and where can you wind up?"

Mark looked at her and smiled slowly. "Front Royal, Virginia," he said.

Colleen and Megan nodded.

"And, of course, he thinks we're all idiots who would never get it," Colleen said.

"Well," Mark admitted dryly, "most of us were idiots who didn't get it. I mean, we're still looking for a needle in a haystack." He turned to Megan and added, "But a much smaller haystack thanks to you."

"I don't have a scientific guarantee," Megan said. "But from his determination to send letters to the media, and the way he talked to Colleen, I'm pretty sure that's what his taunting meant. I'm not a mind reader, just an interpreter, I guess."

"It puts us on a better path than anything we've had before," Mark assured her. "We can get Angela on local police and forest rangers and tell them we're looking for any kind of cabin or retreat in that area. That will help a lot," he said, looking at Megan curiously again. "A lot. It may be the puzzle piece we've been missing."

"Well, I hope I've helped," Megan said. She glanced at her watch. "I really do need to get to that meeting tomorrow. If you'd be so kind —"

Ragnar spoke to Mark, saying, "I'm going to head over to Sally's place. I'm going to

292

knock on the door and ask her if Brant is there, and if not, find out where he might be. She has to understand we are worried about her and will be looking out for her — including where Brant Pickering is involved."

"All right. We'll get Megan to the train. I'll call Angela and have her and Jackson contact anyone they can in the Front Royal area and see what we can learn. And if we have enough agents and police covering Sally's home and Dierdre's place, I'm going to get Colleen home and we'll call it a night and start out for Front Royal for some in-person searches and discussions in the morning."

"I'll join you," Ragnar promised. He turned to Megan. "Thank you, Miss Law. Your agreement to help on this will hopefully prove to be incredibly important."

He didn't wait for an answer from her; he stooped down to pet Red goodbye and was gone.

Mark realized then that they hadn't told the guard to go ahead and take Jim Carver back to his cell.

He smiled.

The man was ranting.

"Hey! Hey! Talk to me. All right, you all just wait. There is going to be a lawsuit that

is going to make your stupid heads spin."
He paused to laugh. "Yeah, your royal ass
heads are going to spin, right in front of
you!"

His words were garbled at the end because
he was laughing so hard.

But then his laughter stopped as his
temper soared.

"Get me out of here! Lawsuit! Cruel and
inhumane punishment when a man is still
innocent until proven guilty, and you will
not prove me guilty!"

A guard opened the door to the observation room.

"Have you finished with what you need
for today?" he asked him.

"Yes, I'm sorry. We should have informed
you right away."

The guard gave them a hard grimace.

"Not at all. I love watching him; he's
tormenting himself far more than any of us.
Maybe I'll give him another minute."

"You do that," Mark said. "We are going
to leave. Thank you."

"Just nail him," the guard said, and left.

"I guess he's not a particularly beloved
prisoner," Megan said.

"Nope. Now, come on, we'll get you to
your train station."

They talked on the way, the triplets' curious abilities again the topic of conversation. All of them had an ability, and every ability was different.

"Colleen hears, you interpret meaning . . . What does Patrick do?"

"Our brother is a criminal psychologist," Megan said.

"But what does he do — hear . . . see . . ."

Megan winced, glancing over at Colleen. "He . . . um . . ."

"He's psychic," Colleen said. "The real deal."

"You mean he can hold something and find someone that way?" Mark asked.

"Not exactly. He can go somewhere — say a crime scene — and see it unfold in his mind. Or he can be with someone and get a feel for where they've been or what they've done. I thought about suggesting his help before, except I knew he was just finishing up a major case in Philadelphia."

"He should have been a detective," Mark commented.

"Well, he loves what he does. He is professional with everyone he's asked to interview, but he also knows . . . He just can't tell people he knows —"

"Back to Salem. No spectral evidence, and thank God," Mark said.

"Right. But it helps everything move in

295

the right direction. He can also figure whether something was an accident or premeditated . . . He's good," Colleen said. She glanced at Megan.

"If you're going to be weird and spend your life trying not to appear to be weird, it's a good thing to have weird siblings who understand you," Megan said. "People you can talk to when you need help or need to vent."

"True," Mark murmured.

They had reached the train station. They had arrived after the rush hour crunch, but the station was still busy.

"I'm going in with you," Colleen told Megan.

"There are a zillion people here —"

"I'll see you buy your ticket and get out to the platform."

"Mark, I'm sure I'll see you again. Thank you!" Megan said, stepping out of the car.

"No, thank you," he said. He realized he was already scanning the area, especially not knowing where Brant Pickering was.

Megan waved. Colleen followed her into the station.

Mark found he was suspicious as he looked around the station. That might have been ridiculous. No one could have known when they'd get Megan to the train station

— they hadn't known themselves.

There were plenty of people at the station. He could even see two police officers, watching over the scene.

Colleen reappeared from the station entrance after about ten minutes, heading straight for the car.

She gave him a grimace as she got in.

"We can wait — see that she gets on the train," Mark told her.

Colleen smiled.

"I saw her to the platform, and I could hear the train coming in."

"Ah. I guess that works."

"Ugh, you're right, though. I didn't see her get on it."

"I'm sure it's fine."

"I don't know. My parents worry about every little thing, of course. My mom says that at least we all picked the same time zone, so she can get some sleep. Patrick is, well, I wouldn't mess with Patrick. But I do worry about Megan."

"You think she's too trusting?"

"I think she gets enthused about certain projects and people."

"And Brant Pickering is out there," Mark muttered.

"He couldn't know what train she's on," Colleen said.

"We didn't know what train she'd be on."

"Right. There are thousands of possible victims out there," Colleen murmured. "Where are we going now?"

"I'm taking you home. Tomorrow, we'll check out Front Royal and surrounding areas."

"Okay. A thought — maybe we can get Patrick down here? Let him meet with Jim Carver."

"Maybe that's not a bad idea."

"I'll talk to him tomorrow. He can hop on a train, same as Megan."

"All right. We'll look into it."

When they reached her house, he found a space in front where his special plates would allow him to park.

He turned off the engine.

"I'm walking you to your door," he said.

"I carry a big Glock and know how to use it."

"I know."

She shrugged and got out of the car. He was around to her side quickly and they walked to the door of her row house together, Red naturally trailing along.

At the door, she looked at him curiously.

He smiled and asked her, "So, should I ask you on a real date? Or, as Megan suggested, should we just get right to it?"

Hardly a question a professional asks a partner. And, of course, she might be horrified, she might report him . . .

But she didn't. Her smile hit her eyes before her lips.

"Well, we have already been to a supper club," she told him. "So . . . I guess you should come on in!"

CHAPTER ELEVEN

It was absurd, of course.

She'd never . . .

But she was going to.

Maybe Megan was right — they weren't destined to have normal relationships. And maybe in life something just seemed extreme, something that was what she wanted, and maybe even what she really needed.

But along with the way she had been steadily feeling her attraction to him grow on a physical level, she had learned to love the light in his eyes when he smiled, and the way he could make her laugh, and even . . .

The way he had come right to the point, right now, and . . .

She caught his hand and drew him into the house, closing the door, wincing as Red scurried through.

She'd almost forgotten the dog.

But Red trotted in, leapt on the sofa, and

curled up with Jensen. And as she watched, Mark caught her gently, swung her around, and pressed her against the door, catching her hands above her head.

She'd asked him in to sleep with her.

They'd barely shared civil words, and certainly not a kiss.

But now they did.

She felt the pressure of his body against her, a searing heat in his mouth and form that seemed to make the world melt away. They stayed there, lingering there, just tasting the hunger in one another, feeling the intimate connection of being locked together.

Then, at last, he moved back slightly, smiling. "Well, at least we went to that supper club."

"There you go. Almost a date. Actually, didn't the federal government buy me dinner?"

"You mean I didn't even buy you dinner?"

"Well . . ."

"You didn't even buy *me* dinner," he reminded her. "And yet . . ."

She laughed softly. "I want your body without springing for dinner? I know I have some peanut butter in the kitchen!"

"And what are you suggesting with that?" he asked warily.

He moved agilely to sweep her off her feet and into his arms.

She smiled, curving her arms around his neck.

"Well, at least you didn't drop me!" she said.

"Hey, have some faith!" he said, but then he frowned slightly. "I don't know where to go from here."

"Really? Usually, it has to do with taking one's clothing off, all at once, bit by bit . . ."

He started to laugh. "I mean, I don't know your place. Where am I carrying you?"

"Am I getting heavy already?"

"Define 'heavy.' Hmm, from the moment I met you . . ."

"Hey! I've been a good agent."

"Yes, you have. And I . . ."

"Are you trying to apologize?" she asked him.

"I think I have apologized. No, you're not heavy — but which way am I going?"

She laughed softly and nodded her head toward the sofa where Jensen and Red were curled together.

"The children seem to have the living room. We could go up to my bedroom. But please don't drop me on the stairs."

"I should drop you just for being a wiseass."

"Then I'd make you kiss every tiny little injury!"

"Sounds good. Maybe I should drop you for that reason."

She laughed, amazed they could be so close, so easy, so free. She pointed around the entry to the stairs, and he easily moved in that direction. Red let out a woof as they reached the bottom.

Mark paused.

"Feels like we have chaperones," he said. "Red, stay!"

Red stayed.

Red and Jensen both watched them head up the stairs. Neither animal moved.

Colleen indicated the doorway to her room, and they went in. He went to set her on the bed, tripped on one of her slippers, and laughed as he crashed down with her.

She let out a feigned cry of protest that turned into a laugh as he rose above her and straddled over her, reminding her, "Now, there's this thing with clothing, so you say."

She smiled, half rose against him, and tugged off her jacket. She had to wriggle beneath him to get to her holster and gun.

He didn't help any, taking off his jacket and reaching to his back for his own leather holster and gun, then lying over her to set them on the bedside table, just as she had done.

She sighed with mock impatience. "Let me help you with your shirt . . ."

She reached for his buttons. He reached for hers. Feeling his fingers brush against her flesh as he undid buttons seemed so simple and so erotic. And in the end, she wound up ripping off one of his buttons in her haste to feel more of his flesh against her own.

As she had felt with that first kiss, the tension, fear, anger, worry, work, all slipped away. Because there was nothing more important than feeling the muscles tense in his chest, reveling in the caress of his fingers upon her.

They were still half-entwined in their clothing when he kissed her again. The kiss was hot, a fiery blaze that ignited everything within her. They laughed, struggling out of more and more clothing. Some of it was tossed to the floor, some just tangled with the comforter on the bed.

He pulled away from her, tossing off his own shoes and socks, then shedding his trousers and briefs.

He turned for her skirt, shimmying it from her body, then tossed her heels to the floor and crawled up slowly along her legs, murmuring softly as he planted kisses against her calves, knees, and thighs.

"If I had dropped you, it might hurt here . . . or here," he said.

"Oh, it might. And I could have clung to you, stroking your shoulders, working my fingers over your flesh . . ."

"And . . ."

He stopped talking and rose against her, pulling her into his arms again, engaging in another deep, wet kiss, mouths open, tongues . . .

The kiss ended.

This time, he moved down her body, caresses and kisses falling upon her shoulders, throat, breasts, abdomen . . . and below.

The world had melted away.

Now, it exploded, and she drew him back to her, falling into a kiss again, then pinning him beneath her, and reminding him in a muffled whisper that she probably would have dropped him had she attempted to carry him up the stairs, and he would have hurt here . . . and there . . . and everywhere.

Then he rose, pulling her into his arms again. This time, when he kissed her, he thrust inside her, and she felt as if the universe burst apart in sparks, and then they moved together.

It was passionate and wild and tender all in one, and she wondered how she hadn't realized from the second she'd met him that . . .

He could become her world.

She tried to tell herself it was sex. Just sex. People had sex all the time.

But this was . . .

Different. And she didn't believe he was the kind of man who just didn't care, who slept around, who . . .

She didn't think at all.

She felt as if the world and universe and heavens all seemed to collide.

Then they lay together.

Air seemed good. Lying there was good.

Everything was good. For now.

She breathed, afraid to speak.

He didn't speak either. He pulled her against him and held her gently.

Eventually, he spoke softly.

"Your sister is extremely smart."

That, of course, made her smile. And it allowed her to rise on an elbow to look at him.

"See, there are benefits to an attractive partner!"

He smiled, but then a serious look came over his face.

"If you had continued to despise me, I'd

306

have had to admit you were an amazing asset to the Krewe."

"I never despised you."

"I behaved very badly."

"Yes, but Red loves you. There had to be something redeemable in you."

"Hopefully, I've proved myself redeemable."

"You'll . . . pass," she said lightly.

They both laughed and fell into one another's arms.

This was new, exhilarating, incredible . . .

But later, as they lay together, he rolled over and said, "Dog food. I have to give Red something. He's a hardworking dude. I'm a hardworking dude too. Food."

"Well, I do have that peanut butter!"

"So, Megan made the omelets?"

Colleen laughed. "We create together. I'm just not sure what I have in the kitchen. I haven't been shopping in a while."

"Delivery!" he said. "Little effort. I guess I will have to put pants back on to go downstairs."

"Well, one of us should."

He started searching around the bed.

"What are you doing?" Colleen asked him.

"My phone is in my pants."

"Ah, mine is downstairs. Dropped my bag when I came in."

"Aha! Success."

He dug his phone out of his pants. They sat together and looked at the offerings that could be delivered.

They chose a barbecue place. Mark could order a couple plain burgers for Red.

"You don't have dog food?" Colleen asked.

"I don't carry it with me," he told her.

She grinned. "So, you're staying?"

"If you don't mind."

She shook her head. "No, I'm . . ."

She paused, remembering how Megan had said she'd thought she was being watched and how she had felt uneasy herself.

But it had been nothing.

"No. I'm glad you're staying."

He smiled. For a minute they sat, looking at one another. She loved the blue of his eyes and his hair against the bronze of his flesh. She loved the shape of his face.

And, she thought dryly, the shape of the rest of him.

"You can protect me," he told her lightly.

"Ha ha."

She was surprised by how serious he grew.

"Don't kid yourself. I know you'd be fine under any circumstances. We all need each other."

She nodded. "It's good to have you — and

Ragnar and Red."

The barbecue place was near; the food arrived quickly.

They had their late-night dinner in bed.

Colleen remained surprised Jensen and Red got along as well as they did. Jensen had always accepted dogs — he'd known his "cousin" wolfhound and shepherd since he'd been a kitten. But he seemed to have a special acceptance for Red.

Maybe Red was just that special.

They slept that night, late and entwined.

And it seemed an amazing oasis in the harsh sands of the lives they were living.

No matter what hours he kept, Mark had an annoying inner alarm clock.

He woke at six.

He dressed quickly, glad he kept a clean shirt in his car, ran out and got it, ran Red out quickly, and then ran back in to shower and dress again with his clean shirt.

He didn't wake Colleen until then. She was far too angelic-looking, lean, shapely body curled against the tangle of the sheets, the fire of her hair spilled wildly out on a pillow.

How had they been together so long without . . . ?

So long? He mocked himself.

Sex was sex, a friend had told him once. Another football player, a friend who had meant to go all the way to the big leagues, if he could. And he had excelled at the game.

But for him, that had also meant he'd excelled at life. Women weren't expendable, but there were so many of them, and his friend had thought so many were worthy of him.

But while sex might be a biological function, his friend had been so wrong.

Even throwing basic chemistry into the mix didn't make sex — sex.

He didn't ever want to leave. It was crazy. They hadn't been together a week. But he wanted to continue to sleep in the comfort that had claimed him last night, to wake up to see her face . . .

"Colleen," he said, shaking her gently.

Her eyes opened. She stared at him for a minute and then jumped up.

"No, oh, no! I'm sorry! Did I oversleep?"

"Nope. Everything is good. I'm going to go down and make coffee now, while you get ready."

"You just have to press the button — I always have it ready to go. I — I'm quick, really."

"I believe you and we're fine. We can take some time to determine all our best moves, then head out."

"Say we find Carver's cabin — his hidden place to build coffins and torture victims — we still have to figure out who kidnapped Dierdre."

He smiled grimly. "I'm on it," he promised her.

"Then there's the matter of clothing," she said gravely. "We need to get you some over here."

"And vice versa," he said. "I think you'll like my place too."

He hurried downstairs to push the button on the coffee maker. The machine made a little whooshing sound and ticked into action.

His phone rang and he answered it quickly, seeing it was Angela.

"Anything on Brant Pickering yet?" he asked.

"We went through his financials. He bought a ticket for a train ride back to New York. But none of our people — locally or in NYC — have eyes on him yet. Sally is at her house; we've had our own agents watching. They've been able to see her moving around in the dining room. Ragnar is going to head out there to speak with her."

"This early?"

"Our observers know she's awake."

311

"All right. Strange, isn't it — he was so loyal at the hospital. Now he's gone. And without a word to us. I'd have expected a heads-up, since he seemed like a good guy at the hospital."

"This doesn't mean he isn't a good guy."

"He left her alone. Without a word to law enforcement."

"He may feel she's safe, Mark. He may even know we're watching the house. Until we know more, we can't judge him to be a killer."

"Yeah, I know. We're coming in. I have a plan for today — though I want to get out to the Front Royal area quickly."

"Want to let me in on the plan?" Angela asked.

He described what he wanted to do and then asked, "Any word from law enforcement in the Front Royal area?"

"Yes — acres and acres of woods. Dozens of old cabins out there. But they're starting a search."

"Thanks. We'll be in shortly."

"I'll be here to help with your plan in any way. And Jackson is in the office today too."

He thanked her and hung up.

It was early — probably still too early to call a musician.

Screw it. He asked Vince to come in,

promising him he'd get him into a conference room. He wouldn't have to see Rory Ayers, and it could help if he and Dierdre put their heads together.

"But there is no one currently missing that we know of?" Vince asked him.

"We'd really like to get this guy before there is another woman in trouble," Mark told him.

Vince agreed to come in. Mark ended the call and stood, just staring at the coffee.

Their investigations now had to be twofold he knew. They needed to find where Carver had built his coffins.

And they needed to find the second would-be killer.

He gripped the counter for a minute, remembering the night he and Red had discovered the coffin holding Lainie Nowak. Red barking, him calling it in and frantically digging . . .

The media had received an "Embracer" note. He'd just hoped against hope they would find her in time.

The medical examiner told Mark that Lainie had been dead for hours; she'd been assaulted and had internal injuries and had died almost immediately after being put in the cheap coffin in the dirt. While the earth had leaked through, her lungs were clear of having inhaled dirt. She had suffocated before the dirt had sifted into the coffin.

"Hey! You all right?"

Startled, he turned around.

Colleen had been true to her word. She was already up, showered, and dressed, ready to head out for the day.

And the coffee had brewed.

"I'm going to have you bring Dierdre to the office," he told her.

"And you think she'll just come with me? Gary will be there, her folks will be there, and I doubt they'll let her go anywhere alone."

"That's fine. Bring Gary. When you get in, I'll have Vince Monroe there already. We'll get them split up. Ragnar can talk to Gary and pretend we desperately need his help."

"What about Brant Pickering. Have you heard anything? Does anyone have eyes on him yet?"

He shook his head. "Law enforcement is still looking."

"Okay. This could mean we need a lot of coffee!"

They filled travel containers with coffee and headed for the door. Mark called Red.

The dog and the cat were once again curled together on the sofa.

"Red!"

Red jumped up obediently. Jensen followed him to the door.

"Jensen, you can't come! You're not a service cat. But Red will be back."

She looked at Mark and smiled when she said it.

"Red will be back," he assured Jensen.

As they walked to the car, he said, "I have never seen anything like that. The two of them act as if they're puppies from the same litter."

"Jensen is accustomed to dogs."

"Right. Your sister and brother have dogs."

"Yep. So, it's okay if Gary insists on coming in with Dierdre?"

"It will be fine. I've talked to Angela. We're keeping them in separate conference rooms. I want to see Dierdre and Vince together. I want to get them talking about when they were dating, who else might have been around when they were together, if they saw or met anyone who might have been watching them, interested in them, and so on."

"And you want to see Dierdre with Vince," Colleen said.

"Exactly." He shook his head. "It's not my concern either, but it just angers me a man judges another man on his stock portfolio."

"Right. But remember —"

315

"We can't bring our opinions into it, and I don't really have the right to judge Rory Ayers."

"Hey, but we're all human," she said cheerfully. "You do get to dislike him!"

He smiled.

"From what I understand, you had the talent to be really rich and famous. Kudos to you that you chose a more altruistic path," she told him sincerely.

"Hey, football players get beat to pieces. I don't even have any broken bones."

"Right. If you'd been a quarterback, you might have gotten sacked. Now, people may just shoot at you."

He shrugged and glanced her way. "You're here, aren't you?"

"Yes. But I don't think I could have been a rich and famous football hero anyway."

"There are all kinds of heroes."

As they neared the office, Colleen said, "Hey, don't park. I'll keep going and drive out to the Ayerses' place. By the time I get there, it won't be too early."

"All right. I'll pull over and we can switch."

"What if she says it's stupid for her to come in, that she's told her story over and over?"

"We haven't done a cognitive interview.

316

She was in the hospital when we spoke with her. Tell her we'll do a cognitive interview — which we will, after I see her with Vince."

"Okay."

He pulled the car over and stepped out, calling to Red as he did. The dog obediently followed.

As Colleen came around the car, she made a face at him and said, "I'm impressed. You're letting me go get Dierdre all by myself!"

"Of course."

"You're not even sending Red."

"Nope."

"Is that because I'm competent, intelligent, and have a gun and know how to use it?"

"Of course. There's that and the Ayerses' house is being watched by cops and agents."

She laughed, shaking her head, and said, "I'll be back soon."

Mark watched her go, pulling out his phone to call Ragnar.

Over the line, Ragnar said, "Angela told me you want to see some interaction. I am going to visit Sally and ask her what's with her and Brant Pickering, and then I think my most useful action will be to head to Front Royal, talk with the police and the rangers."

"We'll meet you there as soon as possible," Mark promised.

"I'd love to be a fly on the wall there, but even if Megan Law is as annoying as all hell, I think she was reading Carver just right. That shack or cabin is out there, and while we know that Carver used it, his copycat may have used it too."

"And we may find evidence," Mark agreed. "We'll play this out and be there soon."

"Yes. I need you guys — at least, we need Red!"

"Yeah. We'll get Red out there quickly."

He ended the call and walked the rest of the way to the building that housed the Krewe offices. He went to Angela's office first.

"Colleen is on her way to get Dierdre."

"And Vince Monroe has beaten you in," Angela told him. "I have him in the far conference room. We can keep him there until anyone who comes in with Dierdre has gone past. And don't worry, no matter what questions have been asked so far to either Gary Boynton or Rory Ayers, I can come up with more."

"We haven't heard anything further on Brant Pickering, right?"

"Not yet."

"Thank you. I'll go in with Vince. Ragnar is going to visit Sally, and then he'll be heading toward Front Royal."

"We've informed the main Bureau offices there, and they're sending out agents to comb the woods as well."

"We can use all the help we can get," Mark assured her.

He walked down the hall to the conference room. Vince Monroe was seated at the table, staring at his hands.

"Hello," he said, greeting Mark.

"You're early," Mark noted. "Colleen has gone for Dierdre, but it will take a bit."

Monroe shook his head. "It's all right. Ever since I talked to you guys, I've been worried. I go over and over everything I can remember from when we were seeing each other."

"And do you come up with anything?"

Monroe grimaced. "Her father is a jerk?"

Mark shrugged.

Monroe laughed, adjusting himself in his chair. "So, you are being polite, but you know he's an ass."

"Ah, well, my position is not to judge people's personalities unless, of course, they're stark raving crazy and a danger to others."

"He's just a danger to common decency,"

Monroe said. "But whatever." He fell quiet. "It will be good to see Dierdre. Just to see for myself she's all right."

"You do still love her."

Monroe smiled. "She's special. How she's his kid, I'll never know. Her mom is all right, though. I guess she was the one home during Dierdre's formative years. Ayers was probably always at work. She didn't matter until she could help in a merger."

There was a tap on the door. It was Angela.

"Excuse me, gentlemen. Mark, may I see you for a minute?"

"Of course. Excuse me, Mr. Monroe."

"Vince, please."

"Vince," he said, frowning slightly at Angela as he headed out.

"I've found some interesting information," she said.

All the homes in the Ayerses' neighborhood sat on at least an acre or so of land. Many of the homes were surrounded by high walls.

The Ayerses' home was not.

There were cars in the circular drive, and all up and down the street, cars in driveways, and legally parked on the road.

Colleen knew a few of the parked cars were police or agents, but she was glad they were not obvious in any way. Of course, she was watched as she entered the Ayerses' driveway and walked to the door of the house.

Mariana came to the door and greeted Colleen politely and courteously, asking her to wait in the expansive parlor while she found Mr. or Mrs. Ayers.

"I'm really here for Miss Ayers," Colleen told her.

Mariana didn't have to find Dierdre Ayers; Dierdre — followed by Gary — was heading out of the wing with the kitchen and dining room as they spoke.

"Hi!" Dierdre said. "Have you caught someone else? Is there news? Please tell me it's not another kidnapping!"

"No, no, nothing like that," Colleen assured her. "And I'm so sorry, but we would appreciate it if you would come back in."

"But I've — I've told everyone dozens of times what happened," Dierdre said.

"We're going to do something we haven't done yet. Down to basics," Colleen said. "We're going to do a cognitive interview."

"Cool," Gary said. He looked at Dierdre. "I've seen it on cop shows. You close your eyes, you think back . . . It's kind of like being with a shrink."

Colleen smiled. "Well, there are four basic

321

aspects to a cognitive interview. Reinstatement of the environment, looking at different perspectives —"

"She was alone. There were no witnesses," Gary said.

"Oh, there was another," Colleen said. "Whoever did this. And then we look at what happened in a different order, and finally, work on finding every last little detail."

"Cool," Gary said, but he looked at Colleen suspiciously. "You want her alone? I'm not sure about that. I'd like to come in with you."

"Oh, you can bring her to the office and wait and bring her right home after if you'd like," Colleen told him. "We do have something of a lounge with a television that gets the *Bloomberg Report*."

"All right. I don't want you coming or going alone, baby," Gary said.

"Okay."

Colleen was about to turn to leave when Rory and Amelia Ayers came down the stairs. "Special Agent Law," Rory said. "To what do we owe the pleasure?"

"It's all right, Rory," Gary said. "They want to ask her a few more questions, but she said I can go with her."

"Maybe I should go," Rory said.

"Dad!" Dierdre protested. "Gary will be with me."

"Sweetheart?" Amelia said, placing a hand on his arm.

Rory still looked distressed — but now knotted up. Gary was supposed to be the man in Dierdre's life, protecting her from all things. And his wife apparently didn't want him interfering.

"Watch her carefully!" he warned Gary.

"Will do," Gary promised. "I'll follow you," he told Colleen.

When they were out of the house and the door closed behind them, he grinned at Colleen.

"I'll follow you and cops will follow me. It will be great."

"Right," she admitted.

"That's good. It will make me obey the speed limit!"

Gary seemed fine with it, even knowing he wouldn't be in with Dierdre during the interview.

"Are you going to hypnotize me or something?" Dierdre asked as they walked to their cars.

"No, no. Just go through it all, the way I said."

Once inside Mark's car, she waited until

she saw Gary behind the wheel before starting out.

As she drove, she called Mark.

"We're on our way in," she said.

"With Gary?"

"With Gary. But I've informed him he'll be watching business news in the lounge."

"And he is okay with that?"

"He was."

"All right. Bring Dierdre to the end conference room. Angela can get Gary settled in the lounge. She's made some interesting discoveries, by the way."

"Oh?"

"I'll show you when we finish. She has the information she gathered and is transferring a file to me. You can look at it during the drive to Front Royal."

"Okay. That's evasive."

"No, it's . . . well, let me put it this way: there was an Embracer at work years ago. We may have just discovered the tip of an iceberg."

Mark was with Vince when Colleen brought Dierdre back to the conference room.

They both stood when the women entered.

"Dierdre!"

Vince spoke her name with reverence.

"Vince!" she said, smiling. "They dragged you in here too? But surely, you let them know it has been some time since . . ." She turned to glare at Mark and Colleen. "You can't possibly think Vince had something to do with this!"

"I don't think Vince is guilty. Not at all," Mark said. And it was true; if he had any instincts at all, Vince Monroe was not guilty.

And Red liked the guy. In fact, Red had happily curled up at Vince Monroe's feet.

"Oh," Dierdre said, confused, and turned to Colleen for clarification.

"We're just looking in every possible direction, and we thought Vince might remember someone who had been too interested in you, given you all a hard time at some point. We have to investigate every possible lead," Colleen told her.

"In fact, it's great you came in for the cognitive," Mark said. "Maybe if you and Vince chat for a few minutes together, you'll think of someone who was sketchy, who paid you too much attention at an event or something. Actually, if you two will excuse us for a minute, I need to bring Colleen up to speed on a few things. We'll be right back, and then we'll just need another thirty minutes or so and you can be on your way."

"Red is here!" Dierdre said.

"You know the dog," Vince said.

"He helped save my life. You bet I know this dog. Can Red stay with us?" she asked.

"Of course," Mark said. "Red, stay."

Mark smiled and indicated the door, and Colleen walked out ahead of him, pausing in the hallway.

"We'll go to Angela's office; the camera and mics are on," he told her.

They walked to Angela's office. Angela was behind her desk, watching the screen.

"Gary Boynton?" Mark asked her.

"Jackson is avidly listening to his tech talk," Angela said, without looking up. "I wanted to make sure we were good on this end."

Dierdre had chosen to sit in the chair next to Vince's. They faced each other, smiling and laughing. They weren't talking about the past; Dierdre wanted to know about his music.

He was excited, telling her about a song he was going to record for the group. They were planning another album.

He asked about her, his concern evident.

"I'm okay. I'm really okay. Gary is wonderful," she assured him. Then she shrugged and said, "He isn't you. I so loved the music! But he's . . . well, he's been great."

She said the last word in a whisper.

"She cares about Gary," Colleen said. "But I think she really loves Vince. They only broke up because of her family."

"What if that family finds out their sterling choice is the man who might have buried their daughter?" Mark said. "There's nothing yet on Brant Pickering?" he asked Angela.

"I believe Ragnar is with Sally right now," she said.

"But there's been no sight of him in the city?"

"No. And he isn't answering his door."

"We need the local police to get his super to open the door, then," Mark said. "With this having gone on, we can fear imminent danger."

"It's only women who have been attacked," Angela noted.

"But we could worry he knows something, and a would-be killer knows he knows it," Mark said.

"True," Angela said.

They fell silent.

Dierdre and Vince were discussing their time together then, places they had been, trying to remember if anyone had looked at them suspiciously or acted strangely toward Dierdre.

"People do look at you. Because you're

beautiful," Vince told her.

"That's so sweet, Vince."

"And you're okay? Really okay?"

"I am. I don't even, well, I stopped for this man. But he was in a hoodie, and then I was knocked out. I never saw his face. I think he had something over it. Like a ski mask. I don't know, I just don't know. But I'm going to do this thing with Colleen called a cognitive and maybe something will come of it."

"I really can't remember anyone who would want to hurt you."

"I wasn't hurt. I was just knocked out and buried alive," she said dryly.

"For that I'm strangely grateful. I mean, we know what happened to Sally and to the women who didn't make it," Vince said softly.

"And I'm so grateful to Red and Mark and Colleen," Dierdre said.

Angela looked up at Mark. "Did you get what you were hoping for?"

"I don't know," Mark said. "I need to let it set in. And then we need to let Colleen know about your discoveries. After the cognitive."

"I think there might have been earlier victims," Angela said.

"But wouldn't we have known? These

murders and kidnappings were highly publicized! And we've searched all law enforcement data banks," Colleen said.

"Just not deeply enough," Angela said. "And I can't be sure, but there are three suspicious cases. You can read all about them on your way out to Front Royal. Right now, I think it's time we get you in with Dierdre so you can do the cognitive questioning, and we can let this trio go."

"Do I close my eyes?" Dierdre asked Colleen.

They were in Angela's office.

Angela had suggested it. She had the customary desk with two chairs in front of it, but she also had a love seat and a plush chair since small meetings were often held in her office while larger meetings took place in one of the conference rooms.

Colleen had taken the chair.

"It's kind of like being with a shrink, huh?" Dierdre had asked, happy enough to take the love seat and lie back.

"Well, I'm not a shrink. We're experienced in this, because it's really pretty basic. The mind is fascinating and it can be helped along with simple questions," Colleen assured her. "Are you comfortable?"

"I am. This is a good love seat!"

"Great. Lie back, relax, close your eyes." Dierdre did as instructed and Colleen continued with, "So, you're still taking college courses, correct?"

"I'm working on my master's degree. My classes are often hard but fun. I was a theater major, but my parents and I figured that a fine arts degree wasn't as useful as a business degree. Anyway, I love my college and I've loved my classes. I'm not back in until the fall, though. But I work part-time as a student assistant in the finance office. And I'm surprisingly good at business. I found out I've done excellently on exams that had to do with taxes. It was not easy, I assure you. I am not going to work for the IRS, but I'm glad I aced the tests. And work is fun. I like the people I work with, and I've been putting in a few hours every week during the summer."

"Did you work that day?"

"I did. Three hours in the morning."

"And you met Gary for dinner?"

"Yes, I love that place! It's great."

"I know — I've been. What did you have to eat?"

"I had fish and he had steak."

"Nice."

"I wasn't thinking I could be in any danger at all when I left. The night was beautiful. The moon was just a sliver, but there were stars out."

"And I think our temperature has been moderate."

"A little hot, but the air in my car works fine. But there wasn't much moonlight. I remember it being very dark, which is probably why the stars looked so pretty."

"And you thought you hit a man?"

"I — I knew I hit something. There was a big bump. And then I saw a man crawling on the ground. And I thought, Oh, my God, I've hit a human being! So, of course, I stopped."

"But it was very dark where you were."

"Yes. At rush hour, you can still drive that road easily. When I was going home, there were no other cars. I left my lights on, of course. But I jumped out of the car and ran over to him and . . ."

She stopped talking.

"Then nothing. I don't know how he did it. They say I wasn't struck with a Taser, but I walked up to him and put my arm on his shoulder and . . ."

"Okay, the night was dark. There were a few stars. Were there any strange smells in the air?"

"The woods I suppose, but . . ."

"But?"

"There was something else. I just . . . I can't pinpoint what it is! Now, that's going to drive me crazy."

"Don't let it drive you crazy. Let it come to you and it will at some point. But remember, you can think with all five senses. There's a small point that's driving you crazy. You saw a man, down on the ground, but you couldn't see his face; he was wearing a hoodie. Did you hear anything?"

"Just the breeze moving through the forests around the road."

"What did the hoodie feel like? You touched his shoulder, right?"

"Soft," she said dryly. "My kidnapper does his laundry well."

"Did you hear anything?"

"Nothing. Not even . . . I never even screamed, it was so fast."

"So, what next?"

"I was in a box. It took me a minute to realize I was in the ground. I was in a box in the ground, and the earth was . . . Dirt was coming through the seams of the box. It was covering me and I screamed and screamed, and it kept coming and I couldn't breathe."

Her eyes were closed, but her expression was pained.

"At first, there were just snatches of

things. I knew I was on a stretcher, and I knew there was a dog there."

"Red," Colleen said.

"Yes, Red, you, and Special Agent Gallagher."

"Okay, from the guy's point of view . . . he meant to kidnap someone."

"I guess. Yeah. But it was weird he was on that road. Or maybe not. Maybe I was a victim of circumstance. Maybe he wanted anyone who came along."

She frowned.

"But maybe not. I mean . . . now, I'm pretty sure he put something in the road. Something I drove over, which I thought had been him. And if he did that, he had to think it was a woman alone. My lights were on of course, but the night was dark, and he couldn't have known who was in the car —"

"Unless he knew," Colleen said.

"He followed me from the restaurant maybe. I don't drive fast. Anyone could have passed me while we were still in the city. Yes," Dierdre said softly, "there was a guy watching me —"

"Gary told us. We interviewed the guy. He was still at work when we found you — dozens of witnesses verify that, but there could have been someone else, someone else neither of you noticed. Let's back up. You hit the bump."

"Yeah. And it felt like I'd gone over a body. Or a log. I mean, obviously, it could have been a log in the road. But then I saw the man hunched over on the ground, and I thought of what a horrible person I was and what a horrible thing I had done."

"And you went to the man. And you don't remember anything else."

"I touched his shoulder," Dierdre said, and paused. "I felt the softness of the hoodie, and he whirled around, but his face was black . . . like a ski mask, I guess. But I only saw it for a second. He moved so fast. He had his arms around me, like one arm crooked around my neck, and I couldn't breathe and that was all . . . until the box and the earth."

He'd halfway suffocated her to knock her out to get her into the box, Colleen thought. *But he didn't kill her.*

He'd wanted her to breathe in the dirt and die that way, like The Embracer's victims.

But there had been no letter and no sexual assault . . .

Dierdre started to tremble. She sat up, her eyes opening.

"And they knew, of course, my folks knew right away, thank God! I called home when

I was leaving the restaurant. If I hadn't — if they'd still thought I was with Gary — you wouldn't have found me!"

"You called home from your table?"

"From the table, as we were walking out."

She could have been overheard, Colleen thought.

"Colleen, I . . ." Dierdre began. She was still trembling.

"It's okay. We can be done for today," Colleen assured her.

"Well, I wish I could remember more. More details. That one thing is just going to drive me completely crazy."

"The scent you can't place?"

Dierdre nodded. "It's like something I should know."

"A cologne or aftershave?"

Dierdre shook her head.

"Nothing so . . . obvious. I don't think."

"Don't worry about it and don't even talk about it. Not to Gary, not to your folks, not to anyone. And then it might come to you," Colleen said.

Please don't say anything to Gary — not when we still suspect he might have been your would-be murderer!

She didn't dare say that; Dierdre would be indignant.

Gary was such a good guy.

He loved her. He would never hurt her.

And he was going to be in a giant business deal with her father.

"Just call me, please. If anything comes to you. Anything at all."

"I will." Dierdre let out a sigh. "Even though I want to forget it all, so badly."

"Of course. And hopefully, we'll have the truth soon enough, and you can start to put it all behind you and concentrate on the future."

"The future," she said. "What a strange day. I do want to get to the future." She gave Colleen a weak smile. "Seriously, you don't suspect Vince, do you?"

"No, I don't."

"He's a great guy," she said softly.

"He seems to be."

"Well!" Dierdre gave herself a shake. "I'd better get going. Gary has been waiting and my parents will be waiting. I wish I could help more!"

"You have helped us every time we've talked, Dierdre, honestly," Colleen assured her, rising. She smiled. "I'm sure Red will be happy if you say goodbye on your way out!"

Colleen opened the door to Angela's office.

Angela almost magically appeared in the

hallway and smiled.

"Dierdre, Gary is waiting out front. Come on, I'll show you the way."

Colleen gave her a goodbye smile and sank back into the chair.

She felt that she *had* learned something.

She just wished she knew what.

Pressing someone for a memory could more deeply bury whatever they were seeking even deeper.

She hoped Dierdre would remember what it was about a smell that seemed to tease at the back of her mind.

It could be crucial.

Mark came around the corner with Red as she stood, reflective.

"Well?" he asked.

"I went through the senses. She remembers a smell but can't put her finger on what it was or where it came from."

"You warned her not to tell anyone?"

"Of course."

"Let's hope she listens to you."

"There remains the solid possibility he's not guilty. Remember, guilty until prove —"

"We aren't judges or juries. We're agents. Suspicious is suspicious."

"I know. But, Mark, she phoned home on her way out of the restaurant. Maybe we have to go back and look over what we learned there more carefully."

"Someone other than the man they both remember seeing — who really couldn't have that many people willing to lie for him."

"It's possible."

Mark nodded. "All right, I'll listen to the recording of your session as we drive, and you can study the notes on Angela's discoveries."

"Others — found in similar circumstances?"

"Similar — we think. And going back six years. Scattered along the Eastern Seaboard. Maybe, maybe not. In two instances, decomposition of both the bodies and the coffins was so severe the police reports didn't call the wooden pieces found with the bodies *coffins*. But if these cases are related to what we're looking at —"

"Then maybe The Embracer doesn't have a copycat. Maybe he *is* the copycat," Colleen said.

Chapter Twelve

Mark listened to the recording of Colleen's session with Dierdre as they drove.

Colleen studied the notes on the cases Angela had discovered when diving deeply into old files on unsolved murders.

Angela had widened her search, seeking female victims of any age, found buried with cause of death likely to be asphyxiation.

Brenda Mar, twenty-five, a known prostitute, had disappeared off the streets of New York City. After two years, her badly decomposed body had been found in a wooded region of eastern New Jersey — near the site of a recently demolished cabin.

Nancy Henley, also a known prostitute, had been found in a similar condition in southern New York State. Her body had been reduced to bone and ash; she'd been discovered when firefighters had come to put out a blaze in the forested region.

Candy Gates, a runaway, had been missing four years before her decomposed remains had been discovered in North Carolina along the Blue Ridge. She'd been found surrounded by strange wooden planks.

"We need to find out who was where when," Colleen muttered, barely aware that the recording of her speaking with Dierdre was still going. "I'm sorry," she added quickly.

"It's okay. I've got it. But now that I'm listening to this, I'm curious about Sally. She was down in that basement with Carver a long time. We need to find out if there were any specific smells she remembers."

"But if our guy was out kidnapping Dierdre while Carver was with Sally —"

"Which is what we believe. And if Sally doesn't remember a particular scent, it helps affirm what we believe. Of course, the scent may be something Dierdre remembers because it's a scent she knows."

"You're back to Gary."

"I honestly don't mean to be. But listening to Dierdre during the interview . . . Someone knew she was on that road when she was on that road. They knew she was kindhearted — if she thought she hit someone, she was going to stop."

"It does sound that way. But we can't

ignore the fact someone might have followed her from the restaurant."

"No, we can't ignore that fact, and I don't intend to do so," Mark assured her.

"Front Royal, Virginia," Colleen said. She grinned over at Mark. "I actually kind of know it. We used to come to Harpers Ferry, West Virginia, when I was a kid, and we made a few day trips. It's beautiful. The population is only about fourteen thousand plus, and they say it was named for an old oak tree. Troops used to drill there and the command would be, 'Front the Royal Oak.' Then there's another legend that claims during the American Revolution, sentries would call out 'Front' and the password was 'Royal.' Then there's a third legend explaining the name came from the early days of settlement when the French called it *'le front royal'* meaning the British frontier."

Mark glanced over at her quickly. "Nice you know all that."

"Trivia from growing up with folks who believed you needed to learn about a place you were visiting. Harpers Ferry is fascinating too. I love the area. Beautiful! And fun white water rafting. And of course, the history there with the John Brown raid having taken place is important to me. I mean, it's important we always move forward in our country, right?"

Mark nodded thoughtfully.

"What?" she queried.

"I just wonder about history as far as, well, as far as whacked-out criminals go. Herman Mudgett — aka H. H. Holmes — is often considered to be America's first serial killer," he said. "And they don't know how many people that man killed. He had a 'murder castle' in Chicago, but there were victims at other times in other places. But it makes me fear there was so much we don't know, and of course, in the nineteenth century, we didn't have psychologists and psychiatrists and behavior analysts to try to determine what makes people tick."

"True," Colleen mused. "Then again, way before, they knew Madame Báthory killed hundreds of young women, anywhere from three hundred to six hundred, according to eyewitness reports at her trial. And that was in the sixteen hundreds, so . . ."

"We've always had people willing to harm others."

"But better methods to stop them these days," Colleen said hopefully.

He smiled and nodded.

"We have to find this hideout," he said firmly.

Red barked from the back seat as if he

understood every word.

The drive was only about an hour and ten or twenty minutes — Colleen hadn't really paid attention to the distance they'd been traveling, and still, it was surprising when they arrived at the edge of the only incorporated city in Warren County and met with Detective Oscar Lindberg.

He was a tall man with salt-and-pepper hair and a lean physique. He'd been waiting just outside a city-owned cabin to meet with them. He was quick to welcome Red, and equally quick to tell them that he had been taken aback by the entire affair.

"Always amazes me how close we are to DC, and how places that are less than an hour and a half away — minus traffic, of course — can be so incredibly different. Warren County and the surrounding areas are heavily wooded. Even the Blue Ridge and Shenandoah National Park have acres of land where anything could go on, and West Virginia and the area around the Blue Ridge and the Piedmont Mountains is heavily forested land."

"We're aware of that," Mark assured him.

"But you think there's a cabin near Front Royal where a man has been building coffins to bury women alive?" Lindberg asked. "Because . . . ?"

"Carver likes puzzles and riddles, and he used the words 'front' and 'royal' several times," Mark explained. "We are looking for a needle in a haystack — we realize that. But we were hoping you could direct us to anything you know of."

Lindberg nodded. "That's why I had you meet me here. We have a map of the county and surroundings. I can at least show you where we know there are cabins or shacks and old ruins. Come on in."

Colleen, Mark, and Red followed him into the cabin. It was one big room with a main desk, a computer and printer, two smaller desks, a leather sofa, and walls that were covered with maps of the surrounding regions.

Lindberg approached one, pointing to circles and initials on the image.

"Here, you have woods where colonials tried creating settlements, but too few or . . . I'm not sure. Maybe the terrain just wasn't what they needed. There were people living in the various cabins or homes until the mid-eighteenth century. By the end of the Civil War, most were gone. But you do have ruins in those locations. You have an area right here —" Lindberg paused and pointed "— where some students came out to investigate an old burial ground around several abandoned old home sites about two years ago. Most have been lost, of course — markers, I mean. Markers were often made of wood and you know how time takes care of returning wood to the earth. But some people used stone markers, so there was some research done there. Over here, you have what was once known as the Jones place — a man named Jones brought his family, but they headed west after the Civil War, and it's just a name for an area of forest. There are roads — many of them just earth — that will bring you near most of these places."

"He'd need a road. He'd need a way to get his victims there — and then out in a coffin. Ask your officers if they've seen any kind of truck or van in these areas recently," Mark said. He couldn't say so, but he realized that Alfie would have noticed a car parked in front of Carver's house.

"You know, we haven't —"

"Resources enough to pull a large number of officers? We'll take care of that," Mark assured him.

Lindberg smiled. "I understand. And we have no problem with feds here, I promise."

"Thanks," Mark said lightly.

"Yes, thank you," Colleen added.

"Especially the furry kind!" he said, giving

Red another pat on the head.

Red woofed his approval.

As they spoke, there was a knock at the door. Lindberg went to answer it.

Ragnar had arrived.

Mark quickly introduced him, and Ragnar also assured Lindberg they'd call on more people from their offices to cover the enormous amount of forest space that might be considered close to Front Royal.

Ragnar then looked at Mark.

"Angela is calling out more troops. I'll get images of these maps and then I can start from the east and work toward the west. I figure we'll start with the closest."

"Good plan," Mark said. "Want to take the old 'Jones place'? Colleen and Red and I will start at the ruins where the students were working on the old graveyard and home sites."

Ragnar nodded.

"Angela is pulling up cold cases she discovered that might have something to do with our case, and interviewing anyone she can related to those," Ragnar said.

"And if there is anything, she'll find it," Mark said.

"I do have county and all my officers briefed," Lindberg told them.

"Then we'll get going," Mark said. He

thanked Lindberg again.

As they headed to their cars, Ragnar paused, shaking his head.

"You know, Carver might be laughing at us right now. Thinking he's so clever we listened to him and went off on the entirely wrong track," Ragnar said.

"I really don't think so," Colleen assured him.

"I don't think the man thought he said anything that might be a clue to us," Mark said. "I wouldn't have gotten what he was saying. But in hindsight, after listening to Megan, I can't help but think she's right."

"Yeah," Ragnar said briefly.

"So, onward?" Colleen asked.

"Onward," Ragnar agreed.

With a wave, he went to his own car.

Mark looked at Colleen. "Let's do this."

They got into Mark's car and started out.

"You kind of know where you're going?" she asked him.

"I'm a little familiar with the area. I've driven through it. But of course, I've never driven through it while searching for crumbling old homes through the trees."

"Ah, but we have the maps!"

They had pictures on their phones of what the wall had displayed at the police cabin.

"Yeah, and I'm grateful too that we're in

an SUV with good shocks," Mark said.

The roads were bad with tree roots growing across them.

But as he spoke, Colleen saw the remnants of structures through the trees.

"There!" she called.

They saw a small stretch of drive that led to the left — and the remains of scattered cabins that had once been homes.

After Mark made the turn, they noticed the frame of an old chapel.

"That's got to be the old burial ground, where the students were studying, right around the chapel," Colleen said.

"Yeah, and look there. That old structure appears to have had work done recently. I'm thinking whoever was in charge of the student on-site work saw to it the place was safe enough for them to set their work area."

"Seems kind of sad, doesn't it? I mean, once people lived and worked and had hope here. It had to have been large enough at one time to have a chapel and graveyard," Colleen said.

There was an open space in front of the cabin and chapel that was now filled with tall grass, but it wasn't as overgrown as the rest of the surrounding area.

"They must have had it mowed down back when they were studying this place,"

Colleen said.

"Yeah. They parked their cars here. When this study went on, they must have had the area cleared. That's why it's just overgrown grass now," Mark said.

Colleen turned back to the dog.

"Let's see what we've got, eh, Red?" she asked. She stepped out of the car, letting Red out.

Mark emerged from the other side.

"One would think, though, if someone was building coffins here and closing women into them, one of the students might have noticed," Mark said dryly.

"Ah, but they were here before Emily was killed," Colleen said, studying the notes she had on her phone.

"True," he agreed. "So . . ."

"I'm going to check out the chapel," Colleen said.

"I'll take that old house," Mark said. "Red — go with Colleen."

She smiled. "Now, would you have sent Red with Ragnar?"

"No. But I haven't slept with Ragnar," he said, grinning.

Colleen laughed. "You'll never get over how attracted you are to me," she said.

"Nope. Never will. Nor will I get over just how much I like it."

She grinned and walked off — accompanied by Red.

The old chapel seemed as sad to her as the rest of the decaying little compound. The area had probably been too rocky and overgrown for the settlers to sustain any kind of farming, though. From what she understood, people had lived here until after the Civil War.

There were a few broken and rotting pews left in the chapel. Rain had come through. The altar, though, had been made of stone and remained.

It was one room.

And there was nothing in that one room to indicate anyone had used it recently — to build coffins or do anything else.

The roof was only partially there.

Leaves and bracken covered just about everything.

She went back outside. Her cell phone rang. It was Mark.

"This is the place the students were using," he told her. "Whoever was in charge of the study group definitely made sure the foundation of these ruins was solid. There's a torn tarp still covering an area where the roof leaks. The wood is deteriorating in the whole of the place, but I can see where an area was swept and cleared at one time for tents and bedrolls for the researchers out here."

"Anything else?"

"There isn't much to the cabin here. It's one big room."

"The chapel is one big room too. I've just started out to the graveyard. I think I can see a few of the old stone markers Lindberg was telling us about."

"Okay, meet you there. I believe there are still a few of these cabin remnants we'll need to go through, but I'll meet you in the graveyard first."

"I'll be there."

She hung up.

At her side, Red began to growl.

"What is it, boy?" she asked the dog.

He barked and ran through the overgrown profusion of weeds and stones.

Colleen followed him and then stopped as the dog dug furiously at the ground.

"Red, it's an old graveyard. There's going to be —" She broke off.

Where he was digging, pieces of broken wood began to appear.

An old coffin. A very old coffin.

But it wasn't. The pieces of wood were treated pine.

And in the mix, there were bones. What appeared to be disarticulated finger bones.

"Colleen?"

She looked up. Mark had come out of the old cabin. He was staring at her, frowning.

"Someone has been here," she said, her voice soft across the distance.

"The students —"

"Not the students," she said. "Mark, we have another victim."

The medical examiner was Dr. Jerome Bailey, early forties, competent, and serious. He arrived skeptical they had found a body from the current century, but he quickly changed his mind.

The remains were that of a young woman, midtwenties to early thirties. She had been dead a year to eighteen months. He would know more when he had her at autopsy, where he could determine all he could from the bone and soft tissue that remained.

Colleen, Mark, and Red stood stoically waiting as his assistants gingerly removed the corpse with tatters of synthetic clothing from the broken pine coffin and earth.

Ragnar arrived; headquarters was called. Forensic evidence would be gathered by the federal authorities since they were amassing the discoveries from the previous victims.

Finally, the crime scene team were left to discover what clues they could find. Mark,

Colleen, Ragnar, and Red were together at their cars.

"There was no letter to the media on this victim," Colleen commented.

"None that we know of," Ragnar said.

"If anyone had received anything, I believe they would have let us know by now. The murders of our victims and the kidnappings of Dierdre and Sally were widely publicized. Along with the arrest of Jim Carver," Mark said.

"But you don't think Carver did this," Ragnar said.

"Any sign of Brant Pickering?" Colleen asked.

Ragnar shook his head. "Sally said he was finishing some research. But he insisted on asking a friend to stay with her, an aunt of his, to make sure she's okay and with someone. The woman's name is Carol Hughes. I've checked her out. She doesn't even have parking tickets. Mother of three, grandmother of five, and beloved by everyone who knows her, from what I can tell. I asked Sally to call Brant and she did, but it went straight to voice mail. She insists he's legitimately working. They're back together and making the decision now as to where they want to live. Oh, I had her leave a message that he needs to call one of us. So far, no, I haven't heard back. She says, though, Brant has all our phone numbers and she's convinced he will get back to us."

"Was his research supposed to be in New York? And if so, why wouldn't he go to his own home?" Colleen asked.

As she spoke, Ragnar's phone rang. He cast Mark and Colleen a curious glance and answered the call. "Mr. Pickering," he said. "Hey, my colleagues are with me. I'm putting you on speakerphone."

Mark heard the man say, "Sure."

Then Ragnar said, "Sorry to bother you, but we've just been concerned you haven't been with Sally."

"And you're wondering if I'm off kidnapping another woman?" Pickering said over the speaker. "I'm up in the Bronx. I'm doing research on the Edgar Allan Poe cottage here and the life of Poe. Yes, I'm in the city, but it's just been easier to stay here. I'm at a bed-and-breakfast. I can text you the name and number of the owner and you can check on me."

"It's just that, well, Sally just got out of the hospital and you left her," Colleen said.

"Special Agent Law! Nice to hear your voice. And by the way, your sister is going to love this book when it's finished!"

"I'm sure she will," Colleen said. "But —"

"I've been trying to finish this and get it in to editorial, so my slate is clear — and all my time can go to Sally." He hesitated. "Also, I think she needed time away from . . . from a physical relationship. Don't worry! I love Sally. And this doesn't change anything about that love, except I want her to be well physically and emotionally. My aunt and Sally have always had a great relationship. I wasn't worried about anyone going after her. I know you guys are watching the house night and day. I guess I should have reported to you what was going on with me. Except I honestly didn't think I was on a list of suspects. I never met Dierdre Ayers or anyone in her family and, well, you know Carver was holding Sally."

"Right," Mark said. "Thank you for calling in. It's part of the territory. We just like to know where everyone is. But no, you had no responsibility to call in."

"Thanks. I'll be here about another twenty-four hours, and then I'll be heading back to Sally. I'll get the information to Special Agent Johansen, and I know he'll share it with you."

"Right," Ragnar said. "Thank you."

"By the way, I want to get Sally a dog. A great dog like Red!" Pickering said. "Where did you get him? Off a special law enforcement site?"

Mark smiled. "Off the street. Someone dumped him. Do some research or go to a shelter. You can find a great dog almost anywhere."

They heard Pickering laugh softly over the phone. "A shelter it is! That's the responsible thing to do. Anyway, I'm here, and I'm sorry I missed your calls. I've been interviewing docents and the like. But I will pay attention from here on out."

They all thanked him again and Ragnar ended the call.

He immediately checked his messages.

"Bobbie's B and B in the Bronx," Ragnar said, dialing the number.

When his call was answered, Ragnar said, "Hi, I'm trying to confirm a guest is staying with you, the writer Brant Pickering?"

Ragnar listened as the person on the other end of the call went on at some length, then he thanked them and ended it.

"Brant Pickering is a registered guest. He checked in right after he left Sally's."

Mark had his phone out. Colleen looked at him, frowning.

Ragnar grimaced at Mark and quickly explained to Colleen, "He's going to have people discreetly watch the bed-and-breakfast. The guy who owned the place was shocked I knew Pickering was there. The owner is a fan of Pickering's work too. But Mark is making the right move. The owner explained to me — as a bit of an advertisement really — that all rooms had an outside access. Guests didn't need to come through the parlor. He and his wife work the place, and they don't like to get woken up at all hours."

Mark heard their conversation as he managed his own with Angela. They'd be pulling their people off the NYC apartment and move them to discreetly watch the B and B and Brant Pickering's movements.

"We need a real timeline," Colleen said. She shook her head. "We think Carver killed the two victims who were discovered, and he sent letters to the media. We know he kidnapped Sally. But with this murder and the murders Angela discovered, there were no letters to the media."

"Well, a killer sometimes refines his methods," Ragnar said.

"Right," Mark agreed. "Except there was no letter when Dierdre was taken. I think this leads to the fact that Jim Carver is not the only guilty party. We need to finish searching this area, but I'll bet it was used — and abandoned — by our killer already. I don't think he kept to one place."

"I think you're right," Colleen said.

"Let's do it," Ragnar agreed, looking back toward the ruins of the rest of the old cabins and cottages that had once housed a small community. "Divide and conquer?"

"Yes. I'll take Red, not to worry," Colleen said.

Mark smiled. "Thanks."

He pointed left, straight, and right.

They all took off in different directions.

He had reached the third of the ruins in his path, an old place with just two walls — a front wall, and a side wall to the west — when he found pine planks.

They were rotting. Time, rain, and the elements taking their toll.

But a killer had been there; he had used the old ruins. The remnants of the grisly tools of his trade remained.

He had probably been amused, burying a girl in a graveyard.

She would die . . . among the dead.

And no one would ever find her.

He pulled out his phone and conference called Colleen and Ragnar.

"Found it," he said. "I'm almost into reclaimed forest area — third place behind the main remaining cottage."

Both said they were on their way.

And a minute later, they arrived with Red

loyally and obediently following Colleen.

"We can have forensics look," Ragnar said. "But I doubt they're going to get anything. Time and nature have taken their toll. But there it is — the same pine."

"Well, the same pine available at home and garden stores in every city in every state in the country," Colleen said. She looked at Ragnar. "So, the first murder — possibly — was four years ago. Or perhaps there was another even earlier that we don't know about. I'm thinking about our suspects and age."

"Serial killers have started as young as fourteen years old," Mark said.

"But are they able to travel at that age?" Colleen asked. "Then again, if we're only looking at three years, I don't know . . . Brant Pickering could still be a suspect, but it sounds as if he's been telling the truth. And none of us like Gary, but —"

"It's hard to like an elitist," Ragnar said. "But it doesn't make him bad — or should I say evil?"

"And according to those watching, he's been at the Ayerses' home," Mark said. He looked at the sky. Night was falling fast.

"Time to leave others working at their posts. I have to get some sleep. Angela got us all rooms at a place in Front Royal," Ragnar said. He pulled out his phone. "Yeah, she texted us the information." He sighed, shoving his phone into his pocket. "Guys, I'm having room service. You do what you want. She got us three rooms." He grinned suddenly. "Not sure why she bothered, but we must keep up professional standards."

Colleen stared at him.

Ragnar grinned at her. "Oh, come on — sparks fly off you two. Hey, whatever. I'm heading back. I'll be in my room if you need me!"

He turned to leave, waving as he got in his car.

Mark stared after him.

"But I disliked you!" Colleen said.

Mark laughed. "It's been a long day. Let's turn in too. And if everyone thinks we're up to something, well hell, might as well be guilty as charged."

He was glad she smiled.

"What the hell?" she said, grinning. "It will be good to forget again, if only for a —"

"Don't you dare say 'moment,' " Mark said, matching her smile.

"If only for the night," she said softly.

He laughed again, setting his arm around her shoulders as they walked to the car.

"Oh, yes. Let's say for the night!"

CHAPTER THIRTEEN

The Krewe of Hunters' offices often used several of the large chain hotels and had business accounts with them.

In Front Royal, they'd chosen a local establishment, which was once an old tavern that had welcomed travelers as far back as the early seventeen hundreds.

It wasn't elegant or new; it didn't offer a dozen showerheads or any other luxuries.

But it was nestled on a grassy slope surrounded by lush pines and flower gardens lovingly tended by the owners.

And the rooms offered fireplaces with carved mantels and beds with plush mattresses.

Red immediately found himself a spot in front of the mantel, where he curled up on a soft rug in front of two rocking chairs.

His back was to them, as if even the dog wanted to offer privacy and time alone for just the two of them.

The baths had been remodeled in the 1980s and as Mark and Colleen quickly discovered, they were something to manipulate.

They'd been digging.

They'd found a corpse.

Showers were a mental necessity as well as a physical one.

But they crawled over the awkwardly high rim of the tub to step in together. He stood behind her with his arms around her, as they first let hot water spray over them, easing muscles and minds. Then he found the soap and slid it along the slick beauty of her body. She turned to him, and as their arousal grew, they moved more, eager to stroke and touch and kiss one another.

But when he took a step back to allow the spray to fall over his well-soaped chest, he slid and wound up sinking down to his butt with Colleen falling backward on top of him.

"Are you all right?" she asked quickly, twisting in his arms as best she could in the confines of the tub.

He laughed. "Butt bruised, but fine, and maybe . . ."

"I think we're clean," she said.

"As clean as we can get."

She struggled up with both of them laughing. They crawled out of the tub, grabbed the deliciously fluffy yellow towels the owners kept, and tried drying in the bathroom. They were drying themselves and one another, and laughing again at the lack of space, finally moving into the bedroom and falling on the bed to finish the task — or half finish the task.

"Bruised butt!" Colleen teased, her eyes an emerald fire. "Poor baby!"

"Hey! Not a poor baby here."

"Ah, and I was going to try to make it all better, Mr. Macho."

"Not a Mr. Macho either," he protested.

She laughed, crawled over him, found his mouth for a deep, rich kiss as hot and sultry as the cascade of water had been. She slid against the length of his body to continue erotic kisses here, there, and all about. She teased him and then became erotically intimate until he twisted, pulled her into his arms and to his side, savored the sweet slick feel of her, tasted her, breathed her, fell into a realm of desire that seemed to encompass his soul as well as his flesh.

They made love, laughing at first, the laughter fading as passion took over, and then holding each other tight in silence.

He loved just holding her, he realized, as much as he loved making love to her.

And he wondered about himself.

He knew his past had marred his relationships before; his past and his present. It just didn't make sense to get too close to someone when his work constantly took him away, when his work wasn't something that could always be explained.

He knew Krewe members often wound up together. They had working relationships and personal relationships. When their spouses or significant others had work in other fields, they at least still saw the dead. They were never forced to live a lie. And maybe . . .

He didn't want to think. It was too soon. It was better to take time away from the deadly tension of the case they were on and let the future come. But as he held her, he thought about his biological mother and father. And he hoped somewhere in the great beyond, they had both found peace and happiness. He liked to think his father had seen his mother as a beautiful human being rather than just a stripper.

He wished he could have known him.

In whatever Mark's relationships had been, he had never been anything but monogamous.

He'd seen the lives of strippers, even if he'd been too young to understand what some did for a real income at the time.

Colleen came up on her elbows at his side, looking down at him worriedly.

"Are you okay?"

He smiled. "With you? Always," he told her.

"Who would have thought?" she asked.

"Right. Because I'm —"

"Superior?" she said.

"What?"

She laughed. "Well, you were not particularly welcoming at first."

He arched a brow. "Am I welcoming enough now?"

"You'll do," she teased. "For the —"

He laughed. "Don't you dare say 'moment.' I swear, I'm not Mr. Macho, but a man does have an ego in there somewhere."

She laughed again. "And I sincerely doubt you lack confidence, Special Agent Gallagher."

"Aw, well, I doubt you lack it either."

She lay her head down, her eyes meeting his.

"Honestly? I was horribly nervous. Working with Jackson? He's determined to draw the best out in everyone. And then you and Ragnar and Red have worked together awhile; you know how each other thinks.

Then I was thrown into the mix."

He was silent a minute and then he told her, "I think you're amazing."

"Really?" She laughed and a light of mischief touched the emerald beauty of her eyes. "You mean, just now, or . . ."

She could be erotically passionate — and make him laugh. And ease away the tension a day could create.

"Amazing all around," he assured her.

He pulled her into his arms. It was a while before they spoke again.

Then she lay by his side, and he knew after a moment they were both thinking about the events of the day.

"We know she was killed about a year and a half ago," Colleen said.

"And Carver and our second killer possibly both made use of the area for coffin building," he said.

"Now we have to find out where his latest workshop is located," Colleen said.

He hesitated.

"You said sometimes you hear the dead. But you didn't hear anything from her."

"No. I think that means she is at peace; she's gone on."

"I like to assume that. Have you —"

"Yes."

"You don't know what I was going to say,"

he told her.

She smiled. "There was a woman in our local cemetery. She waited for her husband to pass and he stayed a bit until he found her. And they seemed to disappear in a ray of sunlight right as dusk was falling. I think most people do just go on. I mean, if not, we wouldn't be able to walk down a street without bumping into a spirit. The world of the human being has now gone on for so long. I do like it. But it's nice to think there is a better place and to get to believe it without having to rely on faith, like most people do."

"Or don't."

"Or don't," she agreed. "But, with this new young woman . . ."

"You heard nothing."

"Nothing."

"And that's for the best, I guess," he said. "Though it would be nice if, every now and then, a ghost did stick around to tell us who did it!"

She smiled. "It's great we do have Sergeant Parker."

"Even as a ghost — he's only human."

"True. So, where —"

"We keep up the search. We know a killer used the old ramshackle cabin at one time. He possibly went on to find a new one."

Colleen nodded.

He pulled her closer.

"Tomorrow," he said softly.

She eased against him.

Because tomorrow would come early.

Colleen was proud to wake up before Mark. She wasn't sure why she woke up so early, but the remnants of a dream were playing in her head, and she wondered if her last hours of sleep hadn't been restless.

But she didn't think she'd had a nightmare. She wasn't prone to nightmares, and the few times she'd had them, she'd woken right up. And waking up assured her she'd had a dream — just a dream and nothing more.

Once she'd dreamed about an alien invasion.

But instantly awake, she'd known it hadn't happened. And she was glad she hadn't shared her dream with anyone, though she always thought she'd tell Megan about it one day, maybe for one of her authors to write up.

Now she'd awakened, but she hadn't had a nightmare. There was just something that seemed disconnected in her mind and she didn't know what. And so she dressed quickly, aware Red was waiting politely for her to take him out.

Which, of course, she did.

She didn't see Ragnar downstairs yet, but it was barely light. And it made sense he and Mark were both still sleeping. It was easier seeking a wooden piece of needle in a wooden haystack by the light of day than by the remnants of darkness.

When she returned to the room with Red, Mark was up.

"Hey, thanks," he said, referring to Red.

"No problem," she returned. "I've got the back of all my partners," she assured him.

"I know Red appreciates it."

"He does." She grinned. "As the saying goes, poor fellow peed like a racehorse."

"He does do that. Anyway, Ragnar just called. He's heading down now. We'll meet up with him and discuss our plans for the day."

She shook her head and grimaced. "I'm hoping we find a cabin and not another victim. Any word on the woman we found?"

"I'm expecting a call from Angela. She's been tracing possible suspects, their movements, credit cards, and so on. Naturally, she has a Bureau ME going out to politely observe with the local ME. But the autopsy isn't scheduled until nine, and it's barely seven thirty. And . . ." His voice trailed for a minute. "We're talking about distances someone could have traveled relatively quickly. So, we need to find the cabin, and either find the forensic clues to identify a killer or get a stakeout set up."

"Right," Colleen said. "Okay, then. Breakfast sounds good."

They stepped out and almost ran right into Ragnar, who was heading down as well.

"Good timing," Ragnar said cheerfully. He didn't murmur a word about the two of them coming out of the same door. But then, he was the one who had implied they hadn't really needed a third room.

And it was as if it was nothing or simply accepted.

"Is Red joining us?" he asked.

"I've got his service coat on him. He'll be fine. And he loves bacon. Naturally, his vet does not approve of a lot of bacon, but now and then, well, the doctor told me the same thing."

Ragnar grinned, setting his arm around Colleen as they headed to the elevator.

"Another long day," he said. "And all these extra eyes — three agents and the dog, that's actually eight eyes, plus four pairs of great ears, and one stupendous nose — are better than just me. Angela is sending another agent out to work with me, and the

Bureau has a couple pairs already driving around."

"Good," she said.

"And if you do hear anything . . ."

"You know we'll call you immediately," Colleen assured him.

They were seated at the diner-style restaurant when Ragnar asked innocently, "Everyone sleep all right?"

"Almost overslept," Mark said. "Colleen was up bright and early."

"I think I was dreaming," she said.

"Oh?" Ragnar teased. "That's not the man of your dreams — or nightmares — next to you?"

She grinned.

"If I were any younger," Mark warned, "I'd kick you under the table."

Colleen shrugged. "I don't know. It was strange. I woke up with the feeling I could almost touch something at the back of my mind, and then it was gone."

Ragnar leaned forward. "With you, that could be relevant."

She shook her head. "No, it was just strange. Snatches from being a kid. My folks barbecuing, playing at a park . . . stuff like that."

"Hmm. Anyway, I'm going for the Combo-Combo," Ragnar said. "Did I ever eat last night? I don't even remember. I do know I'm hungry now!"

"Yeah, looks good," Mark agreed. "I can share with Red. The vet really wouldn't approve of pancakes, but Red loves a taste now and then."

"Veggie omelet," Colleen said. "And Red is welcome to share."

She glanced at her phone for the first time and noted she'd made the idiotic mistake of not charging it the night before. Then again, she'd dug up a corpse, showered a little desperately, and then desperately in a different way fallen into bed with Mark.

"Can I charge my phone in the car?" she asked him.

"Of course. But my charger is up in the room."

"So is mine. I'll just run up and get both," she said, rising. "Excuse me. Order for me, please. Oh, yeah, and coffee!"

"A bucket of it," Ragnar promised solemnly.

She grinned and left them, returning to the elevator and taking it back up to the third floor. She entered the room, found her charger, and started back out again when she paused.

Her dream was coming back to her.

Such a strange thing to have a dream

about. She hadn't dreamed snatches of different days and different places.

She'd dreamed of one day. She'd been with her folks at the park and her father had brought them all out for a barbecue.

They'd been maybe fourteen at the time.

Different personalities, but triplets, close by birth.

And by being . . . strange.

They knew about each other's abilities, which had shown up in each of them by the time they were ten.

But that day, they'd been young teenagers, complaining quietly to each other they really had places to go and people to see, their different sets of friends. Megan had wandered off toward the mangrove trees at the park, Patrick had just been sitting with his handheld video game playing, and she had been wandering a little aimlessly after picking up family trash and recycling when she heard her sister's voice.

Looking around, she saw that Megan was nowhere near her.

And she knew she was hearing with her mind.

Megan was asking for help.

She'd concentrated as hard as she could, whispering, "Where are you, Meg? Where are you?"

"By the trees! My foot is stuck! Can't say I was crawling around in here. Dad would be so mad. Please, please, come quickly! There are snakes here, Colleen!"

She'd run to the edge of the pond where the mangrove growth began and carefully sloshed her way over the climbing and curving roots, through the shallow water and over land.

Her sister's voice came closer and closer. And she found her.

Megan was indeed stuck.

"What the heck were you doing out here?" she'd demanded.

"I — I don't know. I was just curious looking at the little things in the water, and I didn't realize I was going so far or —"

"You were thinking about boys!" Colleen had accused her. "Maybe Brian Appletree?"

"Maybe. He asked me out. And here I am in the mangroves!"

It had taken some doing. They'd had to chip away at a root to free Megan's foot, but she was fine and they'd never had to tell their parents.

Why dream about that occasion?

She wondered if her sister was calling to her — either for real or perhaps in her mind?

I don't read minds, I just hear . . .

Her phone rang. She didn't recognize the

374

number, but with everything going on, she answered it quickly.

"Special Agent Law."

There was a slight hesitance on the other end. Then a female voice she recognized asked, "Colleen?"

"Yes, is this Casey?"

Casey Johnstone was an editorial assistant at the publishing house where Megan worked and was one of Megan's friends.

"Yes, Casey. I was just concerned. I know Megan was with you, but she said she was coming back for the meeting yesterday. Then she didn't show up. Megan isn't like that, and I was wondering if she stayed with you or if she'd left a message as to where she might be and if she's coming back in today."

Megan.

Fear shot through her, curling into her with an icy grip.

"Megan left the night before last," Colleen said. "She hasn't contacted you at all?"

"No."

She tried to keep from panicking.

Something might have happened that was entirely innocent. Another author might have called for help, and being Megan, she might have decided on a personal visit if she was in the area. Megan might have missed her train and just stayed by the station rather than bother her or even call because she knew Colleen was on a case.

Yes, something might have happened.

But there was only one reason she had dreamed about her sister being in trouble.

Her sister *was* in trouble.

"I've got to go. I need to file a report and start finding out what happened," Colleen said. She didn't want to cause a cold and crippling fear in another person, but Casey knew Megan as well as Colleen did.

She was never irresponsible. She would have called someone.

"Please! Call me back. Please, I'm worried."

"I will, Casey. I'll call you back."

Colleen didn't wait for a reply. She hung up and started down the hall.

Her phone rang again. She thought it was going to be Casey, but it was not. And while she didn't know the number, she would answer anything at that moment.

It might be Megan.

"Special Agent Law," she said, answering as she always did.

"Special Agent Law!" came a voice. "How delightful. I hope you're alone. I'm not actually looking at you right now."

"Who is this? And why would you be looking at me?"

"I am someone you want to talk to. Trust me. So, let me start off by again saying, I hope you're alone. Because if I see either of those men you work with or that stupid dog, your sister is dead. I'll kill her on the spot, no negotiation, no chance. I have a gun at her head right now."

Colleen froze. The whole of her body seemed to be comprised of ice and fear.

"Who is this? And why should I believe you?"

"Talk to her!" she heard him command someone roughly.

"Colleen?"

It was her sister's terrified voice that came to her then.

"Megan, stay calm," she said softly.

"Don't come. He has a gun. He's claiming the stupid man got the wrong girl. He wants to kill you. He'll just kill us both —"

She broke off with a little scream and Colleen winced, knowing Megan's captor had struck her hard and sent her flying.

What stupid guy? Who —

She realized she knew the voice on the phone.

Carver. It was Jim Carver.

But Carver was being held . . .

She heard his laughter next.

"Ah, you know who this is! But you hadn't heard yet? I escaped during the transfer! It wound up being delayed and the stupid cops in charge were anxious to get home, and they can be so damned careless. My buddy Dean is adept with his hands — fashioned a pick out of a spoon, can you believe that? You know, when people work together, they can do incredible things. There were four of us in on it, and we were brilliant I must say! Marty did some of the best spastic choking I've ever seen. The guard went to help him, and well . . . I'm damned good with a knockout punch. Got his gun, freed the others . . . Oh, we didn't even kill the driver. Just tied them up good, away from all radios, took their phones . . . they didn't miss us forever! Of course, bulletins are going out now, but anyway . . . Do you want your sister to live?"

"Don't give in to him!" she heard Megan cry.

"Do you want your sister to live?" he repeated angrily.

"What do you want?"

"If you're alone, come. I do have a gun, and this time — though we all know how I relish using and 'embracing' my lovelies — I'll shoot her straight between the eyes." He half covered the phone to yell at someone

378

else in the room.

Not Megan this time.

Of course, there was someone else. Carver wouldn't have had time to take Megan if he'd just escaped custody. He had an accomplice.

He thought he'd muffled the call, but he didn't realize Colleen could more than *hear.*

"For now, leave her the hell alone! You took the wrong one! Why the hell do you think it was so easy? Leave her alone. She's how we get the right one!"

He unmuffled the phone and said, "I really hope you're alone. I'll give you directions. Don't be followed — I'll know. Don't call your buddies. I'll know. And I'll shoot the dog on sight after I shoot Megan. Got it? I mean, sure, you can call down the entire Bureau and every cop on the Eastern Seaboard. But do so, and your sister dies, got it?"

"What do you want?" Colleen demanded icily. "And how do I know you will let Megan go, that you won't just kill us both?"

"You don't. But if you don't come, I guarantee she'll die. And if I know you, you'll figure out a way to make me free her before you hand yourself over."

"Just what the hell is it you want?"

He started to laugh. "You haven't figured

that out? Oh, come on. There's just one thing I really want."

"What?" Colleen shouted.

"You," he said softly, very softly. "I just want you."

The call from Angela came just as the television screen in the hotel's coffee shop showed the police arriving at a wooded section of road where a corrections bus was slammed against the trees at an odd angle.

"Mark, he's out — Jim Carver is out. He and other inmates being transferred managed to take out the guards and escape. The police just found the bus. They had lost communications, and there had been some flooding in the area they had to travel. You and Ragnar must take extreme care. He's going to be out for your blood."

"What the hell?" Mark demanded, standing, almost knocking the table over. "They had a man who was possibly — no, probably — a dangerous serial killer —"

"And several other inmates. They didn't kill the guards. From what they've gleaned, Carver wanted to kill them. But one of the other inmates was in for armed robbery and wasn't adding murder to his charges. Thank God for small favors. Anyway, it's all over the news. Direct order from Jackson. Stay together today and be on the lookout. He is holding a terrible grudge against the two of you — and Red."

"And Colleen. She questioned him. She just went upstairs to get something. I'm hanging up, Angela. I'm going to look for her."

"What the hell?" Ragnar said.

"Yeah, what the hell? Stay here in case she comes back. She's been up there a long time to just get a phone charger."

"Got it," Ragnar said, standing, throwing bills on the table for the food they wouldn't eat, and then walking with Mark toward the entrance.

"Red, come," Mark said, and he hurried out, too anxious for the elevator. If she came down that way, Ragnar would see her. He bounded up the stairs to the third floor.

Colleen wasn't in the hallway.

And she wasn't in the room.

"Colleen!" he shouted her name.

There was no reply.

He didn't even know if she'd actually been to the room or not.

Yes. She had been there, he thought. His keys had been on the bedside table.

They were gone.

"Colleen!" he said again, knowing it was useless.

But why would she have just disappeared? She was competent. She carried a gun, and she knew how to use it.

Could someone have surprised her in the room?

No, not with her hearing.

Then what was going on?

"Red?" he asked, not sure in what way the dog could answer.

Red whined; he knew something was terribly wrong.

Mark took the stairs two at a time again back to the hallway by the diner. Ragnar was in the hall waiting for him.

"I talked to one of the bellmen. He saw Colleen leave."

"He knows it was Colleen?"

"Yes, he recognized her. And she waved and said good morning to him politely as she exited the hotel. That's all I know."

"She walked out of her own volition?" Mark asked, bewildered.

"No one near her, according to the bellman. Let's get to the cars."

"My keys were gone."

"She took your car then. Mark, what the hell could have made her leave like that? She's a smart woman."

Mark's phone was ringing. It was Angela and he answered it quickly.

"Angela, she's gone. He's gotten to her somehow. Ragnar and I are going to follow, but I have no idea how . . . She just walked out. Alone. Did she call in?"

"No, Colleen didn't call in. But I know why she's gone."

"What? How? Why?"

"I just received a call from a young woman named Casey at Megan Law's publishing house. Colleen was supposed to call her right back — and she didn't. She had called Colleen because Megan Law never came back to work after her trip to the DC area."

"She still wouldn't have gone off on her own. She would have come to us and given us that information!" Mark said.

"Not if someone else called her."

"Carver!"

"Possibly, but I've made a few other discoveries."

"Angela!"

"Your second killer or copycat or original or whatever isn't who you suspected, not if what I've discovered is true."

"What? Someone not associated with the families? Angela —"

"Oh, he's associated all right," Angela said. "Get going and I'll explain."

Mark nodded to Ragnar and they headed out. Behind the wheel of his navy SUV, Ragnar asked, "LoJack?"

"LoJack," Mark agreed. "Angela, pipe it through!"

She did.

And she began to explain.

He had been close.

So close . . .

But not close enough.

CHAPTER FOURTEEN

Colleen knew Jim Carver had to be an extremely sick and demented human being.

But he wasn't a stupid one.

His directions came by phone and then by notes left under rocks or squirreled between roots in the trees by the roadside. He had her drive south just to turn and drive north, then west, and then east.

Her first instinct had just been to find her sister. If she traded herself for Megan, that would be all right.

But Megan had been correct in her thinking. Carver would just kill them both. Unless she could find a way to save them.

Eventually, her training and sense of logic began to kick in.

There was a second person involved. The man had to have been watching them — somehow.

Who?

Brant Pickering? She had the oddest feeling she would have somehow known through Megan if the second killer had been Brant Pickering.

Gary Boynton?

Did it matter who? One of them had gotten his hands on Megan and met up with Carver after he'd escaped the corrections bus!

It was Carver who had Megan, and Carver who wanted her.

But what she was doing was reckless. He'd asked if she was alone. Obviously, he and this person were wherever it was that she was going.

And she was foolish not to report in.

But even as she knew she needed to call, she feared Ragnar or Mark — or even Red — might be so determined to take the men down that they'd give themselves away.

And Megan would wind up being collateral damage.

That was unacceptable.

If she didn't have a plan, Megan would die along with her.

She'd stopped by a huge oak in the forest — bigger than the others — just as she had been told in the last instructions.

The note she found there led her to a fork in the road where she'd receive further instructions.

Two men. Both with Megan. They

couldn't see her. And they didn't have a trace on her phone.

She was being irresponsible. Fear for her sister was taking control. She couldn't let it — not if she wanted to save her sister.

And herself.

Back in the car, she set her phone down on the seat beside her, hesitated only one more minute, and then called Mark.

He answered the phone frantically.

"You're all right?"

"Yes."

"Carver —"

"Escaped, yes."

"And you took off on a dangerous solo mission without a word. Colleen —"

"He has —"

"Your sister. I know. But you're trained to work as a team, to understand —"

"It's my sister! Listen, please, listen. I called you because I know what you're saying. But he promised to shoot her — even if it meant his own death — if he saw you, Ragnar, or Red."

"And you didn't think we could stay back? Colleen —"

"I've called you now. I'm about ten miles east of —"

"I know where you are."

"How?"

"GPS on the car. We've been following you."

"Stop! Please, you can't follow me. If he sees you —"

"He won't see me."

Colleen pulled the phone away from her ear and realized she could hear Megan speaking.

"Wait, wait!" she said to Mark. "Hold on — please!"

She pushed the phone away and closed her eyes.

"This is where you build coffins," Megan was saying.

"One of my many hideouts. My dear, you would be quite surprised what secrets old forests can hold!" It was Carver speaking then. His voice was fainter.

She could always hear her siblings more clearly.

But Megan knew that. And she couldn't know where Colleen was — Megan didn't have a map of the area in her head — but she was making him talk because *she knew* Colleen might hear them.

She picked up the phone quickly, knowing Mark was going out of his head.

"I can hear them. I'll call back as soon as I've figured out what Megan is trying to get him to say."

"How clo—" Mark began.

But she ended the call.

She had to listen.

Carver kept talking. "This cabin, that cabin. I go place to place. You know, if this idiot here hadn't gotten through to me via code that he'd gotten the girl I wanted, I wouldn't have broken out of that bus. I could have beat the rap. Sally was such a sweet whore! I could have made a judge believe she begged me for exciting sex! And those creeps you worked with — they entered illegally. And in court that would have stood up."

"Quit calling me an idiot," another voice said.

Colleen frowned, trying to recognize the speaker.

She knew the voice.

"They look alike!"

"They look alike — from a distance!"

"I'm The Embracer. I'm the mentor. You came to me. I taught you —"

"You were crude and stupid. I thought of the letters. I drove the police insane! You just got stupider and stupider and —"

"You ass. I'll walk out of here. When they catch you, I'll deny anything you say about me and call you a crazy person. People will believe me."

"I have a witness."

"You're going to kill both girls and you know it."

"I have to agree with him — you were stupid," Megan said in a calm voice.

And before she spoke again, Colleen *knew*. She recognized the voice of the man with Carver. Knew why she knew the voice and she wondered — should she have guessed something before?

But who would have thought the man would have done what he did to . . .

Her phone was ringing again.

"You know, I know this area. We used to drive here all the time when I was a kid," Megan said aloud. "My parents loved to come through Front Royal on their way up to Harpers Ferry. And there are woods here, right, but . . . you do like to live dangerously. Civilization is not far!"

Colleen quickly hit Answer and Speaker on her phone.

It was Mark, of course.

"The cabin is between Front Royal and Harpers Ferry! I can hear Megan, her voice is becoming clearer and clearer! I'm near her. I can hear her clearly and even the faint voices with her are coming through. Carver had me driving all over for his clues, but I think I even know the little woodsy turnoff where he found a cabin. It's state land now, but for years there were hunters' cabins on it. With reclamation by the park service, they've cleared people out. But you have to let me get in there first. He can't see you —"

"He won't see us. Neither will his partner."

"Mark, I know who it is! And I saw pictures, but I'd never have suspected, even though I should have asked more questions . . ."

"So do we. Angela pulled up some magic. And it was easy to figure out from there."

Colleen realized she was almost there.

The trail now winding through the forest would lead her to whatever structure it was Carver was making use of then.

"Colleen, if you just barge in —"

"I'm not barging in. I have a plan."

"And that is . . . ?"

"Slowing down enough for you to get here. Entering armed so I can negotiate with a gun. Keeping them occupied so they don't realize you're out there, and you can take them down while I'm trying to get Megan out."

"Colleen, that's —"

He was going to say "risky." She hung up on him before he could.

She didn't park right in front of the old cabin, which just about blended into the trees, nestled into what couldn't even be defined as a clearing anymore.

She studied the cabin as she approached it. She was in the open; they could see her from the house and she knew it.

But the door to the cabin didn't open until she was almost at it.

By then, her Glock was drawn.

And she took aim at Carver.

"Shoot me and my buddy shoots Megan!" Carver said.

"Buddy? You've been calling him an idiot all day," Colleen said. "Back up. Get inside."

"Give me the gun or —"

"Back up. Megan is safe, or you die. That simple."

"I give you Megan and you've still got a gun —"

"Your 'buddy' has a gun on my sister. She goes out — then you get my gun."

She'd forced him back and stood solidly, her Glock aimed at him. She was at the threshold to the cabin and could see inside. The light was weak, coming through the trees. If there had ever been electricity to the place, it was long gone now.

But she could see her sister.

Megan was seated in a chair in front of a

crumbling wooden mantel.

And a gun was indeed being held to the side of her head.

Colleen ignored Carver for a minute, frowning and shaking her head at the man holding Megan hostage.

"Seriously stupid," she said.

He frowned at her fiercely.

"Your own daughter! You buried your own daughter alive!"

"Not my daughter!" he snapped back. "My bitch of a wife was pregnant with some dick's kid when I married her."

"But you raised her!" Colleen exclaimed.

"A little Goody Two-shoes like her mother," Rory Ayers said.

"So, why did you marry her mother?" Colleen asked.

He laughed and shrugged, digging the nose of the gun he held too close to Megan's head, just above her ear.

"She was the one with the money!"

"But still, you had to know it would come back on you."

"No, it will not come back on me. You're looking at Gary — and other men my daughter dated. Like that pathetic musician. You would have never —"

"Oh, but we did. They know you're the second Embracer —"

"I am not the second Embracer!" he shouted. "I am the first!"

"But I'm the best," Carver said.

"And they don't know anything!" Ayers cried. "You're lying."

"I'm not lying," Colleen said, waving the Glock in a small semicircle that still kept it trained on Carver. "You see, we have people in our technical departments who can trace people's movements through their credit card purchases and pictures from toll roads. Oh, and Special Agent Hawkins looked into the date of your marriage and the date of your daughter's birth. Now, we all know many babies are conceived before marriage, but it was enough to get her thinking. And now we know. Of course, we believe Carver killed the women when the notes went into the media. The Embracer notes were what he sees as perfecting your crimes. But you are the one who has been killing women for years. We found another one yesterday, by the way. So. Which one of you geniuses found all the cabins?"

"None of this matters," Carver said. "Give me the gun. Give me the gun, or he shoots Megan."

"No. Megan walks out the door, and I give you my gun."

"That's crazy. I won't do it. Shoot me.

Rory will shoot Megan."

She smiled and turned the gun on Rory.

Carver instantly drew a weapon himself.

She'd expected it.

"I shoot Rory; Rory can't shoot Megan. And I'm good. Maybe I can shoot you and Rory. Or you can let Megan just walk out of here and run into the woods. Maybe you'd find her afterward anyway. But Megan walks out of here."

They were standing when Colleen heard a faint rustling in the woods outside. She knew no one else could hear it yet.

Nor could they hear the soft little whine from Red.

Colleen stood pat.

They'd come. Mark and Ragnar were just outside the cabin. They were finding their positions.

That didn't take the danger away from Megan.

But Colleen believed she still had the upper hand.

"How did you get Megan?" she asked.

"They had a puppy, and the puppy was loose, running into the parking lot, and I was helping chase it and then . . ."

"I left you at the train station to get on the train!" Colleen told her sister.

"I know! And I was being wary of people.

I didn't think to be afraid of puppies!"

Megan knew Colleen was trying to keep them talking.

"I told you to get on the train."

"Hey! I'm older than you by two minutes!" Megan returned. "You can't tell me what to do! And I didn't know to be afraid of an old man."

"Old man!" Rory Ayers protested. "Oh, girlie —"

"Wrong girlie!" Carver growled. "If you'd gotten the right damned girl —"

"From a distance they look alike," Ayers said. "And that kind of watching has to be done from a distance."

"You're an idiot."

"Reddish hair —"

"That one has lighter hair! And she doesn't truss it up to try to look like a nun. You're an idiot. Anyone can see that —"

"We are sisters," Megan put in.

"And we do look similar," Colleen said.

Talking. Keeping them talking was good. It was at least a chance for her and Megan to get out alive.

"And, Carver, get serious! Ayers wouldn't have gotten the 'right' damned girl and you know it," Colleen informed him sweetly.

"You think you're that good?"

"I think I'm an agent. Trained."

396

Megan seemed to know they were playing for time.

"But you would have tried to save a puppy too, Colleen. I know you're a trained agent and all, but you would have gone after a puppy —"

"Well, we've got you both now!" Ayers shouted.

"No, you don't," Colleen said. "If you want me, you let Megan go."

"You really are such a superior bitch! But guess what? I know how to play any stupid woman. And I will have you now!" Carver promised.

Colleen trained her gun on him. "Will you?"

Ragnar parked his car on the side of the crooked dirt road a distance behind where Colleen had left Mark's car.

Red had been given the command for secrecy. He'd been on detail before where they sought to take criminals by surprise, and he knew the command well.

Mark hoped it wasn't going to be the one day the dog disobeyed and went against his training.

But he didn't want to leave the dog behind. Neither did Ragnar. There had been too many times when Red had proven himself to be an invaluable member of the team.

Mark knew he shouldn't have been on the detail himself — not according to the books. He was personally involved. Far more involved than he had ever thought he would be.

As they moved along the road toward the cabin, Ragnar shook his head and said quietly, "Her father! Dierdre's father. Or should I say, the man who raised her. How he must have relished calling in the Bureau — certain he'd get away with it. And she was the only one who wasn't held and violated — maybe something of a fatherly instinct kicked in!"

"We should have known," Mark said.

Ragnar looked at him. "You knew all along it was someone connected to one of the girls."

"And we focused on Gary Boynton. And Brant Pickering."

Mark and Ragnar paused. They were approaching the cabin.

He could see Colleen was just inside the doorway, which remained open.

Jim Carver was just a few steps in front of her, staring at her. Her gun was trained on him.

But Carver was also armed.

Luckily, the cabin had been all but reclaimed by the forest. There was rich growth all around it.

He motioned to Ragnar; his partner would move around to the left. He'd go right with Red. They'd stay back, hugging the trees and the foliage right by the empty window frames.

It didn't take long for them to move the distance as they had planned. And when he found his position, Mark could see Rory Ayers was there and armed as well. The nose of what looked like a Smith & Wesson was pressed to the side of Megan's temple.

Megan sat still, ignoring the gun.

"I know you don't want to die," Colleen was telling Carver. "I mean, if you die, what will you have? Nothing. Let my sister go."

"I can't figure out how," Carver said. "You don't trust me enough to put down your gun."

"Damned right," Colleen assured him. "So, let's work on that. You have to let Megan go, and I have to give you the gun. So, how do we do it?"

"We don't let Megan go!" Rory Ayers snapped. "She's a witness against me."

"Mr. Ayers," Megan said, "didn't you hear Colleen? They've already figured out you're the copycat."

"I'm no copycat!" he raged.

Mark saw Megan wince — the nose of the gun had been thrust harder against her skull.

"They've figured out you're a killer, Mr. Ayers," Colleen told him.

"They'll never prove it in court," Rory Ayers said.

"You'd be amazed at what kind of forensic proof they can pull — even after years and years," Colleen said. "We do have some of the best techs and scientists in the world working at the Bureau." She looked at Carver, smiling. "And when they get you — which they will — you won't be walking out of court either. Especially not now that you're part of an escape in which men were injured."

"Not killed — though I'd have loved to have killed that one fat bastard!" Carver said. "Drop the gun. Or I'll shoot you, and Rory will shoot Megan."

"What fun would that be? If you kill me, you can't do what you really want to do to me, right? I mean, you do enjoy the torture and thinking about your victim slowly suffocating to death. Then again, I'll shoot one of you too," Colleen said.

Mark was amazed by the calm she was showing.

And he suspected she knew they were there. She'd probably heard every little rustle of the leaves as they had moved through the brush and the trees.

She'd come here desperately. She'd had to save her sister. But she knew now she wasn't alone. And still . . .

With the nose of the gun against Megan's head, they all had to play it out as far as they could — until they found a way to take out Carver and Ayers.

He couldn't motion or speak to Ragnar from where he was, but Mark knew his partner would follow whatever he started. And it seemed he had only one choice.

He gave Red a silent command to sit, stay, and watch. And he moved around to the front, making an entrance as if he had no idea of what was going on inside. This time, he let himself be heard.

"Colleen!" he said, forcing anger into his voice. "What the hell are you doing? Why in God's name would you just take off with my car like that? I've reported it to — oh!"

He pretended to be shocked, seeing the occupants of the cabin.

Carver turned his gun on Mark.

Colleen edged back, staring at him, keeping her weapon locked on Carver.

"I told you not to bring anyone!" Carver raged.

"I didn't bring him —"

"You ass!" Mark raged. "Didn't you just hear? The bitch stole my car. But now you're here —"

"And I am going to shoot your ass!" Carver swore.

"And I'll shoot yours!" Colleen promised.

"Or you can just surrender right now," Mark said.

"You idiot, you don't even have your gun out," Carver said.

"Last chance," Mark said. "FBI. You're under arrest. Surrender."

"You've got to be kidding me!" Carver said.

And Rory Ayers, watching the action, lost his concentration.

Colleen must have sensed him lower the gun, must have known he was about to turn and take aim at her or Mark.

She suddenly dived low at Rory Ayers's feet, slamming him down on the ground. His Smith & Wesson went flying. And Colleen none-too-gently brought herself down on top of him, ready with a pair of plastic cuffs.

Carver never got a shot off.

Ragnar had made a bull's-eye shot —

hitting the man directly in the wrist causing his gun to fly as well.

The man screamed in pain, falling to his knees, swearing vociferously.

"I will live! I will win in court! I will get you yet, Special Agent Law. You will know The Embracer and then you will know what it's like. You will beg and plead, and I will listen to you as earth caves down on you and dirt fills your lungs! I will —"

He'd stared to rise. To scramble for his gun.

But Red knew when to act, and the dog bounded through the window, landing right on top of the man, taking his injured wrist into his mouth with a terrifying growl.

Red had Carver.

Mark hurried over to help Colleen cuff Ayers.

Ragnar hopped through the empty window opening and shook his head.

"I guess that was something of a plan," he said. He shrugged. "It worked."

"I don't believe it!" Megan whispered. She started to rise.

And then she fell.

Ragnar rushed over, catching her right before she could fall to the ground.

"We need to get this called in," he said,

trying to hold Megan and reach for his phone.

"I've got it," Colleen said, leaving Mark to drag a cuffed Rory Ayers to his feet. Mark's eyes met hers, filled with gratitude and relief — and she was shaking as well.

He knew she was glad he had taken over with Ayers. She didn't trust herself with the man who had held his gun against her sister's head.

He saw she was trembling slightly. She'd held it together; she'd worked it well. But her life — and her sister's life — had been on the line.

Colleen made the call.

Jim Carver started screaming again. "Police brutality!"

"We aren't cops," Ragnar said. He seemed to be more perplexed about what to do with Megan than he was with anything the serial killer might say.

"I will sue you! I will have this wretched mutt put to sleep!"

Red made a sound that was almost like a human laugh.

"Carver, you don't even faze the dog," Mark said, walking over to relieve Red and cuff the man as well.

Carver screamed in rage as Mark dragged

404

him up and tried to put the cuffs above his wound.

"I'm bleeding! I'm injured!"

"Sorry, but you shouldn't have been waving a gun around," Mark said. "I did ask you nicely to surrender. And, sir, you are a dangerous man."

Rory Ayers tried to lunge at Mark.

Mark sidestepped him and let the man fall back to the ground.

He rolled over, staring at Mark.

"You don't know the half of it! You don't know the half of it!"

"They're coming," Colleen said with relief.

Mark heard the sirens moments after she spoke. Relief was coming. Officers had been out in the area searching for a cabin.

Just like this one.

Within minutes, several local sheriff's deputies had arrived, and an ambulance was on its way.

But Megan woke up in Ragnar's arms.

She stared at him in alarm and flailed her arms.

"Hey!" Ragnar protested. "I'm the good guy!"

"Oh. Oh!" Megan said, realizing where she was. "Oh, my God, but —"

She looked around the room, blinking,

shaking, and clinging to Ragnar. She realized the area was filled now with brush, bracken — and officers.

For a moment, she fell back in his arms with relief.

Then she tried to scramble out of his hold. "I'm sorry. I'm so sorry —"

"Oh, Megan, it's all right," Colleen assured her. "You held it together when you needed to. It's fine. You inadvertently helped catch two killers."

She tried to ease to her feet and started to falter again.

But this time, the paramedics were there, ready to catch her and help her out to the ambulance.

Jim Carver and Rory Ayers were taken away with Ayers still screaming they didn't know the half of it.

There were more bodies buried in the woods, Mark thought.

And they might never find them all.

But for now, he looked at Colleen, standing still, trembling inside.

They were professionals.

But he took her into his arms anyway, holding her.

Until her trembling ceased.

CHAPTER FIFTEEN

Harpers Ferry, West Virginia. It was one of the places Colleen had loved most as a child, so when she and Mark — and Red and Ragnar — were ordered to take a few days of vacation time, Mark had suggested it because she'd talked so fondly about it. And they were close.

No travel arrangements had to be made other than the booking of a charming bed-and-breakfast. Colleen's neighbor would check on Jensen while she was on vacation.

To her surprise, Megan had taken a few days off too. Her publisher had insisted, and once everyone at her job got over being grateful Megan was fine — they were also thrilled and intrigued.

Though her publishing house was famous for its sci-fi books, they thought a non-fiction book by a woman who had nearly become a victim of "The Embracer killings" would be an amazing thing to have on their list.

Megan was still undecided.

And she didn't really want to be alone right away. That was natural. So, she came to Harpers Ferry.

Ragnar figured it was an easy jaunt too.

So by day, Mark and Colleen were occasionally joined by the still-bickering pair while white water rafting, hiking, touring, and roaming the shops.

Mark had told Colleen that coming here was an idea — just an idea. Maybe she wanted a beach — far from any woods.

But Colleen had determined she wasn't going to be afraid of the woods or nature, and so they enjoyed the hiking, rafting, and the sights.

She especially loved Jefferson Rock — named after Thomas Jefferson, who had written about the view in his *Notes on the State of Virginia*. The area had been part of the state of Virginia back then. It hadn't split off until the Civil War.

But it didn't matter what the area had been called when — the view was stupendous. The Potomac and the Shenandoah Rivers met there. From the rock, she could see rushing water and rapids and mountains and valleys. It was simply beautiful.

She loved the history of the place too, the

national park plus all there was to be learned.

And she loved the quiet that could be found, the time they spent together, laughing, teasing, being passionate, and discovering more about each other and loving each discovery.

It was while they lay in bed one night, just enjoying the plush comfort of the mattress of their charming nineteenth-century bed-and-breakfast rental, when Mark suddenly turned to her and said, "I think we should just get married."

"What?" Colleen exclaimed.

He shrugged. "Lots of us are couples. It doesn't work that way in the main Bureau. I mean, agents can be together and married, but they're in separate units or areas. In the Krewe, well, we're the weird unit. And we kind of work best together, you know? So . . ."

She smiled. "Honestly, we've barely been together."

"That doesn't matter to me. I've never just . . . known. But I'm sorry. I didn't mean to pressure you in any way. Hey. You said you might want a dog like Red. I think Red would love a second owner like you."

She laughed. "Marriage for a dog! Haven't heard that one yet."

"Couples fight over pets in divorce cases all the time," he said gravely.

She rolled over, edging on top of him. She loved the darkness of his eyes and the way his dark hair, damp now, fell over his forehead. And she loved the strength and life she felt in his body as she pressed against it, grinning.

"I promise I'll never take Red. But I'll never divorce you either."

He frowned slightly. "Is that a yes?"

"For the sake of the child — er, dog — of course."

"Big wedding? You have a family —"

"No. Megan can have the big wedding. I think we should just surprise everyone."

"Courthouse?" he asked her.

"And maybe a small church wedding and reception somewhere along the line."

"It's a plan," he said gravely.

She eased down on him, whispering just above his lips, "Wow. We're engaged, and I guess we should seal the deal, don't you think?"

He smiled.

Engaged was good.

His kiss was hot, wet, passionate . . .

Later, before they slept, she whispered, "Engaged sex is really great."

"Thank you."

"Hey! There were two of us."

"And I thank you," he said softly.

Colleen, Mark, and Red met Ragnar and Megan for breakfast in the B and B's charming dining room the next morning.

Colleen made the announcement.

"Wow!" Megan said. "I — Congratulations! Is that allowed? I mean, does one of you have to quit or transfer or —"

"Not with the Krewe," Ragnar told her.

"Oh, great! Have you told Mom and Dad or Patrick — you'd best tell Patrick. And Mom and Dad, of course —"

"I'll call this afternoon," Colleen said. She smiled. Her parents had wanted her to come to Orlando. She had tried to play down the danger she and Megan had faced, assuring her parents she and her partners had been in control all along.

Patrick had been harder to convince. But then, he was a criminal psychologist and was never surprised by the way a demented killer's mind might work.

They didn't need the truth. Patrick knew the truth but was convinced not to drop everything and rush down because the trauma was over. He might just show up anyway, Colleen thought, when the weekend arrived.

"So, when? Weddings take time to plan —"

"Quickie marriage," Colleen said.

"We should have gone to Vegas," Ragnar put in.

"Ah, too late!" Mark said. "But, hey, if you hang around until we get back, maybe you and Megan can be our witnesses."

"Um, sure," Megan said. She frowned. "I'll hang around. If you'll help me."

"Help you — do what?" Colleen asked.

"Bring me back to the cemetery. I want to see Sergeant Parker again. And I want everything you have on him and the girl he was trying to save. And in your free time, you have to help me work on it!"

"We won't mind doing that in the least," Mark assured her.

Ragnar let out a long breath. "We're going to have to try to get Ayers to talk too. Both men are going up on federal charges, and the attorneys want to go for the death penalty. Ayers said we didn't know the half of it. The families of any other potential victims deserve to know."

"I don't think that's what he meant," Megan said.

"He screamed it twice," Ragnar told her.

"Oh, that's right. You were passed out the first time."

Megan gave him a condemning glare. "I may not be an agent!" she snapped. She shook her head. "But that's not what he meant."

"What do you think he meant?" Mark asked her.

Megan inhaled a deep breath and looked at each of them before speaking.

"Well, it seems as if Rory Ayers was something of a mentor to Jim Carver. He's a brilliant technical guy — and I figure that's how he and Carver were communicating without being discovered. He kidnapped me — thinking I was you, Colleen — in order to bring me to Carver, so he knew Carver had planned an escape. They both knew where to go."

"That's what we've all figured, yes," Colleen said.

Megan shrugged. "I'm thinking Ayers might have had a mentor too. Or worse, they were schooling someone else."

"And you do usually know what people mean," Colleen said.

"I'm just afraid you're going to find lots of old victims," she said. She winced. "And maybe some fresh ones."

"We're on vacation," Ragnar said. "And the Krewe is now a nice-sized agency. Others are working on finding cabins in the woods. The three McFadden brothers, who know the area, are on it along with others. I'm going to enjoy the view, the breeze, and time off." He smiled pleasantly at Megan. "I'm going to enjoy it, no matter what clouds some might see!"

Megan shook her head. "I think I'm going to go back down and do another of the tours. They have a great ghost tour here tonight by the way." She grinned. "I'll see who I can meet!"

"Or see again," Colleen reminded her.

"And who might that be?" Mark asked.

"Father Michael Costello. He was a priest here at St. Peter's Catholic Church during the days of John Brown's raid at Harpers Ferry. The poor man witnessed everything. And the church became a hospital and the city changed hands again and again. We met a pair of Civil War soldiers — one who had been with the Union and the other with the Confederacy — who became best friends. They were both killed in battle," Colleen said.

"They're wonderful!" Megan said. "Patrick talked with them endlessly. He was always trying to get into people's minds! Anyway, they try to make sure we understand history now. Guides who mess up might be pinched! Private Rickie Naughton

— CSA — and Sergeant Ryan Huntington — USA — try to make sure we understand the war proved what our Constitution says — that *all* men are created equal. Well, men and women," she added sweetly, glaring at Ragnar.

"I'd love to meet them," Ragnar said, ignoring the look she gave him. "Maybe I'll go on this tour too, and see who we see. You guys in?"

"Maybe," Mark said. He glanced at Colleen. "What does my *fiancée* have to say about that?"

"She really should have a ring, you know," Megan told him.

"I really don't need a ring. Being together is something we choose to be," Colleen said. "A ring is jewelry. Even a wedding certificate is paper. Legal or not — we're together."

"That was beautiful. But we will get a ring!" Mark promised.

"But what about the ghost tour?" Ragnar asked, indicating Megan with a twitch of his head.

"We'll go," Colleen agreed.

But as it turned out, they didn't have to wait for the ghost tour for her to run into an old friend.

Ragnar had told them he wouldn't really be reading and relaxing; he'd be following

Megan. That had pleased Colleen. Her sister's words troubled her. Megan saw true meaning.

Even with her hearing, Colleen could only know what was said.

"You don't know the half of it."

But the Krewe was on it. And she felt they had earned their vacation time.

She and Mark were casually strolling along a hiking trail with Red when Colleen heard a voice.

"It is you, Miss Colleen! All grown up now. Oh, and I'm sorry, you don't need to respond, young woman. Not now. I see you're with —"

"Rickie!" she cried out with pleasure.

Private Rickie Naughton stood in the center of the path, still in his full uniform.

"It's all right, Miss —"

"Private Richard Naughton," Mark said. "A pleasure to meet you, sir."

"Ah, another!" Rickie said. "Sir, I cannot tell you — the pleasure is uniquely mine. Your — kind — is rare. In fact, we first met this lovely young woman when she was barely a teenager. And we met her siblings as well. I see your arm about the lady, sir. I do expect —"

"We're engaged," Colleen assured him.

"Congratulations, then. Sir, you are gainfully employed and a good man who appreciates we are a great human family."

"Most certainly, sir," Mark promised.

"Alas, many of us foolishly learned the hard way, but you see, once death claims us, a human soul has no color. We are one, and alive and dead, we are beautiful in all that we are."

"Indeed, sir!" Mark said.

"And you are gainfully employed?" Rickie asked Colleen.

She laughed. "We work together, Rickie. We work for the government in the FBI."

"It's an agency that —" Mark began.

Rickie cut him off.

"Sir, I have strolled over these hills a great many days. I am well aware of the agency of which you speak." He paused, shaking his head. "War, sir, is ugly and horrible. And yet, perhaps, I died in one that had to be fought. Still, like this young lady, I was from the great state of Florida; I followed my state, as did many a man. But through the years, I have also seen man's terrible toll upon other men when war is not in the picture, and I am honored I walk with those who seek justice for all men."

"Colleen and Megan spoke of you this morning," Mark told him. "It is I who am honored to walk with you."

417

"And what a beautiful dog!"

"Red," Mark said. "He is a very good dog."

"And he senses me too," Rickie said. "You said your sister is here as well?" he asked Colleen.

"She is. Shopping, I believe. But she's going on the ghost tour tonight."

"Ah, then a ghost shall join the ghost tour!" Rickie said. "And I'll bring my best friend with me. It's sad to realize the enemy is just as human after a war has been fought, right? Or even accept the fact that you were wrong." He hesitated and shrugged. "Maybe I stayed to learn I was wrong. And maybe I'll be around longer to see the decade when everyone from everywhere is really free and equal. Anyway, you two keep up the good work!"

"Thanks!" they said in unison, waving as Rickie hurried on.

They walked a few trails and returned to town, ate a light dinner in the commercial section of the area, and went back to the B and B to freshen up and head out on the ghost tour.

They were supposed to meet downstairs at twenty after eight to go to the ghost tour. She and Megan knew about most of the sad stories. They'd been on the tours before.

The guide would talk about Screaming Jenny who, sad and poor, had cooked out in the open, and when the fire caught hold of her dress, she'd run screaming down the railroad tracks right into an oncoming train. It was said there were nights when her apparition might be seen, and the sounds of her screams echoed through the darkness. There was the ghost of a soldier who haunted St. Peter's Church; he had died because no one realized the severity of his wounds when the church had been used as a hospital. Saddest maybe was the story about the ghost of a little Civil War drummer boy who had fallen out of a window when soldiers were playing around — soldiers who supposedly loved him.

The stories always differed a little. But the guides were usually excellent, and it was forecast to be a beautiful night.

Mark's phone rang as they were about to leave. Colleen looked at him curiously. He gave her a grimace and covered the phone.

"Ragnar. He has followed Megan all day. He wanted us to know they're both back at the hotel, and we'll meet downstairs as planned."

"Great."

They went down.

Ragnar was there, waiting.

419

Megan was not.

"I'll run up and get her," Colleen told the two men.

Red woofed as if he were offering to go up to the second floor with her.

"It's okay. I've got this, Red!" she said, setting her hand on his head and then going up the stairs.

Megan was at her door.

"Am I late?" she asked. "I'm sorry. I just —"

"Is something wrong?" Colleen asked her.

"Other than the Viking following me around all day? I mean, he's probably fine when he's really working, but the guy is taller than most other human beings and, anyway, I guess it was good he was worried, but I don't think I was in danger in the souvenir shops — or the bookstore! Oh, I do love national park bookstores!"

"I do too."

"I was back in plenty of time. I admit I was glad the Viking was following me at times. Because I can't get Rory Ayers's words out of my head."

"I've been thinking about them too," Colleen admitted. "But come on! Let's go. We're all on vacation. And you deserve it. My making fun of you for trying to save a puppy was —"

"I know. I'm amazed I was as calm as I was." Megan gave Colleen a sudden hug. "I knew you would come for me."

"With help. Anyway, let's go down. We already ran into Rickie, and he's going to 'haunt' the tour tonight so he can see you."

"Great! Let's go."

There was a lot of walking to be done at Harpers Ferry, and much of it up and down. But for their ghost tour, they headed to the area known as the Lower Town. It was downhill. There was some traffic on the road, but there seemed to be heavier foot traffic that night. And there was plenty of space for Red to sniff about and wag his tail and behave like any dog might.

Their tour met near the old arsenal.

Their guide was good. He laughed. He explained history, legend — and what folks said happened here and there that could be taken as truth — or not.

They heard again about John Brown's raid on Harpers Ferry and how the first man killed was Dangerfield Newby, an African American man with Brown. The frightened townspeople had stuffed their weapons with anything, and he'd been hit with a barrage of spikes and nails.

After the raid, they had viciously desecrated the man's body.

Now it was said there were nights when he ran through the streets screaming.

"Poor fellow has the right to run around screaming," Ragnar muttered.

Colleen grinned at the comment and then frowned, not sure if she was hearing something strange at the back of her mind or not.

"Yes, I heard them whispering about you, you freak," a voice said. "Some of the cops think you're crazy. I just think you're the monster who brought good men down. Go ahead! Nod if you can hear me."

She frowned.

The guide was talking.

Even Red seemed to be paying attention to him.

But she nodded.

The voice went on, "Look to your left. To the far end of the street. It's dark . . . not on the tour. But this lady is finished with the tour and . . . are you going to make her pay for what you did?"

Colleen turned to her left. She was looking far up the street, away from the tours, away from what remained open at night.

There was someone there — barely discernible in the darkness up the street. But he held something that glinted in what pale light reached him.

A knife.

And it was held against the throat of a young woman.

"Taking a note from my buddy's playbook, Special Agent Law. This blade is at this woman's throat. Come now, or I'll slide it right through her. Just slip away. I'm sorry it's an uphill distance into the darkness, but I couldn't get closer to your co-creeps. Come on, come on, come on, or she'll die, and I'll disappear into the darkness. You'll find this sweet young thing with her life's blood spilling out on this hallowed ground!"

Not again.

She couldn't play this again, not without telling the others, and yet . . .

He was watching. If anyone turned in that direction . . .

It wasn't Megan, but it didn't matter. She couldn't have a young woman's death on her conscience, not when she could have acted.

And she believed she knew who it was.

Mark had been right all along.

Nothing like having a mentor!

The voice entered her head again.

"Slip away, and I mean, slip away. There will always be another chance. But this girl will die."

There was one thing she could do. She

believed it would work. She took her sister's arm lightly and spoke to her in a whisper.

"I'm going to find the ladies' room," she told Megan, slipping back. Both Ragnar and Mark were staring straight ahead, listening.

But Megan would understand.

And carefully relay the message.

"But this gentleman is talking —" Megan began. "Um . . ."

"I have to go!" Colleen said.

She backed away, and then hurried toward the hill as everyone around her paid her no heed.

They really had a good guide.

Of course, in a minute, Mark and Ragnar would know she was gone. But with any luck, Megan would say the right things.

"Don't turn around," Megan Law said, staring at their guide as he told the story of a park ranger who had seen strange things. "I mean it — don't turn around."

Mark didn't turn. Neither did Ragnar.

"What?"

"Something is happening. Someone has another girl. Whoever it is, he knew Colleen, and he 'talked' to her. Don't be obvious; we're talking just seconds. She went up toward town, but she took the higher road there, where there are bushes, homes."

424

"She left again without her team!"

Another Embracer acolyte was moving more quickly than they had thought.

More closely than they had imagined.

"No. She left knowing I was here, and that I would tell you what's going on," Megan said. "And if this guy has taken someone as I was taken, she did what she had to do. Don't turn. Laugh, talk to the guide, then get to the stone steps there and circle around and find her!"

"Right," Mark said, still feeling the ice around his heart invading his soul. "But you stay with this tour, with people. Do not leave."

"Right. I swear," Megan vowed.

Mark and Ragnar started to make their way to the edge of the crowd, pretending to laugh at the tour guide's jokes.

It was only then he realized that Red wasn't with him either.

Red had become as loyal to Colleen as he was to Mark.

He prayed the dog was following his training by instinct, and he'd save both Colleen and this killer's victim . . .

And himself.

At the far end of their tour group, he looked back at Megan, who nodded.

They couldn't be seen from the road Colleen had taken.

They headed for the stone steps and the upper levels of the town, desperate to move quickly, circle back around, and cut off the killer before he could whisk another young woman and Colleen off into the darkness.

"Seriously? You walked through town like that?" Colleen said.

Gary Boynton was wearing a ski mask, black cap, and hoodie. He looked as if he was about to climb Everest.

All she could see against all the black covering his face were his eyes.

But she knew who it was.

"I didn't walk through town. I caught this little cutie when she was just going down to join your group. We've been hugging the shadows, right, cutie?" he asked the girl he held close to his body with his left hand.

In his right, he held the knife that had glinted so briefly in the moonlight. The blade was touching her skin beneath the jaw.

With a thrust, he could push it through soft tissue, her mouth and on upward.

"I'm here. Let her go," Colleen said.

"First, I need your gun," he told her.

"I was on a tour. I'm on vacation!"

"Oh, right! Yes, the brilliant, gifted agent who dug Dierdre out of the woods. But that hearing thing of yours must be real. You heard me!" He pressed the knife closer to the terrified young woman's throat drawing a trickle of blood. She let out a little sob, caught quickly. "Your gun. Or she dies."

The woman he held was young, maybe in her early twenties, if that. She had shoulder-length, honey-colored hair and enormous dark eyes that were filled with terrified tears.

Boynton had probably warned her to silence, and only the pain and fear had allowed her to make the little squeaking sound.

"I have to admit, you guys are way sicker than I'd imagined. Because it was Ayers who put his own daughter in the box, right?" Colleen said. "And I'm starting to think that while you may not be as . . . talented at torture and murder as your mentors, you are a bigger idiot. Two people have been captured. Cops and agents are every-where."

"No, I am not an idiot. I am the best — I'm young and able and I'm the best and I will prove it. Yes, Ayers put Dierdre in the box, but he hasn't half the talent I have. We should have gone on and on except . . . you! You just had to find her!" Boynton said.

"But it was all a business deal. For a business deal, didn't you need to marry her?"

"No. My relationship with Dierdre . . . just a performance. I am an amazing performer. Rory and me, well, we just hit it right off when we met. And the relationship with Dierdre seemed like a good reason for me to be around so much. I mean, naturally, her husband-to-be and father could join in a partnership. Rory really hates Dierdre. His wife too, but it was the kid he hated most. But that's the thing. We all need to be careful. Play the game. I really am the boy next door! Rich, charming . . . never mind. You screwed it all up. This will be my crowning achievement. Where they failed, I will prevail. And they'll get to know. Okay. I'll take that Glock."

She lifted her arms.

She really wasn't carrying the Glock. She was, however, armed. She had a tiny 9 millimeter Ruger at her back, but it was so small, it was in its holster beneath her jeans and the tunic she was wearing — a truly concealed weapon.

And this time . . .

It was Gary. Just Gary.

"What in the good Lord's name?" she heard.

Looking past Gary, she knew the man hadn't heard the words. They were being spoken by a dead man.

Rickie.

"You let her go, you despicable coward!" Rickie cried, throwing a punch at Boynton's neck.

Boynton flinched and shivered — but didn't stop staring hard at Colleen.

"There's solid help on the way!" Rickie warned.

"I know you're armed. Let me cut her a little more deeply," Boynton said.

"No!" Colleen protested, spinning around. "I have nothing on me. Just my ID and a credit card in my pocket. I don't carry things when I'm going on a two-hour walking tour! I told you — I'm on vacation. Let her go! You've got me."

"Can't do that," he said. "She'll start screaming and bring people too close. I have a plan; we're going away, but go figure — I lied. I have to kill her."

Colleen shook her head. "I'm faster than you. Let her go — or I run."

"I'll bring you down like a hawk on a pigeon, bitch."

"Okay. We can see who is right. Or you can let her go. Tie her up. Or are you too stupid a newbie Embracer to have brought along rope?" she demanded.

The blonde girl was, of course, absolutely terrified.

429

And she was bleeding.

Not badly . . .

And yet enough. Every time Boynton became animated, the knife cut into her more deeply.

She had to act and now.

But then . . .

Something flew out of the darkness, and she thought at first that another spirit had joined them, one determined to throw Boynton off if nothing else.

But it was no spirit.

It was Red.

He slammed into Boynton with such force the young woman he'd been holding fell to the ground, crying out. Colleen quickly dragged her away and reached around her back, seeking her little Ruger.

Boynton was screaming; Red had a grip on his left wrist.

But Boynton's right wrist was free, and the blade was still in his right hand, bearing down toward Red.

"No!" Colleen screamed.

She ran forward, thundering toward the man, determined she could slam his arm even as she reached desperately and instinctively back with her left hand to seize hold of the little Ruger she was carrying.

Boynton threw his arm back; Red ripped

half his skin away but lost his grip.

The knife aimed toward Colleen with just inches to spare. She fumbled briefly then found the Ruger. His knife was bearing down hard for the top of her head.

But she didn't need her gun.

The sound of a shot exploded in the night.

For a split second, Gary Boynton seemed as posed as a historical statue.

Then he fell. Dead. Shot through the back of his head.

And a man stepped from out of the darkness. Mark.

Red barked and jumped away from the dead man, and Ragnar joined the group, coming up behind Mark with his weapon in his hand as well.

"So. Boynton," Ragnar said. "Go figure. He was in on it too, huh? Thankfully, the stupidest in the group."

The woman on the ground was sobbing, and Colleen hurried to her. But the gunshot had been heard in the Lower Town where tours were going on, where *life* was going on in such a historic town. And soon, there were officers, and a medical examiner, and an ambulance for the young woman, who wasn't so badly injured, other than the trauma that had been *her* life for those moments.

Traumatized and terrified, she was tearful and grateful, thanking Colleen over and over again and then Red and Mark and Ragnar. She was finally taken away.

And the body of Gary Boynton was taken away.

They reported to the local and county police; more agents arrived.

They were, at last, free to go. Naturally, Colleen wanted to know about Megan.

"She swore she would stay with the tour group," Ragnar said, agitated.

"The tour must have ended a long time ago now!" Colleen said.

"But she promised she'd stay . . ."

"I'm here!" Megan cried, joining them on the darkened height where Boynton had thought he could trap Colleen. "And I'm not alone! Jessie stayed with me."

She indicated their guide, who walked behind her.

"Thank you!" Colleen said.

"My pleasure," the guide said. "Megan is going to look at my first effort at a science fiction novel. I intend to mix it up with some history, which is my area of expertise. I mean, what if an alien had been around — and he'd swept down and taken John Brown away?"

Colleen looked downward, wincing. Historical purists wouldn't like that one bit!

But their guide started to laugh.

"Just kidding. I have a group of Alpha soldiers heading out on the first Mars landing. Not so far from reality. But Megan really knows her history for a science fiction editor —"

He suddenly stopped talking, looking past them at the place where Boynton had lain after Mark had shot him.

"Um, sorry. Anyway, tonight is, well, good for another ghost story," he said. "Thankfully, that of a dead killer and not an innocent woman. I should get going now. Megan has my information."

"Thank you again!" Colleen and Megan called together. Mark and Ragnar echoed their words.

"Rickie!" Megan cried then.

And turning, Colleen saw the ghost who had tried so hard to help her.

"I really must learn to move something more than air," Rickie said.

"You did," Mark said. "You moved through time and space to warn Ragnar and me exactly where to go to find Colleen and the girl and Boynton. Colleen might have gotten off a shot but maybe not. We might have been on time but maybe not."

"So, I might have saved a life," Rickie said happily.

"Most probably," Colleen told him.

And the ghost of the soldier smiled.

"I like that. I like that so much. A soldier has his duty. But it's much better saving lives than taking them!"

"Much better," Megan said, hugging the air, and yet knowing the soldier's soul could feel the touch. "Much better and thank you!"

"So, um, maybe you'll really take the ghost tour tomorrow night?" Rickie asked.

"No!" The word sounded unanimously from all of them.

"But we'll be back! We love you guys," Colleen promised.

"And I may be getting into some nonfiction soon, and you and your friends here have so very much to give! Discreetly, of course!" Megan told him.

He nodded. "That will do. Well then, children," Rickie teased. "Off to bed. And I will look forward to our next meeting."

He disappeared into the darkness.

Colleen knelt down to cuddle Red. Mark came to hold them both. Megan had to join in and Ragnar encompassed them all.

"To sleep, for what of the night is left," Mark said. "And let's pray Rory Ayers was referring to Gary Boynton as his protégé, and The Embracer story has finally come to an end."

"Yes," Megan said. "We can focus on the courthouse tomorrow. And then, I'm leaving you people! I love my quiet and peaceful NYC. And who in their right mind would ever think that anyone could say something like that?"

Colleen smiled. She looked at Mark.

Yes, it was insane. Their lives would continue to be crazy. But Mark and Red and Ragnar would always have her back.

And she would have theirs.

She wouldn't change Mark if she could.

And that night, she knew he wouldn't change her.

Crazy.

But she loved him.

It was the wee hours of the morning when they were finally back in their rooms.

They slept late.

Even Red.

But they were back in the Alexandria area by three, and thanks to a few machinations by their Krewe founder, Adam Harrison, they had a license by five.

Crazy.

They were married that night.

And as they lay together when midnight

435

rolled around again, Colleen knew, yes, it was all crazy, but she was also *madly* in love and neither one of them would change it. This was the way she wanted to live the rest of her life, lying with him every night.

"No regrets?" he whispered to her, rising above her.

"None. After all, we had to make it all legal for Red and Jensen!"

Red and Jensen were happy to move in together.

They both laughed and fell back.

They had a few days to bask in their newlywed bliss.

They may have been back home, but they'd still make use of those days.

ABOUT THE AUTHOR

New York Times and USA Today bestselling author **Heather Graham** has written more than a hundred novels. She's a winner of the RWA's Lifetime Achievement Award, and the Thriller Writers' Silver Bullet. She is an active member of International Thriller Writers and Mystery Writers of America. For more information, check out her websites: TheOriginalHeatherGraham.com, eHeatherGraham.com, and HeatherGraham .tv. You can also find Heather on Facebook.